CLOAK and MIRRORS

CLOAK AND MIRRORS
by p.m.terrell
Published by
Drake Valley Press
USA

This novel is a work of fiction. Any resemblance to actual persons, living or dead, is entirely coincidental. The characters, names (except as noted under "Special Thanks"), plots and incidents are the product of the author's imagination. References to actual events, public figures, locales or businesses are included only to give this work of fiction a sense of reality.

ISBN 978-1-935970-39-2 (eBook)
ISBN 978-1-935970-38-5 (Trade Paperback)

Author's website: www.pmterrell.com

CLOAK AND MIRRORS
by p.m.terrell

Book 6 of the award-winning Black Swamp Mysteries Series

What reviewers are saying about the Black Swamp Mysteries Series:

"Riveting, spellbinding... sexy, intense, stay-up-all-night until you are done thriller... terrell's best book yet!" - Marcia Freespirit, Bengal Book Reviews

"Page-turning action, unforgettable characters, breathtaking descriptions and unexpected plot twists" - Richard R. Blake, Midwest Book Reviews

"An elegantly penned, fast-paced thriller" - syndicated reviewer Simon Barrett

"A soaring start... enough tension and electricity to keep us coming back for more... and quality page-turning excitement" - Donna Coomer, Between the Lines Reviews

"The author has created a cast of characters that are realistic and complex, their intensity and interactions make the story that much more compelling and powerful. I was fascinated by Vicki's psychic abilities, her tenacity and strength peaked my interest, it felt like I was right by her side during her remote mental journeys. I absolutely fell in love with the handsome Dylan Maguire, who wouldn't fall for an Irishman with a lilting Irish brogue? I really liked how the author balanced the suspense thriller with a passionate romantic twist, it left me completely satisfied." – Jersey Girl Sizzling Book Reviews

"The action is non-stop and the reader barely has time to catch her breathe from one crisis before being plunged right into another one. Reading these books reminds me of being on a roller-coaster ride... and I love roller-coasters!!!" – It's Raining Books

"The author is truly skilled and, with her apt descriptions and well chosen words, she really amps up the suspense... There are a lot of twists and turns in the story and Ms. terrell keeps you guessing to the end." – Long and Short Reviews

"an exciting mystery that has romance, danger, modern technology along with the beauty of Ireland and it's culture that will please any reader… I loved the suspense and the wonderful love between Dylan and Vicki and the snarkiness of Brenda. I could just picture the village portrayed in the story and feel the mists and smell the peat from the bogs. I highly recommend this series." – Reviewer Kathleen Kelly

"It is pm terrell that makes it come together so magically, making us a part of their world. pm is most definitely a master wordsmith, plying her craft so well as to make us fall under her spell and never ever want to come back out. See I have a secret, I am not a big fan of suspense or mysteries and pm has made me a huge fan of her books. That alone speaks of her talent. I highly recommend her books." – Reviewer KJ Partridge

During the Cold War, the United States Government discovered that the Soviet Union had begun a psychic spy program. The goal was to infiltrate our most secure facilities and obtain information about our newest weapons and our deepest secrets. The United States intelligence community began its own psychic spy program to determine whether human beings had the capability to remotely view events occurring halfway around the world.

According to some reports, the United States Government discontinued their psychic spy initiative a few decades later.

But according to others, the program is alive and well…

And in the southeastern corner of North Carolina, the black water of the Lumber River snakes its way through Robeson County. And when it recedes, as it so often does, it leaves behind almost impenetrable black swampland, the perfect place to hide a body…

Welcome to the continuation of Black Swamp Mysteries…

1

The room was stark and cold, the dull white walls and pristine floors reflecting the character of the inhospitable Siberian winter. Vicki Boyd shivered as she watched Alexei Volkov, despite the fact that she was thousands of miles away and witnessing events unfolding only through her experienced psychic eye. The frigid temperature did not appear to affect him, however, as he stood with his back against the wall, obliquely watching through the partially opened door. The seconds ticked past as her mind's eye scoured the adjacent hallways for any sign of movement.

"All clear," she said, her voice solid and authoritative as it carried from her headset to his remote location.

"Five doors," he whispered in English laced with a heavy Russian accent before darting out of the room and down the wide, glaring corridor. At each end of the hallway were the skeletal remains of antiquated closed circuit cameras; dismantled and off-line, they had just a few short hours before a newer, highly sophisticated system would be set in place. It was this window of opportunity that had presented itself suddenly and without forewarning, setting in motion a stream of players that reached from Siberia across Europe and into the United States.

Five doors later, Alexei hesitated, his hand mere inches from the doorknob.

"Clear," Vicki said.

A shadow appeared at the end of the hall, and she added, "Hurry."

The door opened silently, Alexei slipped inside, and it closed with a quiet click just as two men rounded the corner at the far end of the hallway.

"Remain still," she ordered.

She could hear his breath in her headset; it was steady and slow despite the danger. Though she lay on a couch in a darkened room half a world away, she could clearly see him in her mind's eye: his dark hair cut so short it appeared almost shaved, his cornflower blue eyes hidden behind rimless glasses, the slightest shadow across his upper lip… His shoulders were squared and she knew underneath the button-downed shirt lurked the tensed muscles of one prepared to be captured but hoping he would never be.

"They're heading your way," Vicki said, watching the two men as they made their way toward the room in which Alexei hid.

He did not answer but his breathing slowed further until it was almost imperceptible.

One of the men laughed loudly and the other joined in as they strolled past the frosted glass door. She waited until they were nearing the opposite end of the hall before she said, "Across the room to the left is a door and immediately inside that room is another door on the left. Take it now."

It was silent on the other end, though she knew he was making his way past the desks that were conspicuously lacking any papers or activity. The slightest sound of a door opening reached her ears before she heard the unmistakable sound of computers humming.

"It's the second server on the right," she said.

They had rehearsed this countless times and now her brain buzzed with a jumble of psychic knowledge and a desire for the information that felt so close and yet so far. She could see him in her mind's eye removing the flash drive from the temporary pocket basted inside his pants, just beneath the belt. She knew he was attaching it to the server and she could hear him counting the seconds as he searched the drive.

She also knew the servers in that room were so highly guarded and classified that they were hard-wired to only two computers: those belonging to Russia's head of the Main Intelligence Directorate and the Russian President himself. They did not rely on a local area network and were certainly not connected to the Internet. Unauthorized entry to any of them would mean certain, slow and tortuous death.

"Two minutes," she said.

She heard the stopwatch at her side and knew Sam was anxiously watching the seconds tick. She felt an uneasiness begin to surface inside her, a queasiness that she first attempted to fight before she realized what was happening. Quickly, she turned her focus outward beyond the tiny room, past the inner office, through the outer office and into the hallway.

"Mlakar is returning early." The words rushed from her.

"Where is he?" Alexei's voice was curt.

"He just stepped off the elevator."

"There it is. Copying now."

Their intelligence had suggested the file was likely to be several gigabytes and the process of copying it now felt woefully sluggish.

"He's moving down the adjacent hall."

"I can't rush it."

"Ah!"

Vicki heard the man's voice as if in stereo—it boomed through her mind at the precise time that she heard a more muffled version through her headset. There was silence on the other end and for a long moment, she was afraid to speak. Then with a whoosh of air, she realized the man was outside the outer door, calling to Mlakar, the software technician, as he rounded the far corner.

"Hurry," she instructed.

"I can't rush it," he repeated. His voice was calm despite the urgency.

She could sense the sweat forming across his brow. There was only one file; to remove the drive prematurely would mean they had nothing and years of preparation would be lost.

She quickly scanned the rooms and the adjacent hallways. There was one way in and one way out. Mlakar hesitated a few doors away as the man who had been searching for him spoke in a rapid Russian dialect that she could not understand.

"Almost there." Alexei's voice remained steady despite the fact that his heartbeat had increased.

Mlakar said a few words dismissively and continued down the hallway, pausing at his office door. He placed his hand on the doorknob as the other man continued speaking.

"Agh," he interrupted, his irritation evident.

"He's coming in," Vicki said.

"I'm done."

She sensed Alexei removing the flash drive before diving behind a stack of boxes along the far wall. It was a woefully inept hiding place but there was none that was better.

Mlakar placed a lunch bag on the desk in the outer office. Though she did not understand the Russian language, his tone of voice was brusque. The other man was now cajoling as he followed him into the inner office and then the room housing the servers.

He moved to the first server and jiggled the mouse to awaken the screen from its sleep mode. The server whirred as the screen came to life. His thigh bumped the table next to him where the second server's screen still glowed from Alexei's activity, but he didn't seem to notice. He was intent on looking something up for the man who now stood sheepishly alongside him and it was now apparent that he felt his lunch had been rudely interrupted.

Finding the screen he was searching for, he jotted down a few words and handed the paper to the man.

After a tense exchange, Mlakar puffed out a stream of air. Then half-wadding the paper within his hand, he brushed past the first man and strode through the server room and past his desk to the outer door. The door was whirled open and he made no effort to hide his displeasure as he stalked down the hall, the second man on his heels.

"Almost clear," Vicki said.

She could see Alexei rushing forward to set the screen saver on the second server, causing it to go blank once more. The flash drive was tucked back into the pocket just beneath his belt. "When?" he asked.

"Now," she answered as the two men rounded the corner at the far end of the hall.

He rushed through the server room and through the open door into the hall, turning in the opposite direction.

Vicki took a deep breath. Her job felt as if it was only just beginning. Like climbing Mount Everest, getting there was presumed to be the easier part. It was while getting back that most spies were trapped and in Alexei's case, he would be caught red-handed. The flash drive was now the most important property in the world, even if only a handful of people knew about it.

"Three doors down, duck inside," she said as she spotted a uniformed officer making his rounds.

Alexei ducked inside the room, his back against the wall, as he watched the officer's darkened form move past the frosted glass.

A pain shot through Vicki's abdomen and instinctively, she sucked in her breath. The hallway began to blur as though she was peering at it from underwater. She drew her hand to her abdomen and pressed against it while she struggled to focus.

"Vicki?" Sam's voice was calm but the deeper timber reminded her of just how high the stakes were. Though he sat in a chair next to the couch, taking notes and recording the mission, she struggled to avoid focusing on him. Her concentration was required with Alexei.

"The corridor is clear to the last door," Vicki said. "Stop there."

As Alexei made his way down the corridor, she directed her focus to the adjoining hall. Two stairwell doors beckoned, though she knew from earlier Intel that the cameras had not been disconnected, as they had been elsewhere. He would have to use the elevator to descend one floor, where his presence and his security clearance would not be questioned.

She honed in on the single elevator shaft. It had stopped on the third floor. She felt herself descending into the shaft to the top of the compartment, where a grate allowed her to peer inside. A form moved toward the open doorway and then was gone.

"Get to the elevator," she directed to Alexei. "It's clear."

She could hear Alexei's breathing through her ear bud as he rushed down the wide vacant corridor toward the elevator.

The pain shot through her abdomen once more and instinctively, she cried out before she could stop herself. Perspiration broke out across her upper lip as she struggled to see through the grate into the shaft, but her vision had blurred. She squeezed her eyes shut against the throbbing as she pressed her hand more firmly against herself.

"Vicki." Sam's voice was firm. "Report."

Was someone inside the elevator? She couldn't be sure. She thought she'd seen a flash of skin but her vision had become like an impressionist painting. Focus, she told herself sternly. Focus.

"Do I press the button?" Alexei's voice was low and strained. He had undoubtedly heard her cry out; he knew something was amiss but could not know how it would impact the mission.

She hesitated. Then, "Yes."

Almost before the word escaped her lips, the doors opened. She could hear Alexei as he inhaled sharply.

"What are you doing here?" the man asked in Russian.

"Mlakar," Alexei answered. "Where the hell have you been?"

Mlakar stepped off the elevator. "How did you get here?"

"I've been looking for you."

"You don't have security access to this floor."

Alexei's voice became insistent. "Did you know your office door is standing wide open?"

"What? Oh—" Mlakar's voice broke off. Vicki listened to the sound of rapid footsteps. The pain in her belly was becoming excruciating. "Damn that idiot," he continued. "He interrupted me with his stupid problems."

"Do you know what would have happened if a supervisor had been here?" Alexei continued, his voice rising in indignation. "It's the worst kind of protocol lapse."

The footsteps stopped abruptly. "Alexei, don't, please, don't tell anyone. I know you're supposed to fill out a report, but—"

"Mlakar, what the hell? You know better than this." His voice grew louder before it became grudgingly softer. "I won't report it. But just don't let it happen again, Mlakar. God knows what could happen to you."

"Oh, thank God it was you." The footsteps began again. As they continued back down the corridor Alexei had just traversed, Vicki pulled her ear bud out of her ear.

"He's—"

"I know," Sam said. "I heard." He adjusted his own ear bud, listening for another moment to the men's conversation as he eyed Vicki. "I understand Russian, even if you do not."

"I'm sorry, Sam," she said as she struggled to stand up. "I know that was close."

"Damn near close enough to cost the man his life." He turned off the ear bud and removed it. Heavy brows that were once black were now mottled with gray and deeply furrowed. His eyes were such a deep brown that it was impossible to detect his mood by looking into them. "What's going on?"

"Nothing," she lied as she held her stomach with both hands. She swung her legs over the side of the couch and sat up, though the room swam with the effort. "I'm just feeling ill all the sudden, is all."

"You said you could do this."

"I thought I could. I did. He made it, Sam."

"He hasn't 'made it' until he's out of Siberia and out of Russia." He turned off the audio equipment. "Anyway, it's your last mission." He waved in the direction of her stomach. "You're officially on maternity leave."

2

It was only half past four but already the sun was dipping close to the horizon against the backdrop of a spectacular ombré sky. The street lamps began to flicker before turning to a continuous glow, casting a cozy muted yellow light through the bedroom windows on the third floor of the Victorian home.

Dylan Maguire paused in his packing long enough to switch on the nightstand lamp, instantly transforming the large room into the warm, welcoming place he'd grown to love. He caught his reflection in the dresser mirror; the sleeves on his red and black plaid shirt had been rolled up, revealing the hint of muscled biceps, while faded jeans hid his long legs. A lock of dark hair had fallen across his brow and though he pushed it to the side with the back of his hand, it reappeared instantly.

The television hummed across the room with a 24-hour news station, but he paid it little attention. Christmas was a mere two weeks away, but even more importantly, his marriage to Vicki Boyd would take place in Ireland in less than 48 hours. Vicki's bags were already packed and waiting at the top of the stairs like a couple of impatient children, though their plane wouldn't leave until morning.

Despite his best intentions, Dylan was just now beginning to pack, though he knew it wouldn't take long. The day had slipped past too rapidly as he worked alongside Sam, who had agreed to take care of the freshwater angelfish business they used as a front to cover their CIA activities. The last time he cared for them had been just a few months earlier, which had nearly ended in catastrophe. He hoped the man had acquired a bit of fish sense since then, though in all honesty, Sam was a CIA section chief accustomed to sitting behind a desk. Rolling up his sleeves and diving an arm into a tank didn't come easily for him.

Ah, but at least he would do better with the dog, Shep. His border collie had taken an instant liking to Sam and even to Sam's fluffy white Persian, Chloe, and truth be told, Sam had bonded with Shep as well.

As Dylan added the last bit of clothing to his luggage, he mentally rehearsed the next few days for the hundredth time. Red sky at night, sailor's delight, he thought with a glance toward the sunset. Though they would be flying, it was still a good omen. He and Vicki would leave at first light for the Fayetteville Airport just thirty minutes away from their home in Lumberton, North Carolina, which would take them to Atlanta. They would have several hours to kill before boarding a red-eye to Ireland. By the time the sun was rising over the Emerald Isle, they would be landing.

Sam would also fly over, but he was taking a private flight to Dublin, where he had some business to conduct before making the drive to the wedding. As Vicki's adoptive father, he would, of course, give away her hand in marriage. Then he'd return to North Carolina, his duties with the Agency, and to hopefully ensure none of the breeder fish died in their absence. It might only be a front, but Dylan had grown partial to the beautiful angels and their wee eggs.

Dylan's boyhood friend Thomas Rowan—now known as Father Thomas, he reminded himself with a smile—would perform the ceremony. He'd left the arrangements to Vicki, who had promptly drafted Thomas' mother into assisting, something he suspected the woman was rather excited to be doing as she had no daughters herself. He assumed half the village would be present and while he preferred something more private and simple, well, if asking half of Eire to attend made Vicki happy, that was all that mattered, now wasn't it?

He recognized Sam's heavy steps as he climbed the stairs from the first floor. Vicki's mission must be over. He was relieved that it was to be her last one. Between the wedding, a honeymoon, and the baby's birth less than five months away, it was a lot to consume the woman without the thought of psychic missions weighing on her as well.

The sound of Sam's voice wafted up the stairs. Cocking his head, he concluded the man was on the phone. He cut his eyes back to the telly. Hundreds of people were standing beneath the famous St. Louis arch, pointing at the skies.

He turned the sound up as Sam reached the bedroom door, switching off his phone.

"What's up?" Sam said, stopping just inside the door to watch the television screen.

Dylan chuckled. "It appears some are seein' UFO's now." He turned it off. "No doubt we'll find out in time that a remake o' 'War o' the Worlds' was underway and it wasn't wee green men after all."

"Yeah, Dylan, listen," Sam started, growing somber. "I need for you—"

"No work. Not today." He zipped his luggage closed and carried it to the top of the steps, where he deposited it alongside Vicki's.

"So," Sam said almost too casually, "it's almost time." His voice sounded bored, something Dylan suspected he worked quite hard at perfecting. He'd seen the man in some precarious situations and his tone rarely changed.

"Aye," Dylan replied, "and so it is."

"You nervous?"

He shook his head. "No. Well, perhaps a wee bit. Where's Vicki?"

"Downstairs. This pregnancy's been hard on her."

"That it has. Her mornin' sickness hasn't subsided yet." He waved his hand in mock dismissal. "Ah, truth be told, it isn't mornin' sickness at'al but all-day and all-night sickness."

"She's lost weight, I think."

"Aye, and she's none to spare… She has nausea and backaches and 'er feet 'ave ballooned and her kidneys 'ave shrunk…" He sighed.

"And she's got more than four months to go."

"Ooohhh." He couldn't imagine her climbing two flights of steps to their bedroom as he envisioned her waddling like a penguin on a couple of stick legs, her hands constantly rubbing her bloated belly. "We'll muddle through it. For sure, it'll all be sorted and in the end, we'll have the child we both want."

Almost on cue, he heard the rail straining and her soft but rapid steps on the stairs. They grew faster as they cleared the first landing and he nodded to Sam. "Best get out o' the path to the facilities," he said, his eyes cutting over to the master bathroom.

Sam side-stepped closer to the bed. "Listen, Dylan," he said, his voice growing low, "I need for you to do something for me while you're in Ireland."

"You'd not be givin' me an assignment, I can tell y' that," he responded. "I'm about to be married and then I'll be on me honeymoon with only one thought in this head o' mine."

"I just need to—"

"—bugger off," he finished for him. Vicki's feet cleared the top landing. He opened his mouth to greet her but she whirled past them both in a flash of long strawberry blond hair, the bathroom door closing behind her in an urgent slam.

"What—?" Sam began.

Dylan shook his head. "Like y' said, Sam, she's had a tough time o' it, she has."

"Hhmm." He stood awkwardly, one arm limp at his side while the other clutched a file. Dylan eyed the manila envelope suspiciously. Work was not happening on this trip.

"So, anyway," Sam continued, clearing his throat and shifting his feet, "as I was saying—"

He was interrupted by the sounds of a painful thud, shattered glass and Vicki's startled cry. In two long, quick steps, Dylan had cleared the opposite edge of the bed and in two more, he was at the bathroom door. "Vicki?" he shouted, the insistence in his voice matching the urgency of his heartbeat. Without waiting for an answer, he threw open the door.

Vicki lay in a heap on the bathroom floor. A china figurine and bottles of cologne that had been carefully arranged on the dressing table were scattered across the floor, as if she'd thrown her arm out to break her fall but succeeded only in tumbling the table's contents along with her. The tile was covered in blood and as he bent to pick her up, his eyes raced over her. But the fleeting thought that she'd cut herself on the glass was instantly replaced by a realization that grabbed his chest like a vise. She lay in a pool of blood that was growing thicker by the moment.

His hands were upon her arms almost ready to pull her to her feet when something stopped him. It took only a split second to register her hands on her belly, her incoherent moaning, and her blood-soaked clothing.

"Sam!" he shouted. He whirled his head in the older man's direction. Sam had followed him to the door, where he stood frozen; his face ashen. "Call for an ambulance!"

Before he had finished speaking, Sam was dialing 9-1-1, the phone rising to his ear even as his eyes remained riveted on the scene before him.

3

The sky was as black as a bucket of coal. Dylan was vaguely aware of a heavy downpour that had ended just moments before, leaving the parking lot outside the hospital drenched in inky pools. The melancholy atmosphere matched the heavy weight in Dylan's chest as he stood at the window at the end of a hall that reeked of antiseptic.

His eyes drifted downward but his mind barely registered the activity below. Regularly spaced utility lights fought vainly against the darkness and he found his attention wandering back to the sky where presumably God lived.

It was impossible not to recall another day and another time half a world away, when he stood at another window with this same vacant feeling washing over him. It had been raining then too; the ground below swallowed in water as black as the skies while his wife and his child had both lain lifeless at the end of a morbidly impersonal corridor. It had smelled the same, as if there was but one sterile solution for all hospitals and they all competed for the strongest stench.

But it had also been different, he reminded himself. Alana had been nine months pregnant, her labor anticipated with the naïve delight of first-time parents. They'd mapped out their child's progress until they knew exactly where he or she would attend school—even which university—what vocations would be best, as well as what sacrifices they would make to ensure their child's imminent success.

Failure had not been anticipated and certainly not addressed. Women had given birth through time immemorial and only a midwife would be required. The child would be born healthy—ten little fingers and ten little toes, as his grandmother, Mam, liked to say. And when she'd gone into labor at home, they both thought it would be a matter of hours before they held their child in their arms.

He placed an arm against the glass and leaned into it, his forehead resting against his forearm as his eyes continued peering at the ground below without really seeing it. His mind was three thousand miles away, remembering his frantic calls to the midwife, a woman who lived in the next village over—a village, as it turned out, that was too far removed in the end. But how were they to have known that a driving rainstorm—the worst in decades— would eventually cut off access to their tiny cottage? How were they to have known the baby would breech? Or that Alana—my Alana—

His hand balled into a fist and he closed his eyes against the images. She'd never made it to a proper hospital; she'd died in his arms. He still remembered—he would always remember—the look of panic on his friend Thomas' broad face as he helped to hold the rowboat steady while Dylan lifted his wife into it, her belly swollen and her cries agonizing against any movement—or no movement at all. Yet she'd hung in there for the boat ride to a rain-swollen hill, where Thomas had left his car for them. She'd tried valiantly to survive despite a frenzied drive through the countryside, a ride on narrow, winding roads that too often had been sliced in half by the gale-force winds and driving rains.

Beads of perspiration broke out against his brow, just as it had back then. He remembered all too well how Alana's silence had begun to worry him even more than her cries had; how he'd begged her to hang on as time and again, he was forced by rising waters to turn back and try another route, hoping against hope that the next one would lead him to someone who could help deliver their child and end her suffering.

No, he thought. It was different then. She'd never made it to a hospital.

She'd died in his arms, her sweat and his tears merging into one. She'd known she was dying when the last physical exertion she would ever make was to reach to his shirt sleeve and tug on it. Her lips had been cracked and dry when she asked him to stop the car. He hadn't wanted to; he had wanted to keep driving. But there had been something about her voice, something about her eyes; something left unsaid that caused him to stop the car right there in the middle of the roadway. She'd asked him to hold her and she'd told him that she loved him. And then she'd closed her eyes.

Had she heard him when he told her how much he loved her? How much he needed her? Or was she gone before the words could escape his lips?

He felt his fist tighten against the glass as his other hand stiffened against his leg. What were the odds, he wondered, of impregnating two women and of both of them losing the child? What message could God have been intending to make, and certainly with the power the church said He had, He could have found a different way to impart it?

He heard the sound of a throat clearing behind him and of feet shuffling against the tile. It was only then that he realized his sleeve was wet. He wondered briefly whether his sobs had been audible before quickly deciding that he didn't give a wee rat's arse.

"I went by Vicki's room." Sam's voice was subdued.

Dylan gave a half-nod without turning around.

"I wasn't allowed to see her," Sam continued. He cleared his throat again. "The nurses were in with her… They said you'd come down this way, toward the chapel…"

He could feel Sam's presence behind him but he didn't respond. An awkward moment of silence passed and then Sam inhaled.

"I guess—if you need me—"

"She lost the baby." The words sounded brusque and for a moment Dylan wished he could take them back, as if the child wouldn't have passed away if he hadn't have spoken the words aloud. He felt more than heard Sam's stunned reaction. After a moment, he wiped his eyes against an area of his shirt sleeve that had until then miraculously managed to remain dry, and he turned around.

Sam's lips moved but no words managed to escape. His eyes were locked briefly on Dylan's before they skittered as if he was trying to think of something to say. He moved to a nearby bench and sat heavily. "Are you sure?"

Dylan joined him before answering. "She miscarried."

"But—but she was nearly five months along. It was too late to miscarry."

"Apparently not."

"I don't understand."

"You're not about makin' this any easier on me, are y' now?" Before waiting for an answer, he continued, "They called it placental abruption."

"What the hell does that mean?"

He shrugged. At least the conversation was helping to alleviate some of the tension. He waved his hands. "It means 'er female parts separated."

"What?"

He shook his head. "They couldn't do anythin'. 'God's will,' the nurse said."

"God's will, my ass."

"My thoughts precisely."

They sat in relative silence, each with their own thoughts against the backdrop of call buttons sounding at the nurses' station and occasional moans from rooms down the hall. A man swore gruffly and the elevator dinged as the doors opened down an adjoining corridor.

"How's Vicki?" Sam asked finally.

"I haven't yet spoken to 'er." He waved a hand toward the nurse's station. "They're to get me when it's time."

"Time for what?"

"Time to take 'er home, I suppose."

"They're not keeping her overnight?"

"They said she's better off at home, away from the germs o' the hospital…"

Sam stared at the floor. "Do you know if she's—I mean—"

"Physically, she should be fine. But they're yet to know whether she can conceive again."

Sam shook his head. "Dylan, I'm sorry."

He nodded wordlessly.

"I—I know what you've been through. And I know this is tough on you."

"Aye. Well."

Another moment of silence passed before Sam asked quietly, "Do you think you'll postpone…?" His voice drifted off as if he was reluctant to speak the words.

Dylan met his eyes. "I'll be marryin' Vicki Boyd if she's able to travel, day after the morrow in Ireland. And if she's not," he added, his voice growing firm, "I'll be weddin' 'er 'ere as quickly as I can be procurin' the license."

A small smile tugged at Sam's lips. But before he could respond, the sound of footsteps brought both men to their feet.

"You can see her now," the nurse announced.

~~~

Vicki was standing at the window, her back to the door as Dylan entered. He hesitated at the doorway and out of the corner of his eye he spotted Sam hanging back in an effort to give them privacy.

Her hair, normally sleek and shiny, was unkempt and hanging in folds as if it had been drenched in perspiration. She was a petite woman—barely five foot three—but now she appeared even smaller, even more fragile. Though he was fairly certain that she sensed his presence, she did not turn around. Glancing beyond her, he saw the same black sky and the same forlorn parking lot he'd been staring at just moments before.

He quietly stepped behind her and slipped his arms around her waist. "Should you be out o' bed now, darlin'?"

She sighed deeply as her palms moved to his forearms. He glanced down at her small hands on his strong arms. They looked dainty and pale. "I'm sorry, Dylan."

He pressed his face against her strawberry blond hair
~~~

where it cascaded past her neck. "It's no matter."

She whirled around. "How can you—?"

"There will be others," he interrupted. "I promise y' that."

"But how can you be sure? The doctors—"

"I'm sure."

"And what if I can't?"

"Then we'll 'ave one another."

Her eyes looked tired; they were puffy and lined; the outer edges downturned.

"Should y' be standin'?"

"What? Yes. I'm fine."

"And the doctor—he said it was safe to travel, did he?"

"Do you—?" She hesitated. "Do you still want to marry me?"

"What? Certainly I do." He guided her to the bed and eased her onto the coarse white sheet. Keeping his fingers locked in hers, he gently sat beside her. He thought his heart was going to break in two. He wanted to bury his face in her hair and cry the tears that were right at the brink. Like drops of water at the edge of a waterfall, all he had to do was stop struggling and simply allow himself to plummet over the precipice. He smiled weakly. "I've already got the ring." His feeble attempt at a joke did not elicit the smile for which he longed; that tender smile that could stop him in his tracks, cause him to fall in love with her all over again; that smile to which even the moon and the sun appeared lackluster in comparison.

Her fingers traced the dimple in his cheek. "Now you don't have to, you know."

"I didn't need to before. I wanted to. The fact that y' were with child was just the *Meisterstuck,* wouldn't y' know." He wrapped his arm around her and pulled her close. He rested his chin atop her head and when he continued his voice was strong; thankfully, it did not betray his inner angst. "We'll have wee ones someday, darlin'. We've plenty o' time."

"It's just that—I really wanted to have this child."

"I know." He squeezed his eyes shut. "I did as well."

"You'd make such a great father."

He swallowed, tamping down his emotions. "There'll be time enough for that. Right now," he said, squeezing her tighter, "it's the time for us. You and me, Vicki. We'll go to Ireland if you're up to it—"

"I am. I'm always up for it."

"Aye, then."

"And Father Thomas will marry us?" She tilted her head back where she could look him in the eye.

He smiled. "Aye. And Father Thomas will marry us."

4

Vicki studied her image in the full-length mirror. It was a picture-perfect day with delicate blue skies and cottony clouds, no doubt brought about by the Child of Prague. The tiny statue had been placed at the church earlier in the day—a superstition that didn't really matter, as rain on a wedding day also was considered good luck by the Irish as if it simply was not acceptable to have bad luck on one's wedding day.

The sun shone optimistically through the church window, so ancient that the dimpled glass morphed the rays into shimmering shapes as it spread across the room like fairy dust. They illuminated a dainty gold strand that had been braided alongside her head before being caught up in a delicate chignon at the nape of her neck. Her hair, she had to admit, looked radiant. At intervals along the braid were carefully positioned shamrocks; barely the size of a thumbnail apiece, they were just enough to provide an added dose of good luck.

Father Thomas' mother, Mrs. Rowan, clucked beside her in admiration, her hands folded demurely atop a burgeoning middle. She'd meticulously applied Vicki's cosmetics and she had to admit, the woman had done a wonderful job. Somehow she had managed to hide the dark circles under her eyes that had appeared from lack of sleep combined with the shadows left by the loss of the baby.

She skimmed her hands over her abdomen. Her gown was the most subtle shade of blue she'd ever seen and the matching lace was nothing short of angelic. It had been fashioned for a larger belly and though the extra fabric had been expertly gathered and pinned beneath a light tan sash, she felt the baby's absence with a fresh, razor-sharp pain.

It was her wedding day. It was supposed to be one of the most joyous occasions in her life. So why did she feel like crawling under a rock? Had it really been less than 48 hours since she'd miscarried?

She'd stood at the window in the hospital room, staring at the parking lot below; in a fleeting moment of desperation and anguish, she'd wished that she had died along with her child. She'd wondered what it might feel like to open the window wide and leap out; she'd pondered whether six stories and an asphalt pavement would kill, and not just maim. In an insanely grief-stricken moment, she'd even had her hand on the lock handle when Dylan had entered the room.

He'd interrupted her, and she'd pretended that she was stronger than she really was.

"Marry in blue, lover be true," Mrs. Rowan crowed with a wide smile and a twinkle in her merry eyes, mistaking Vicki's attention to her gown as admiration of the color. She stepped forward and adjusted the sash's elaborate bow at the small of her back. "And marry in tan, he'll be a loved man. Ah, but the colors bring out your amber eyes. Such gorgeous eyes y' have."

"You've been wonderful to me," Vicki said, turning toward her.

"Mick is a second son to me," she said, using the name by which Dylan had been known before leaving Ireland for America. "He always has been and always will be. And any wife o' his is a daughter o' mine."

"I wish my mother could see me," she murmured. "You know that my parents passed away when I was young?"

"Ah, I did. First time Mick brought y' home, I asked all about y'. But dear, both yer parents are lookin' down upon y' this day, wouldn't y' know it now? I feel their pride in y', I do."

Vicki's lips curled into a shy smile. "I hope you're right." She turned back to admire her reflection once more. "They would have loved Dylan—Mick."

"There's a lot to love there, for sure. What a man he's grown into… Oh," she added, "I have a couple o' items for y' still." She waddled to a corner table and returned with a dainty handkerchief. "It's pure Irish linen," she said, beaming. "Only the best for y'. See the lace there? Hand-sewn, it was. In Belfast, no less. It's known as a 'magic hanky', dear. When yer child comes—for surely y' will conceive again, and more than once—w' just a couple o' stitches it turns into a christenin' cap. It's a family heirloom, y' see. It was worn by Mick's mother and then by Mick hisself at his christenin'…"

Vicki grasped the elegant handkerchief and tried to envision something so small fitting on Dylan's head. "Where did you find this?" she murmured.

"Ah, my dear friend Bonnie O'Sullivan had it, y' know," she said.

Vicki smiled. Bonnie O'Sullivan had been Dylan's grandmother but they both referred to her as Mam. It sounded a bit odd to hear her full name spoken now.

"She'd worn it at her own marriage as well," Mrs. Rowan continued. "I still miss that woman. She was my dearest friend in all the world. Though she pays me a visit every now and again, she does."

Vicki jerked her head up. Dylan's grandmother had passed away only a few months before. Mam had raised him after his return from America. He'd been perhaps all of three years old when he came to live with her. His father, apparently overwhelmed with the duties of fatherhood, left them without a word while in New York; not even a simple good-bye. Mam had scraped together enough money to get her daughter and her young grandson back home, and then Dylan's mother had succumbed to an alcohol addiction and left, leaving her son behind.

"I wish Dylan's mother could be here," she said quietly as she fingered the lace.

"Yes, dear. Don't y' know, we all wish she'd been more o' a mother to that child… But who knows where she's about, or what she's been doin' to fill her time. It'll be a grand day nonetheless. Focus on the positive, dear." She took the handkerchief from her and carefully folded it, tucking and pinning it neatly behind the sash.

A knock at the door interrupted her work.

"Aye?" Mrs. Rowan called out.

"It's Sam," came a gruff voice. Before they could respond, he cracked the door open. "They're waiting."

"It's time." Vicki felt her heart beat faster and she suddenly had a shortness of breath.

"You're beautiful," he said. He stepped just inside the door, his eyes taking in Vicki's appearance from her satin shoes to the braid in her hair as she admired him in return. She was so accustomed to seeing him in casual attire or in a standard business suit when the occasion warranted. Now he was dressed in a tux that fit him so well that he appeared twenty years younger. His face was softened, his eyes almost dewy.

"Dylan—?" she asked.

"He's beside himself." He chuckled. "Kept Thomas and me up half the night. The boy's a bundle of nerves."

She smiled. She hadn't seen him since they had arrived in the village. She'd been whisked off to the cottage they'd rented on their first visit to Ireland, and Dylan had been taken in the opposite direction by the village men. She'd been concerned at first, afraid of spending an entire night alone with the memories of her first journey there with Dylan and her sister Brenda, who had been unable to attend the wedding due to a rather lengthy prison sentence. But Mrs. Rowan had never left her side. There was enough food to feed an army in the tiny cottage, and it seemed like every surface contained a fresh bouquet of flowers. After she'd arisen the next morning, the woman had even replaced the sheets with a special set of "wedding linen". There certainly seemed like an unending array of Irish traditions and Mrs. Rowan apparently remembered each and every one.

Now the older woman hurried to Vicki's side with a bouquet of white flowers. The Lily-of-the-Valley, Sweet William, Myrtle and Hyacinth were surrounded by delicate shamrocks and two satin ribbons—one blue to match Vicki's dress and the other tan, to match her sash.

She held it slightly aloft, and Vicki sucked in her breath at the sight of a porcelain horseshoe underneath.

"Hold the horseshoe like a handle," Mrs. Rowan instructed. "When the ceremony is done, Mick can hang the horseshoe above yer front door. It's always pointed up, so the luck won't run out, y' know."

Sam held out his arm and Vicki slipped her hand into the crook of his elbow. He patted her hand and when she looked up at him, surprised at his tenderness, he winked.

As they left the room at the end of the hallway, she could hear the sound of Irish pipes playing. Lighter in sound than a Scottish bagpipe, they sounded almost like flutes. The music was haunting, melodic and hypnotizing.

She would have been content with a simple ceremony. She'd always thought that a woman either looked forward to the wedding or looked forward to the marriage, and she'd been the practical type that preferred the latter. But Mrs. Rowan would hear none of it, and now as they entered the narthex, she caught her first glimpse of the nave through the open door. The tiny cathedral was filled.

They stopped just short of the door. Time stood still and time snaked past, an unending parade of seconds in which her breath caught in her throat and her hand clamped shut against Sam's arm. He stood ramrod straight as if unaware that her fingers were digging into him; instead, he peered down the aisle toward the altar table like an impassive statue. Her eyes darted through the audience; most she vaguely recognized as villagers who had attended Mam's wake. No doubt they had known Dylan throughout his entire life. She felt tears begin to form as it dawned on her that they now recognized her as one of their own.

She didn't realize the tempo of the music had changed until Sam began to move forward. He rested his free hand atop hers, patting it encouragingly as they calmly, sedately, made their way down an aisle that appeared as though it would go on and on forever. As the mournful chords of the uilleann began to play at her heartstrings, she came dreadfully close to bursting into tears. In an instant, everything seemed to collide: the difficult pregnancy, the cruel miscarriage, her flat belly, the long plane ride over the Atlantic and two sleepless nights.

Then her eyes came to rest upon Dylan.

He stood in front of the altar, a sheen on his dark hair cast by the sunlight that wound its way through the towering stained-glass windows. She locked her gaze onto his. His normally hazel eyes appeared sea green and as she drew nearer, she realized they were moist. Though he remained immobile, his hands folded neatly in front of him, his eyes offered the encouragement she longed for; the knowledge that she would be alright. She drew strength from his eyes and felt her own tears slip away as her heart began to soar.

She'd never seen him appear so sophisticated. His black tuxedo seemed to be tailored for his body. The high collar of his white shirt and the black bow tie accentuated his features and she realized as she came within a few steps of him, that his five o'clock shadow was gone. She wanted to reach out and touch his cheeks, to run her finger along his dimples… His lips turned up and she realized he'd been watching her expression in amusement. As he stepped forward, it was as if no one else existed.

She vaguely heard Father Thomas' voice and Sam's deeper one responding, but she didn't remember Sam leaving her side. In one moment, she was walking down the aisle, holding onto his arm as if her life depended on it. Then in the next, she was holding onto Dylan's more muscular arm and turning to face the priest.

Thomas was as tall as Dylan and broad-shouldered, but there the similarities ended. His hair was light brown with golden highlights and it was long, brushing past his collar as if in defiance of the solemnity of his cleric's robe. His sideburns reached toward his jawbone in a style reminiscent of bygone years but which somehow looked perfectly modern on him, and he sported a trim mustache. His eyes reminded her of Mam's—sharp as a tack, as her mother used to say—and as blue and sparkling as an ocean on a clear summer day.

If there was ever a time in which she wanted to memorize every word, every detail and each breath she took, it was now. Yet she found herself unable to decipher all the Latin that Father Thomas uttered and her heart began to beat erratically as she struggled to remember all that she was expected to do.

She hadn't realized that she'd missed a cue until the priest leaned toward her, smiling. He winked as he whispered, "Take the ribbon and encircle Mick's—Dylan's—hand."

A young woman stepped quietly to her side, easing her wedding bouquet from her hands. Out of the corner of her eye, she saw a beautiful little girl with copper curls holding a tiny tufted pillow. She reminded her of her younger sister Brenda when she was a child. Dutifully, Vicki received the ornate gold ribbon from Thomas and encircled Dylan's hand with quivering fingers. When she looked up, she found his eyes on her. He half-nodded, unable to stop a crooked smile. Then he accepted the portion of the ribbon not yet tied and encircled one of her hands with it. His own hands were steady and firm as he squeezed hers in reassurance. Father Thomas began encircling them both as he recited in a voice that resonated through the sanctuary,

"Do you, Michael Dylan Maguire, take Victoria Freeman Boyd, to be your wife, to be her constant friend, her partner in life, and her true love? To love her without reservation, honor and respect her, protect her from harm, comfort her in times of distress, and to grow with her in mind and spirit?"

Without taking his eyes from Vicki's, his voice rang out solid and strong. "I do indeed."

The priest turned to her. "And do you, Victoria Freeman Boyd, take Michael Dylan Maguire to be your husband, to be his constant friend, his partner in life, and his true love? To love him without reservation, honor and respect him, protect him from harm, comfort him in times of distress, and to grow with him in mind and spirit?"

She parted her lips to respond, knowing that her voice would ring through the cathedral with the conviction she felt in her heart. She felt Dylan's hands grasp her more tightly under the confines of the ribbon as she answered, "I do."

When the priest placed his hands atop theirs, she felt the heat emanate from them both. Their hands felt heavy yet supportive against hers as Father Thomas recited in his lilting Irish brogue:

"Happy is the bride that rain falls on
May your mornings bring joy and your evenings bring peace.
May your troubles grow few as your blessings increase.
May the saddest day of your future
Be no worse than the happiest day of your past.
May your hands be forever clasped in friendship
And your hearts joined forever in love.
Your lives are very special,
God has touched you in many ways.
May his blessings rest upon you
And fill all your coming days.
We swear by peace and love to stand,
Heart to heart and hand to hand.
Hark, O Spirit, and hear us now,
Confirming this Sacred Vow."

Carefully, he unwrapped the ribbon and with a flourish, he laid it atop the pillow held by the young girl.

"The ring," Father Thomas said.

Dylan turned to a young boy who looked like he

would rather be anywhere else but there. When the boy failed to produce the ring, he bent down and whispered to him. He stuck his little hand in his pocket, pulling it inside out until the ring was visible. Chuckling, Dylan picked it out and blew off the fuzz from the pocket before handing it to the priest amid quiet laughter from the pews.

As the priest's blessing commenced, Vicki's eyes locked onto the dainty ring. It was the Claddagh he had given her just a few months before when he'd asked her to marry him. She remembered now, taking the ring off as they arrived in Dublin and just before Dylan was whisked away in one direction and she in another.

When she had accepted his proposal, he had placed the ring on her left hand with the heart facing outward, explaining that it meant they were engaged. Now as the priest handed the ring back to him, he turned it so the heart would face inward.

"Repeat after me," Father Thomas said.

He took a breath but before he could continue, Dylan interjected in a voice that resonated through the church, "I take you my heart at the risin' o' the moon and the settin' o' the stars. To love and to honour through all that may come. Through all our lives together, in all our lives, may we be reborn that we may meet and know and love again, and remember."

"Well done," the priest whispered.

Then Vicki turned to the beautiful young girl, who lifted up the pillow with Dylan's ring resting cozily in the middle. "Thank you," Vicki said with a wide smile as she accepted the ring. As she repeated the words to Dylan that he had just said to her, she slipped a more masculine version of the Claddagh onto a thickset finger.

"Do you have the coin?" Father Thomas asked.

Again, Dylan turned to the young boy. Amid chuckles from the audience, the pants pockets were turned inside out again until a once-shiny coin appeared. Turning back to Vicki, he placed it in the palm of her hand. Holding it there against her skin, he said, "I give you this as a token of all I possess, of all that I have, of all I will have."

In response, she drew a breath. She knew that the priest was there to guide her through her reply and she had fully expected to need his help through her wedding day jitters. Yet she spoke from the heart, the words rolling off her tongue as though she had attended a thousand Irish weddings and knew the blessing by heart.

"There are four things," she said, "that you must never do: lie, steal, cheat, or drink. But if you must lie, then lie in my arms. And if you must steal, steal away my heart. If you must cheat, then cheat death. And if you must drink, drink in the moments that take your breath away."

Dylan grasped her hands in both of his. A teardrop formed at the outer corner of his eye and he turned his head away from their audience as he blinked it away. It was Vicki's turn now to clasp his hands in reassurance.

The priest raised both his arms. "By the power that Christ brought from heaven, mayst thou love one another. As the sun follows its course, mayst thou follow each other. As light to the eye, as bread to the hungry, as joy to the heart, may thy presence be with one another forever and through eternity.

"I now pronounce you husband and wife."

Dylan's hands nearly flew from hers to wrap her in his embrace. His smooth cheek swept across hers until his lips discovered her own.

"You may kiss the bride!" Father Thomas announced belatedly amid the laughter of the audience.

Though she heard the laughter and a sob or two, the clamor might have been a world away. In her heart, there was only the two of them, enfolded within one another's arms.

5

It was only half past four but already the clouds were shrouded in Prussian blue. They were moving quickly, Dylan thought. They swooped in from the Atlantic Ocean headed for the Irish Sea. By the time the sun had completely set, they would be carried out to sea, leaving behind a star-filled sky. Unmarred by competing city lights or the haze of pollution, the constellations were always spectacular on the Emerald Isle and with a wee bit of luck, they may even be able to see the aurora borealis on their honeymoon.

The sounds of music and laughter cut through his solitary mood. The reception had been boisterous all afternoon but then, what's an Irish wedding without the celebration? Guinness had been flowing like water, the mandolins had played continuously, and the steady melody of tapping was a tell-tale sign the step-dancers hadn't slowed a bit.

The fellowship hall at the church was nearly full to overflowing and the crush of bodies had left him yearning for the crisp night air and the serenity of the countryside that gently flowed just beyond the church's doors. Just a few yards from the building rested a low stone wall. He stopped when he reached it, placing his glass atop the well-worn granite. From the church's position atop a hill, he could barely make out the twinkling lights of the village below, some two miles away as the crow flies.

It was said if one could see the village lights from the church, it was going to rain. And if the lights weren't visible at all, it was already raining.

"Ah, there you are."

Dylan recognized the voice before turning around to face Sam. He lifted his glass, half-saluted him with it, and downed a swallow. "Sláinte."

"Glad I caught you alone." Sam also had a drink in his hand and now he stopped beside Dylan, sipping his beer and peering in the general direction of the village. His bow tie had been loosened and his shirt sleeves rolled up nearly to his elbows. "Congratulations."

"Thank you."

"So you're heading off on your honeymoon after this?"

"Tomorrow. Tonight we'll be stayin' in a cottage not far from 'ere."

"The one by the pond?"

"That would be the one. Vicki likes it there."

"And tomorrow?"

"Northwest o' here." He chuckled. "For sure, I never thought I'd move to America only to spend m' honeymoon in Ireland."

"Why not stay right here? As you said, Vicki likes it here."

"Ah, but I wanted it to be special." He took another sip and savored the way it slipped smoothly down his throat. "I've let a suite at a manor house. It's not a castle by any means, but it's upper-crust for sure. Horse stables, boating and the like. And it's off season so we're likely to have the place almost to ourselves."

"How close will you be to Donegal?"

"Donegal, 'eh?" He narrowed his eyes suspiciously. "Why?"

Sam looked off into the distance as if something there had garnered his attention. "I need you to pick up something for me."

"Are you talkin' work now, or a sweet tweed cap?"

"Tweed cap would be nice. But there's more."

Dylan sighed. "I'm listenin'."

"There's a pub in Donegal known as Deoch, Ceol agus Craic. Do you know it?"

"Never been there."

"It's away from the tourists, where the locals go."

"So you're away w' the locals now, are y' Sam?"

He glanced at him out of the corner of his eye before continuing. "Tomorrow. One o'clock. Far end of the bar. A table will be reserved for you and Vicki. Lunch is on me."

"That's kind o' you."

Sam turned to face him. "A man at the bar will give you a microchip."

"I'd be knowin' there was a catch in there somewhere."

"After you've left Donegal, text me. The message will be 'had the fish and chips'. I'll know you have it."

"And if I don't?"

"You had steak and Guinness."

Dylan finished off his drink. "And what am I to do w' it?"

"I'll be in touch with instructions."

A sliver of light grew from the church to the wall, encompassing them in a golden hue.

"I've been looking for you," Vicki called as she stepped from the doorway onto the path. The music grew louder, along with the sound of clapping and laughter, briefly invading the courtyard before Vicki pushed the door closed behind her.

"I was just giving Dylan my congratulations," Sam said, spreading out one arm to encompass her within it as she drew near. "And congratulations to you as well."

"Thanks for giving me away."

"It was my pleasure. Something I never thought I'd have the chance to do."

"Will you be staying—?"

He shook his head. "I'm leaving tonight." Over her objections, he added, "I've got some angelfish to care for, remember? And I need to pick up Shep and Chloe from the boarding facility. Anyway, you two need to start your honeymoon. And without your boss hanging around."

"Tonight you're not my boss," Vicki said, smiling. "Tonight you're my dad."

"Next you'll want some sort of dowry," he said gruffly, dropping his arm from her.

"A dowry, y' say?" Dylan said, laughing. "I get money out o' the deal, do I now?"

Sam was already halfway across the lawn to the church. He half-waved but didn't turn back around. "Only when I'm dead and gone."

6

It was still as dark as Hades when the alarm sounded. Jack rolled over, groaning as he fumbled in the dark for the clock button. He might have cursed, had there been a woman there to hear him, but what's the bother since he was alone. He pressed the button but peered, sleepy-eyed, at the clock face until the time registered in his muddled mind. Why he bothered, he didn't know. The alarm sounded each morning at precisely six o'clock and wouldn't you know, it was six o'clock now.

Awkwardly, he swung his legs over the side of the bed and forced himself to sit up. It was freezing cold. Heat must have gone out again. Of course it had. It was buggered more often than not.

He buried his head in his hands, the gnarled fingers combing through his hair as he tried to awaken. His hair was thick and was once as black as a raven; now it sported gray veins that seemed to grow ever more prominent. Truth be told, the gray had begun at the age of twenty-three when he was first picked up off the streets of Belfast and beaten nearly to unconsciousness. Had it not been for his mates happening upon him looking for trouble their own selves, he most certainly would have died that night. And for the millionth time, he wondered if that might not have been such a bad thing after all. It certainly would have saved him a lifetime of agony and the devil the bother of finding him twice.

A tickle in the depths of his throat sent panic through him, causing him to awaken more fully. He swallowed hard, trying to tamp down the urge to cough. Ach, it was the coughing that would punish him the rest of his life, he thought. It could bring him to his knees and cause him to blubber like a baby, even now after all these years. The swallowing was bad; it was always bad. But the coughing was pure torture, a gift from Iron Maggie that just kept on giving.

Still swallowing purposefully, he rose from the side of the bed and crossed to the kitchenette in the corner. He poured water into a dented kettle and set it on a portable camping stove to boil. The tea would relax his throat, for sure. It always did.

Away from the bedcovers now, the chill invaded his bones. He rubbed his fingers together, blowing on them for warmth before holding them a couple of inches from the stove's flame. Ah, but there was a time when the cold didn't bother him at all, there was. His fingers had been long and steady, steady enough to hotwire a car or coldwire a bomb. He'd been tall, nearly six feet, with a ramrod straight spine. He caught a glimpse of himself in the mottled mirror that hung above the bathroom sink beyond an open door. Consciously, he tried to straighten to his full height. His bones creaked and protested under his efforts and watching himself in the mirror, he appeared farcical even to hisself.

Ah, what's the world coming to, he thought. Coming to, my arse. It's already gone there and it must like the torment because it's bound and determined to remain there.

He opened the cabinet and extracted a box of tea bags, fumbling inside to find the last one. No matter. He'd be passing the Dealz on his way into work and passing it on his way home again. He'd drop in and pick up another box and perhaps a scone or a crumpet or two. At least he'd have a supper box from work. Brigit always made sure of that. There were always leftovers from the uppity class and they kept him a pace apart from starving.

The kettle began to whistle and he switched off the stove and poured the boiling water into the cup. He rummaged around the upper shelf, finding the distinctive shape of a honey pot and unceremoniously poured a good-sized dollop into the cup. What the tea didn't soothe, the honey would coat. He wiped the pot clean with his finger before sliding the digit into his mouth, licking the sweet stuff. It had begun to crystallize and he realized he hadn't the slightest notion of how long he might have had it. He sighed. No matter. While the tea steeped, he'd ready hisself for work. It was about to be an arctic day in the stables for sure.

7

Dylan set the kettle on to boil and made his way to the kitchen door. He opened it quietly, lest he awaken Vicki, and stepped outside onto the small stoop. It was half past seven but the skies were still dark; it would be another hour before the sun had fully risen. It had rained during the night, leaving behind a heady perfume of wet sod and sweet winter jasmine.

A small pond was situated down a slight embankment just beyond the house and now a misty shroud had nearly hidden it from view. The air wavered there as if it was alive and if he peered long enough and hard enough, it shifted into creature shapes with soulless faces. The last time he and Vicki had stayed in this cottage, they'd made love there after a balmy dip. He contemplated whether the water would be too frigid to repeat their performance.

His eyes traveled the length of the tree-lined winding drive, watching the branches dip as though bowing to an invisible monarch. He wasn't able to see beyond the far lawn; a person could be standing just on the edge of the grass and the mists would obscure him completely. But that's the way it was here in Ireland, he thought. The mists and the fogs could morph in front of one's eyes and if he allowed himself to go there, they would take his mind into places better left alone.

A sudden gust rounded the corner of the house and struck him fully and for the briefest moment, his weight was shifted to his toes as he fought to keep his balance. Ah, the wind, he thought as he settled again. She was as much a part of Ireland as the rain. Never referred to as *it*, it was always *she*: *She's a blustery one today* or *She must be sleepin', she's so slow. She* because the winds were just like a mistress: they could wrap their cool arms around you and calm your nerves; they could give you that extra push up the hill or propel you down one; or they could change in an instant from cajoling to wicked, catching you when you were least prepared. And then there were the lazy winds; the winds that rolled in from the Atlantic or the North Sea on a bitter winter day; lazy because they wouldn't take the time to go around you, they'd go straight through you instead.

He looked up, registering the gray clouds against the dark skies. She's comin' in from the Atlantic, he thought as he watched them roil and tumble toward the east. But there was no more rain in her, at least not now; perhaps later in the day, there would be a mist or two. Now, she was simply playing; skittering across the fields, rippling the grasses, awakening the sheep and the cows as they were set out to pasture half-groggy with sleep.

The teakettle began to whistle and reluctantly, he moved back inside and removed the kettle from the massive stove. He would keep the stove on for awhile, at least; it helped to chase away the chill that inevitably found its way into every nook and cranny. Besides, there was breakfast to be made.

While his tea steeped in a china cup, he placed another peat brick in the fire. The fireplace was along the wall between the kitchen and the living area and visible from both rooms. His eyes dropped to the bearskin rug that lay rumpled in the living area.

He could still see Vicki lying there as she had last night, the fur soft against her skin, the glow from the fire illuminating her curves, her long hair tumbling over her breasts. He had kissed and licked her nipples until she was writhing under him; he had followed those curves with kisses, spreading her legs to find her filled with desire. She had pulled him down to her, her moans filling the air, her fingers threading through his hair, kneading his back, feeling his want. The world around them ceased to exist, his vision filled only with her: amber eyes radiant, silky skin glistening, legs that wrapped him in a cocoon of love.

She had been uninhibited, just the way he liked it. Insatiable. No sooner had he laid back, spent and heart racing, before she was climbing atop him, smothering him with her lips, wanting more.

He smiled now as he savored the memories. He picked up the wine glasses from the night before and after a moment of quiet reflection returned them to the sink. He found his tongue rolling over his lips; he could still taste the wine from Vicki's mouth, could still feel the burn from her smoldering embrace as if she was there still, begging him for more.

He glanced through the open doorway toward the hall. She had moaned in protest when he had extricated himself from her legs this morning; a drowsy moan with eyes still closed, lips slightly parted and her breath soft. He'd sat on the edge of the bed for a moment and watched her return to her slumber, had gently covered her bare shoulder with the thick down comforter.

She was presumably still sleeping and by the time she awakened, the fire would have extinguished the gloom from the wintry morn; it would feel as warm and cozy and comforting in the house as he had felt in her arms.

He busied himself as he began to prepare the rashers and eggs, fresh from local farms, along with brown soda bread and homemade jams bearing handwritten labels. He sipped his tea while he worked until it grew cold, idly considering the day ahead.

When breakfast was ready, he would take a tray into the bedroom and gently awaken Vicki if she hadn't yet begun to stir. She would take her time getting up and dressed, and perhaps they would make love again, though their lovemaking had continued into the wee hours of the morning already.

And then they'd be off to the manor house, a few hours' drive from the village, where their honeymoon would officially begin.

His mobile phone rang, interrupting his thoughts. It sounded rude and shrill in the morning stillness. He hurried to the living room in an effort to silence it before it awakened Vicki, discovered the phone on the end table and answered.

"Sam," he said.

"How'd you know it was me?"

"I suppose if I'd looked at caller i.d., it might've been a clue, wouldn't y' think." When he was met with silence, he continued, "But I needn't bother. Who else would have the audacity to disturb me on me honeymoon?"

"Sorry," he answered in a tone that left no doubt that he wasn't, "but this is important."

"Not work, Sam."

"Listen. Before you hang up on me, turn on your television. You do have one, don't you?"

"No. Irish homes come without 'em." He grabbed the remote. "Of course I do. What's it about?"

"Turn it to BBC News." As Dylan set the channel, he continued, "You remember before you left the States, how there were sightings of UFO's over St Louis?"

"Don't you go tellin' me there are little green men hoppin' out o' 'em now." He glanced up to find Vicki entering the room. She looked radiant, her hair tussled and her cheeks flushed. She wore his plaid flannel shirt, so large it looked like a nightshirt on her and so sexy he was sorely tempted to hang up the phone.

She sleepily pushed him backward into a chair and straddled him, folding her legs against his thighs for warmth. He could see the outline of her nipples against the fabric; unable and unwilling to stop himself, he leaned forward and grasped it with his teeth through the fabric. He brushed one long, soft leg with his palm, forgetting the cell phone between his chin and his shoulder.

"Are you watching the news?" Sam was saying.

"And yeah, sure," he murmured as he moved upward to capture Vicki's lips in his.

"So you see they're over London?"

"Mm."

"What's over London?" Vicki whispered as their lips parted.

"It's Sam," he said, shaking his head. His eyes darted past the television and then swung back. He sat up straighter, pulling Vicki more tightly against him. Grasping the phone again, he said, "You're not jokin' me."

"Vicki's with you?"

"It would be m' honeymoon, Sam."

"Good. She needs to hear this, too."

She allowed his flannel shirt to gape open on her, revealing her nudity underneath. With a sly grin, she began unzipping his jeans.

"I'm listening," she answered as she leaned toward the phone. She slipped off him, gesturing for him to rise slightly from the chair while she slid his jeans to his ankles. She caught his eye and smiled wickedly. Ah, she'd be the death of him for sure, and he'd never wanted it more.

She straddled him again, sliding him deep inside her. Sam was speaking and for the life of him, he couldn't find a decent reason to remain on the phone.

"Dylan?" Sam was saying. "Our nation's security depends on this."

He tried to force his attention back to Sam. "Don't you go tellin' me there's some sort o' war o' the worlds goin' on here."

"Of course not."

Vicki nuzzled her lips against his neck.

"Then what the hell can't wait?" Dylan asked.

"Before you two left, remember Vicki's last mission?"

He cupped a breast within his hand. "Are y' hearin' this, Vicki?"

"I'm still listening," she said, trying to stifle a giggle.

"She was working with an operative," Sam was saying, "to get information smuggled out of Siberia."

"Aye."

"It's been copied onto a microchip."

"The microchip I'm to pick up in Donegal?"

"That's right."

"And that microchip has somethin' to do with flyin' saucers, does it now?" His thumb circled her nipple.

"You know our military has been working on plasma stealth technology."

Vicki grew still and peered at the phone.

"I wouldn't know what you'd be talkin' about now," Dylan said. He mouthed, *Do you?*

Vicki nodded.

"You're familiar with stealth technology?" Sam asked.

"Like the stealth bomber?" Dylan answered. "The one that can't be detected by radar?"

"Well... yes and no. Once our enemies knew it existed, they began trying to invent advanced radar detection systems. So we began a new generation of research for future aircraft; plasma consists of ionized gas particles and a plasma cloud is a collection of free-charged particles."

"I didn't understand a word you just said, but I'm assumin' these are our own aircraft then?"

Vicki moved back and forth slowly, lowering her hands to his hips.

"Sadly, no," Sam said. "We're trying to employ it as a means of masking our aircraft—making it invisible, both to radar and to the eye. But it isn't perfected."

"But the Russians have succeeded." He cut his eyes back to the television as the aircraft vanished. The show cut to the news anchor and an expert in military technology. As they speculated on what they had just witnessed, he tried to focus on Sam's words. "And just why is this a concern o' mine on m' honeymoon, precisely?"

"The microchip contains the blueprint of the Russians' new technology. What I don't know—what we're trying to figure out now—is why they are choosing to unmask their aircraft."

"Is it a threat, you suppose?"

"That's one agency's assessment. They could be trying to send us a message, showing their might, that sort of thing."

"Ah."

"Or another theory is the uncloaked aircraft caught them off guard. If that's the case, they might have been hovering over our countries and our allies' countries for some time completely without our knowledge."

"So you're tellin' me that I need to get m' hands on that microchip."

"That's right."

Vicki slipped off him. He groaned silently and held out his hand for her to return but she only smiled. His eyes followed her into the kitchen where she poured herself a cup of tea.

"Sometime during your lunch," Sam said, "a man will enter the restaurant, go to the end of the bar and order a Guinness."

He switched to his mobile's speakerphone. "That would be half the men in Donegal, I'd wager."

"This one is going to leave for the men's room and he's going to leave the microchip at the end of the bar. Pick it up."

"And there's no one else in all o' Europe that couldn't do this? You've got to call me off m' honeymoon to pick up a chip?"

"You've the perfect front."

Dylan watched as Vicki spread some jam on a slice of soda bread. Her legs were shapely as they emerged from under his shirt; her feet bare against the cold tile floor. He tore his attention away as Sam continued his instructions.

"When you leave the restaurant, there's a park two blocks away. Go to the center, where you'll see a fountain. Turn right. Head for the horse and carriage ride. Halfway, a man with a newspaper will pass you. Hand him the microchip."

"No password?"

"He'll know you by sight. As he passes, slip the microchip inside the fold of the newspaper. Keep walking. Don't say a word."

"Fine." He felt an odd stirring in his gut as he tried to imagine slipping a microchip inside a folded newspaper while two men walked past one another in a crowded square.

Vicki returned to the living room with her cup of tea. She took a long, sensuous sip of the warm broth before spreading his legs and lowering herself to her knees. The warmth from her lips surrounded him and he leaned back and closed his eyes.

"And Dylan—guard that microchip with your life," Sam said. "Once you've turned it over, the mission is done."

"As simple as that," Dylan murmured.

"As simple as that."

"Fine. Now if it's all the same t' you, I'd like to be returnin' to m' honeymoon." Without waiting for Sam to respond, he clicked off the phone. Tossing it onto the couch across from them, he pulled Vicki to her feet. "Get back up here, wench," he said. "And ride me like the wind."

8

The road stretched out before them like a writhing serpent, the vista nearly identical to what it must have been hundreds of years in the past. It was the western edge of Ireland, a region known for its rugged beauty. Too remote for soldiers during the Dark Ages, it attracted monks fleeing from oppression, torture and death, a place where priceless artifacts and texts were kept in safekeeping as the rest of Europe was burned and sacked. It was life in a remote wilderness long before the discovery of the New World, a place where even Vikings did not venture; the ground alternating between unyielding rock and pliable, burping bog under kaleidoscope skies.

Dylan glanced at the darkening clouds as he turned eastward toward Donegal. They were coming from the northwest and they would bring with them frosty winds and biting cold. Interesting, he thought, how quickly he fell back into the habit of studying the skies and the wind; in North Carolina, he felt more removed somehow whereas in Ireland he considered himself a mere visitor in Mother Nature's home.

His thoughts turned back to the task before him. Picking up a microchip and passing it off to another sounded uncomplicated, nothing more than a minor diversion during a stress-free honeymoon. So why did he feel this unease raring up in his belly, this voice that warned him to turn around?

"Sam's plans never go as intended." Vicki's voice was even, as if she was discussing a grocery list.

"Aye." He drove in silence for another moment before adding, "Anythin' you think I should be knowin' about your mission?"

She hesitated as if thinking. "I'm not sure who originally cultivated the asset, a scientist, in Siberia. Alexei Volkov. That's his name. He has one of the highest clearances in Russia—high enough to get him assigned to one of their most secure facilities."

"Ah."

She was quiet for a moment, her eyes wandering to the Irish countryside. When she turned back to him, she fixed him with soft amber eyes. "There was one area that was off limits to him—off limits to almost everyone. Over a period of years, he established a friendship with the lead engineer, Mlakar Mikhailov. I—traveled—the area in my mind, mapping it out, room by room. Unfortunately, we didn't have anyone on the ground who could confirm the blueprints because the floor was so restricted. Then just before we left America, Alexei contacted his handler in Siberia; the old surveillance system was being replaced. We had only hours to prepare. I walked him through it, and he was able to copy the plans for Russia's latest aircraft onto a flash drive."

He nodded as he pictured the mission in his mind's eye. He turned at a nondescript road that was slightly wider than a car, a lane that most drivers would have breezed past never recognizing it as anything more than a cattle path. Ahead were azure skies dotted with what appeared to be scattered white cotton balls. He glanced into the rearview mirror to see the darker gray clouds roiling behind them against cerulean skies. It would follow them all the way into Donegal, he thought.

"I suppose you heard m' conversation with Sam, that I'm to pick up a wee item?" he said, his voice breaking through the silence. "A microchip."

She nodded. "The plans from Alexei. I heard Sam say that he'd copied it from a flash drive to a microchip. Just imagine if he'd been caught."

"I can only imagine the torture they would have put him through."

"Interesting that Sam would select an out-of-the-way place for us to have lunch on a day that shouldn't involve any schedules at all."

Dylan smiled wanly. "And there's that."

"So tell me your plan."

As he briefed Vicki on the mission, the road widened and in the briefest of moments, became straight. They were nearing Donegal.

~~~

Dylan backed the rental into a parking place parallel to the curb. Turning off the engine, he silently studied the scene before him: the lane curved like the bow of a ship past a row of attached, three-story homes. Even in the dead of winter, there were centuries of moss continuing to grow on slate roofs. At the end was a wider road upon which a medieval cathedral stood like a silent sentinel overlooking all of Donegal.

Peering toward his left at a break between the houses, he noted their location at the top of a hill; a meandering
~~~

canal wound its way lazily through the town, interrupted only by a myriad of bridges that had stood since ancient times. On his right and down a block or two was the center of town and a bustling, vibrant square that was packed to capacity during summer's peak tourism. Today it was the locals' turn; decked out in Christmas lights and decorations, it played host to Victorian horse and carriage rides, hot apple cider and honey meade sold by street vendors that stomped their feet and rubbed their sleeves in an effort to stay warm. Even with the windows raised in the rental, he could detect the distinct crisp aroma of winter air and holly.

He looked back toward the canal, following its length to a quieter, less assuming section of town. The restaurant sat at a tranquil corner, its gothic style a reminder of its age. His eyes scanned the area around it, looking for something or someone that might appear out of place. It was, perhaps, three quarters of a mile to the restaurant and while there were plentiful parking spots available closer to its door, instinct told him to park here on the hill.

"I don't have a good feelin' about this," he said, turning to face Vicki, "and about you accompanyin' me."

"Don't be silly," she answered. "Sam arranged lunch for the both of us, right?"

He nodded.

"Then I'm your front. A couple on their honeymoon," she said, grasping his hand. "What could appear more innocent?"

"It might turn dangerous. You said y'self that Sam's missions never go accordin' to plan."

"I need this," she said, squeezing his hand in both of hers. "I need to work."

Their eyes met; hers, a soft amber that seemed to glow from within and his a hazel color that seemed greener than usual. After a moment, he nodded reluctantly. "We've time to shop," he said.

He reluctantly released her hand and stepped onto the curb. He made his way around to her side of the car, opening the door with a flourish. As she stepped out, he bent to kiss her softly. As he began to pull away, she placed his hand against the side of his neck and pulled him back to her. Murmuring, "We're on our honeymoon, remember?" she kissed him more passionately.

He wanted nothing more than to remain on this cozy little street with her in his arms, feeling her body pressed to his with a myriad of fragrance encircling them; of her perfume that spoke of spring days and fragile flowers to the brisk, cold bouquet of her coat and scarf, to the trees and bushes that had stood nearby for centuries, their winter branches aromatic in the nippy north breeze.

Finally, she shivered and pulled away. "I'm freezing!" she said, rubbing her arms with her hands.

He wrapped an arm around her, pulling her back to the curb and down the lane toward the square.

~~~

Less than an hour later, they emerged from the throngs, their cheeks pink and their eyes glistening from stubborn winds. He carried two bags for her; one filled with lambswool scarves in a variety of plaids and the other, a smaller one, with bottles of Innisfree perfume and lotion. He held her hand in his free one, bending toward her to hear her laughter. A wizened farmer called out to them in an attempt to entice them onto his horse-drawn carriage and Dylan nodded in his direction. "We'll be back after lunch," he called amicably.

"I'm starving," Vicki said, her voice carrying on the wind.
~~~

He pointed in the direction of the restaurant with more of a flourish than he might otherwise have used. "Now there would be a good place, I'd be thinkin'," he said. "A pint and a fireplace to warm you, 'ey?"

They carried on as they made their way out of the town's center and down the meandering road, across one of the bridges over the canal and toward the corner restaurant.

The room was dim and it took a moment for their eyes to adjust. A young woman stepped from behind the bar and made her way toward them. She had dark hair and luminous brown eyes, which set off her alabaster skin. "Two o' yous, then?" she said with a smile.

"Yes," Vicki responded. She giggled. "We're on our honeymoon."

"Honeymooners, are y'? Come here all the way from America, did y'?"

She nodded. "My husband is from Ireland," she said, nodding in Dylan's direction. "How did you know I'm American?"

She laughed. "American accents are easy to pick out, yeah?"

"Would y' mind," Dylan chimed in, "seating us o'er there, nearest the fire?"

"It might get a bit warm for y' there."

"Good," Vicki said. "I'm freezing."

They changed course as their hostess led them to the other side of the restaurant, away from the windows peering onto the street and into a darker section, illuminated only by the hypnotic flames of the fireplace.

"Perfect," Dylan said, helping Vicki remove her coat and scarf.

The hostess set menus onto the table. "M' name's Sinead. I'll be back with water in a moment. Would you be drinkin' anythin' else?"

"Two pints." He loosely folded her coat and scarf. "Would y' mind if I set these here, on the barstool, out o' the way?"

She waved her approval. "It's quiet today for sure. Help y'self."

He laid the clothing across one stool at the far end of the bar, just a few steps from their table. Then he removed his own jacket and placed it on a second stool before pulling out Vicki's chair with a gallant wave of his hand.

~~~

An hour later, Vicki pushed back from the table and held both hands over her belly. "I can't eat another bite," she groaned.

"Surely y' can," Dylan said as he finished off his plate. The steak and potatoes in the tasty Guinness sauce would normally have been sumptuous but he found himself having to force it down. The asset should have arrived by now, he thought as he glanced at his watch, but only two other couples sat in the restaurant and no one had approached the bar. "We've plenty o' time. Perhaps a spot o' tea will finish off the meal nicely?"

"I don't know," Vicki said with a smile that said she could definitely be persuaded.

Sinead, who, as it turned out, was the only server, approached the table. "All done?"

Vicki glanced at the remains of her fish and chips. "It was delicious."

"We'd care for some tea, please," Dylan said, finishing the last morsel. "Perhaps Mandarin orange w' ginger would settle your stomach, dear?"

"Sure, and an excellent choice that would be now," Sinead said, gathering up their used dishes. "Dessert?"
~~~

Dylan and Vicki's eyes met. "Give us a moment," Dylan said as if reluctant. "Perhaps after the tea, we'll have room."

As she left, he reached across the table to hold Vicki's hand. She bent her head toward his. Leaning in with a devious smile, the anxious look in her eye bared her concern. "Where is he?" she whispered.

"Perhaps he didn't feel the time was right," he answered with a couple of kisses in between his words. Though the server was busy across the room and the other patrons had not given any indication that they'd taken notice of them, it was critical that they keep up appearances. "Perhaps he's followin' his instinct."

As if on cue, the door opened, allowing a blast of wind to sweep through the restaurant. A man of medium height and build made his way into the room, removing a tweed cap. "Ach, she's a lazy wind t'day," he said in a thick Irish accent. He wore worn jeans and a leather jacket. A plaid scarf was about his neck, barely brushing the nape of his neck. He ran his hand over dark hair cut so short that it almost appeared to be shaved.

"What have y'?" Sinead asked as she brushed past him to deliver two miniature pots of tea with matching cups to Vicki and Dylan.

"A pint ought to take the chill off, yeah? Ah, and it's warmer by the fire now isn't it?" He moved a bit further down the bar and settled onto a stool but didn't meet their eyes.

Dylan opened the tea bags and settled one in each of the miniscule pots of hot water. "You'll like this, Vicki," he said. "Add a wee bit o' milk to it. Y' won't be needin' the sugar; it's quite sweet enough as it is…" His eyes locked onto hers for the briefest of moments. The message was clear: he's our man. He thought he detected a hint of recognition in her eyes, along with confusion.

"You know what I'd like to do?" she said, her voice calm despite the look in her eye.

"Can't say that I do now."

"I'd like to watch the sunset this evening. I hear that the most brilliant sunsets are in Ireland."

He laughed and glanced at his watch. "Ah, but it'll be sunset in about an hour, lass."

"But it's hardly afternoon!"

"But it's the shortest daylight o' the year. We'll have to hurry and finish this tea if we're to catch the sunset now."

"Jacks in the back?" the man at the bar quipped as Sinead expertly poured a Guinness draft.

"Aye," she said, nodding.

He left his cap on the bar in front of his stool. Fixing his eyes on a point in the narrow hallway beyond the tables and bar, he angled past them. Had Dylan not been watching through his peripheral vision as he sipped the tea, he might have missed the miniscule package dropped into one of Vicki's gaping shopping bags.

"Now isn't that a sweet tea?" Dylan prodded.

"Delicious." Vicki's eyes were downcast, and it was just as well; he wouldn't risk the mission by telling her what he'd seen.

"I hate to rush you, darlin', but if it's the sunset you'd be wantin' to see, we'd best get on with it."

Her eyes opened, locking onto his, revealing surprise. "Yes," she murmured, "I suppose you're right." She pushed her chair farther from the table and began to rise.

Dylan had helped her into her coat and was slipping on his jacket when the bathroom door opened at the end of the hall. He hurriedly snatched up the bags in one hand while reaching for his wallet with the other. By the time they'd stopped to settle their bill and were on their way out the door, the man was just returning to his stool from the men's room.

"Ah, and it's a fine day for a pint," he said in a cheery voice as the chair legs screeched across the floor.

~~~

"Dylan, that man back there—"

"Shh," he admonished, glancing around them. "Not now."

The lights had come on along the street against a hazy winter sky. Two blocks from the restaurant, a maze of trees stood stark against the skies, their branches bending with the mounting winds. Somewhere in the back of his mind, he knew that Vicki had shivered with the chill, and instinctively, he wrapped his free arm around her shoulder, drawing her closer to him.

"Would y' care for one o' your new scarves, perhaps?" he asked suddenly, coming to a halt on the sidewalk.

"I have one already—" she began to protest.

"Ah, but not a Donegal scarf," he interrupted, whipping one of her purchases from the bag. As it grazed the edge of the bag, he reached for the price tag and snared the small package that had been dropped into it. It was wrapped in paper, which he hadn't expected. He slid it under his jacket sleeve at his wrist where a tight cuff secured it. Then he pulled the tag off the scarf. "This will keep the chill away." He made a small show of wrapping the scarf about her neck, pulling it into a loose knot at her throat. Then once again, he grabbed the bags with one hand while his free arm was wrapped about her.

The Irish walk briskly, with a purpose so it's said, and he found himself tamping down his impatience as he forced his legs to move at a more leisurely gait. Vicki's
~~~

legs were shorter and her American shopping sensibilities had already placed her in a window-shopping mode; but he realized as they passed another couple that he probably wore the same expression on his face as the other gent did. Ah, what we do for our womenfolk, he thought. Carrying bags and peering in windows at clothing that all looked the same to him, and there was Vicki carrying on about hot pink and fuchsia and coral and salmon... And salmon was a fish, was it not? Then why the fashion industry would charge top euro for clothing the color of a fish, he'd never know.

His eyes darted toward the park, registering a group of young women laughing in a circle, a man in a business suit on his mobile phone, an elderly couple on a park bench, an older gent reading a newspaper... His view was obstructed by a horse and carriage and as his eyes wandered to the area behind it in an attempt to glimpse his surroundings, a black sedan pulled to the curb.

In an instant, his breathing had calmed. As though he was in slow motion, he felt his heartbeat decelerate, the steady *thump, thump, thump* feeling heavy in his chest. He could hear Vicki's voice droning on but he was no longer focused on her words. She never talked so much, he knew; it was all part of the act.

The horse and carriage began to move and they stopped at the crosswalk diagonally from the park. The walk light was red and in his periphery, he noted cars slowing as the light turned. A chirping akin to a bird sounded the change to a green light.

They stepped from the curb onto the street. The older gentleman stood, shaking out his newspaper and folding it loosely, not quite tucking it under his arm. He turned away from them, making his way toward a fountain barely visible through the dusk. Dylan knew where they would meet; he knew that he and Vicki would approach the fountain from the opposite direction, perhaps tossing a coin into the water at its base. They would come within inches of him and he'd drop the tiny package into a fold in the newspaper. None of them would alter their pace.

Following Sam's instructions, they reached the fountain and turned to the right. Five sidewalks converged at the center fountain, each nearly wide enough for an automobile. The sky was darkening with the combination of heavy clouds and nightfall and he narrowed his eyes to focus. His contact was still a short distance away and as he carried on a nonsensical conversation with Vicki, he instinctively registered his surroundings: a young mother leaning over a stroller, a teenager skateboarding, a maintenance man emptying the wastebaskets, a couple with a small child feeding a wayward duck, an elderly woman walking a Scottish terrier... The black sedan was moving almost imperceptibly, creeping along the road just a few feet behind the contact.

He calculated the distance between them and the speed in which they walked toward one another. They would meet at the intersection of the next sidewalk, and at that moment, the inhabitants of the sedan would have ready access to them all.

They were nearing each other. He could see the man's thinning gray hair and a bad comb-over; his bushy brows as if his hair had migrated there; thin lips pursed; eyes seeming to stare straight ahead. In the blink of an eye, his eyes rolled to Dylan and back. A heavy black wool coat, a plaid scarf, a hand that was red with the cold as it clutched the newspaper, which was loosely folded so that it gaped in the middle... And the black sedan.

With Dylan's arm still around Vicki's shoulder, he suddenly tugged her to another sidewalk. He caught a quick glance at the contact's widened eyes before Dylan called out to the carriage driver they'd spotted earlier.

"Hey, yeah!" he called. "Would you be available now?"

They quickened their pace as the driver answered, "Sure, and hop aboard, why don't you?"

The sedan had stopped and three doors opened simultaneously. Within seconds, they had surrounded the contact.

"And will you be tellin' us about the town as we ride?" Dylan asked, helping Vicki up so quickly that he nearly lifted her like a babe. He slipped the package down from his sleeve wrist to his palm as he climbed up, deftly dropping it into his jacket pocket as he settled in. "We'd be honeymooners, don't y' know," he said genially.

"Honeymooners!" the driver repeated with delight as he spurred the horse into the lane. "Well and that will warrant a very special tour, indeed!"

Dylan avoided Vicki's face as he positioned himself to look straight ahead. He cut his eyes to the side as the three men hustled the contact into the sedan. Within seconds, it had pulled into traffic and swerved around their carriage. The driver didn't seem disturbed by the erratic sedan but was intent on pointing out sites he thought they would find interesting. He could barely concentrate on his words and Vicki's responses as he watched the vehicle careen out of sight.

9

Ah, but there was nothing at all that felt more like freedom than riding bareback on a beautiful beast, giving it her head to go wherever she chose at whatever pace she set for herself. And she was in fine form this afternoon, Jack thought, as he dipped low to avoid the branches that threatened to topple him from his precarious perch. Her head was high, her mane sailing in the wind, her nostrils flaring; he loved the scent of her sweat and the way in which her body glistened. She bolted through the forest, weaving this way and that, knowing the paths and the hazards from a lifetime residing here.

She'd been born here in the stables beyond the forest and Jack had helped deliver her hisself. Gangly and unstable, she'd struggled to her feet in the first minutes after birth and he'd never been so proud in all his life.

Silver in color with a black mane and tail, she was the epitome of perfection.

Her name was Ciara but he didn't remember a time when he didn't call her *A Chara Ciara*, which meant *My Friend Ciara*. They had a special bond, they did; even on the worst of his days, he could forget everything—his past, his heartaches, his pain—when he was atop her broad back.

During the summer months, there were too many tourists and too much to be done and too little time for the two of them alone. He felt a kinship to her, knowing she had no control over her own life, recognizing that her fate was held firmly in the hands of others. He remembered that feeling of cell doors closing, of understanding they would not open again until another, a relative stranger to him, would decide that he should be allowed to step out of it. Perhaps that's why he brought her an apple or a carrot each morning and why he stroked her mane and cooed to her softly; the kindness one showed to another could make all the difference in the world. He knew that well, and knew also the cruelty that could destroy a man and break a spirit.

She burst from the edge of the forest onto an open field, beyond which the Atlantic Ocean crashed against cliffs a hundred feet high. A heady bouquet of saltwater, fish and sea air assaulted them both. Gulls circled overhead and though he couldn't see them from this vantage point, he knew the seals were splashing in the waters below or clumsily climbing onto the rock at the water's edge.

She danced in a wide arc through the meadow, her head tilting higher as if she were trying to breathe as much of the sea air into those wide nostrils as possible. He held onto her mane, his own heart thumping in his chest, the wind crisp against his face.

She slowed as she neared the cliff's edge, her breakneck speed turning into nothing more than a trot until she eventually stopped to nibble on flowers that stubbornly bloomed amid the waning grass, despite the colder weather. Her chest heaved with her exertions and he took advantage of her leisure to lean back, to stretch his aching spine, and to breathe the fresh salty air.

Eventually, he slid off her and made his way to the cliff's edge, where he stared across the water to points that were foreign to him. To the west would lie the Aran Islands and beyond those, some three thousand miles distant, the next parish over was Boston. He wondered how much it had changed in the past thirty-odd years. Ireland, to be sure, had changed in dramatic ways and certainly America had, as well.

When he was there last, Ronald Reagan was President and Maggie Thatcher was Prime Minister and between the two of their huddled shoulders, Northern Ireland's lot was cast. He'd never intended to return to the Emerald Isle, but then a man's fate was often decided by the toss of a die and the whip of a god. His had taken him through unimaginable hell and he was never quite certain whether he was yet beyond the lick of the flames.

The sunset seemed to remind him of his lot; ablaze in red and orange, it leapt from the horizon like a dragon struggling to gain loft while a formidable blackness was determined to tamp it down. It was only mid-afternoon but with Christmas just around the next corner, the days were the shortest of the year.

He liked the darkness, even preferred it, truth be told. He liked the way it cocooned around him, the way the hearth glowed nearly all the time to keep the frost from permeating everything. He liked to read by the fireplace, taken to strange lands and other cultures, places he would never be able to go hisself. He would have traveled more, he thought, had he known that one day his passport would be seized and ne'er reissued; he would have traveled more even if he had barely more than a pence in which to do it.

A memory surfaced briefly before he squelched it; the memory of a young woman with a lithe figure, blond hair and light eyes—had they been green or blue, he wondered? He couldn't believe he'd forgotten. Ah, the memory of her in a cozy kitchen, baking a pie, a babe—their babe—on her hip. He might have forgotten the color of her eyes but he'd ne'er forget the swish of those hips, the gentle curve of her breasts or how she felt all wrapped around him…

No, he thought with an involuntary shiver, memories such as those were best left in the past, gone and buried.

A reflection appeared on the water and he followed its source to a twisting lane along the coast's edge, where the headlights of a lone automobile shone through the growing darkness. There would be only one destination for a vehicle along that way, he thought. It would be heading to the manor house, for sure, and while it was too late and too dark for tourists to ride the horses, its appearance served to remind him that he best return to the stables and to his duties.

The last remnants of the sunset were gone by the time he mounted Ciara and turned her back toward home.

~~~

Vicki stood at the window, peering onto gardens beyond the manor house while the bellhop brought in the luggage. The gardens were haphazardly aglow as lamps inside the house cast fingers of muted butter through open windows. Then one by one, the slithers disappeared as drapes were drawn, leaving only a faint glimmer cast from their room. She heard Dylan's voice as though he was a million miles away, idly chatting
~~~

about their drive from south-central Ireland and the weather, which seemed always to find its way to the top of conversation.

"Well and now," the bellhop was saying, "I know you'll have a grand honeymoon. I'm off until the first of the year, holidays, you know but the Missus and her daughter live here and you'll find their attention the best in all of Eire."

"No other guests then?" Dylan asked.

"No, no. On account o' the season's ended, you know. Just you two so it's like your own private home, I suppose."

As the two chatted behind her, she gazed at the shadowy grounds. A reflecting pond stared back at her, forlorn and neglected. Trees were positioned strategically around it and she wondered how they must look in the spring and summer, filled with blossoms perhaps and green leaves. But tonight they were bare except for a few leaves that stubbornly clung as though evading death's grip, the skeletal branches reflected in the dark pool.

She would have much preferred to have arrived during daylight hours, to drink in the rolling hills that might, to some extent, remain green even during the winter months, to feel her heart calm with the simple act of watching sheep and cattle graze. Now she could barely make out the outlines of the hills and valleys along the horizon and within the next few minutes, she knew they would disappear altogether until the sun found them again in the morn. The meandering drive to the manor house was murky now, the tree line bathed in gloom.

A floodlight some distance from the house was the only spec of brightness and she found herself drawn to it as if it held some surprise. It was mounted at the edge of a large barn-like structure, shedding light across the wide, open doorway and onto the bare open ground around it. She watched as a lone horse sauntered toward it, walking slowly as if reluctant to return to the stable. A figure slipped off its back and as they moved into the brightness cast by the light, she realized he'd been riding bareback. He seemed to glance in her direction but she couldn't be quite sure. A mere moment later he was leading the horse into the barn, closing the doors behind them.

She knew that Sam was waiting for their call, or perhaps they should be waiting for his; after the carriage ride through Donegal and once again in their rental car, Dylan had texted Sam: *Fish and chips but the fish had bones.* They had not received a response and the ride to the manor house had been spent in silence as if both were afraid any mention of the event would be instantly overheard by the enemy.

The door clicked shut behind her and she turned just as Dylan was turning back to face her. They met in the middle of the room beside a fireplace whose warmth chased the chill from her bones. He wrapped his arms around her waist as she raised her arms about his neck.

Somewhere in the back of her mind, she registered the fireplace crackling, the sweet smell of peat so faint it was almost imperceptible; the bed with one corner turned down, chocolates on the pillows; the round table with two chairs between the bed and the double doors, a silver bucket covered in cold droplets announcing the presence of a chilled bottle of champagne…

Without a word, he bent to kiss her, his full lips slipping over her lips so gently that it almost felt like angel wings caressing her. His eyes were dark and for the briefest of moments laugh lines appeared at the outer corners as if he was enjoying a private joke. Then his mouth descended on hers more firmly, his arms crushing her to him.

She felt lost in his embrace. Our honeymoon, she thought with more than a bit of awe. His shoulders were broad and solid, his arms muscular as she raced her hands over his biceps before returning to his neck and the hair that curled ever so slightly over his collar. When he pulled slightly away and she opened her eyes, a lock of his black hair had fallen across his forehead to his brow. His face was flushed and she knew hers was as well; her breathing was rough and shallow.

She tilted her head back as his lips grazed along her jaw before nestling against her neck. She opened her eyes just long enough to spot purple hyacinth and heather intermingling with white roses on a smaller table near the windows, their pleasant perfume wafting toward them on a delicate stream of air. The images felt like parts of a tapestry, gentle, subdued, softly undulating as it wrapped about them.

She wove her fingers through his thick hair as he settled against her neck, his tongue finding her earlobe. She moaned, her voice sounding faint and small.

The suitcases were lined up in a neat row against the wall. For a fleeting moment she visualized the black silk negligee with crotchless panties carefully packed inside as she felt her back laid bare, the unzippered blouse cascading from her shoulders. She wanted to take a moment to change clothes and she didn't want to bother; she just wanted to close her eyes and enjoy the feel of his lips upon her, moving to her shoulders and then deeper...

Her eyes fell on the open window and the flash of the horse and the man at the stables rose unsteadily in her mind.

"Stop," she said weakly.

There was a brief hesitation. He raised his head to look into her eyes.

"The drapes." She swallowed.

He glanced behind him, his brows knitting. "No one can see us, darlin'."

She giggled. "Men always say that."

He leaned back until he was almost an arm's length away. "Just how many men have said that to you, I wonder now?"

She pointed at the window. "Just close the drapes."

"Ach," he muttered under his breath but he reluctantly dropped his arms from her as he stepped toward the window. She felt the warmth disappear with him and she pulled her blouse further up, bundling her palms beneath her chin.

He hesitated for a moment at the window.

"What is it?" she asked.

He was silent for a few seconds before he reached up to pull the drapes closed. "Nothin'," he answered. Turning back around, he added, "Don't you dare go coverin' y'self."

She sat on the bed, sinking into the thick duvet. Still grasping her clothing at her neck, she laughed nervously as he moved toward her, his eyes fixing hers. In an instant, he was upon her, tumbling her backward across the bed, straddling her as he once again found her neck before moving quickly to her shoulder. The blouse was against her skin one minute and at the far end of the bed in the next, her cool flesh warmed once more by his touch.

She unbuttoned Dylan's shirt to bare his brawny shoulders and when he drew away from her, she groaned in protest. Her need was reflected in his eyes as he quickly unsnapped and unzipped her slacks and slid them to her ankles. He lifted each leg, removed her heels and then slipped her clothing the rest of the way until it fell in folds to the Oriental carpet beside the bed.

She sat up to return the favor, and a moment later his boots and pants were scattered alongside her clothing. She grasped his buttocks as he bent over her once again and she smiled as the color darkened along his cheeks. Then she pushed him gently but firmly until he lay on his back and she was left straddling him.

There was nothing as erotic as hearing his breath catch in his throat, of feeling his back arch involuntarily with the pleasure of her lips upon him, at meeting his eyes and seeing his want, his need, his desire reflected within them.

~~~

"Jaysus," he whispered hoarsely, his breath ragged against her ear. She could feel his heart pounding against her breasts as he slumped into her, his body weighted in a way that it had not been during their lovemaking. She wove her fingers through his hair, feeling the dampness at the nape of his neck as he rested against her.

After a moment that seemed only an instant, he slowly slipped to her side. The absence of his weight left her exposed to the chill and she protested feebly, prompting him to drape them both with the bedcovers as he rolled further onto his back.

She had just cuddled against his side, had only just begun to feel his fingers idly strumming along her back, when his mobile phone rang. They both groaned simultaneously as he pulled away from her once more, fishing for the phone on the nightstand.

"Sam."

"What happened?"

Dylan settled back under the covers and she resumed her place beside him, intertwining one leg with his. He relayed the events to him, sticking strictly to the high points in a way that would have prompted Vicki to ask
~~~

a battery of questions, but Sam remained silent until Dylan had finished. "So you have the package?"

"I do."

"Have you confirmed it's the microchip?"

"I haven't confirmed anything." Dylan's eyes drifted to a nearby chair where his jacket lay draped across one arm. As if reading Sam's mind, he slipped out of bed and made his way to his jacket. Cradling the phone against his shoulder, he rifled through his pockets until he found the small package. It was carefully and elaborately wrapped in a single sheet of paper. He described the packaging to Sam as he unraveled it.

"It's a microchip," he confirmed a moment later. Then he looked back at the paper. "Sam, there's more."

"I'm waiting."

"The piece of paper it was wrapped it—it contains a note."

"Read it to me."

"It says, *'I want to defect.'*"

There was silence on the other end of the phone.

"Sam?"

"Can you take a photograph of it and text it to me?"

"Well, sure and I can."

"Good. I'll be waiting."

There was a moment of silence as Dylan waited for additional instructions. When none came, he added, "Is there anythin' more you'd be needin' me to do?"

There was no response.

"Sam?"

"Send me the picture. Save the note; we'll want forensics. And I'll be back in touch."

Before he could reply, the call disconnected. He met Vicki's eyes briefly before he flattened the paper on the table, snapped a picture with his mobile, and texted it to Sam. He waited for a reply but he received only an automated confirmation: delivered.

Sighing, he held up the paper. "Ideas on where to store this?"

"Absolutely." Vicki slid out of bed, wrapping the covers around her to keep the chill away. She grabbed her cosmetics and toiletries bag and opened a box of tampons. She could feel Dylan's eyes upon her as she carefully removed one from a thin plastic wrap and then the cotton from the applicator. She meticulously set the microchip at the tip of the cotton and wrapped the sheet of paper around it before reinserting it into the applicator so only the string remained outside of it. Then she placed it back inside the plastic wrap. She moved to the fireplace, waving it over the fire slowly until the plastic began to soften. Then she squeezed it together, allowing the heat to form a seal in the plastic sheathing, sealing the tampon and the paper inside. Popping it back into the box, she glanced up to find Dylan's eyes still upon her.

"You'd be actin' as though you've done that before," he said. "And I'm not certain whether I should be impressed or horrified."

"You'll never know," she said with a smile. She pushed him back onto the bed.

"You'll be the death o' me, woman," he protested only half-heartedly.

"Your body betrays your words."

"Ah, traitor that it is."

10

Jack rested on the stone wall a short distance from the stables, his eyes glued to the second floor window. He chewed absent-mindedly on the mouthpiece of his pipe. It had been a long time since he'd been able to smoke tobacco, due to his throat being buggered and all, but he enjoyed the smell of it anyway even if he couldn't inhale it. He preferred the deep cherry tobacco in his elaborately carved briar root pipe. The pipe was an expensive item, too expensive for his pocket, to be certain, but it had been given to him years ago by his grandfather and except for that stint in the lock-up, it had rarely left his side.

The sun was long gone and with it, any warmth to be had; the shadows had continued to lengthen until a spot of light was more of an anomaly than the darkness. He found his attention riveted to the second floor, though the light there was dubious now that the drapes had been drawn.

He'd seen her earlier, and what a beauty she was. Her hair had been long and flowing and what he supposed would be called strawberry blond; it was red, to be sure, but blond as well, and it reminded him of another, a long time ago... She'd stood at the window and he could have sworn their eyes met as he was returning with Ciara, but she'd seemed preoccupied as well...

And then he'd been there, a tall man with dark hair, and he'd gathered her into his arms. Ah, it brought back memories, it did: of a time and a place when he was young and tall and fit and ready for his flute to be played at the drop of a hat, and when he'd had a lover willin' to play it...

Unabashed, he'd remained in the shadows watching them and suffered quite the disappointment when the drapes had been pulled to, and he'd wandered to the stone wall to catch the window on the other side but the drapes had been drawn there, too.

He sighed. No matter. It wasn't as if he had a mott at home to quench his thirst, anyways.

But he'd continued to sit there until the winds had grown frigid and his ardor had cooled right alongside it. His workday had been done awhiles before he finally picked hisself off the wall and trudged toward the beat-up piece of shite Skoda, which unequivocally confirmed the Czechs were abject failures at auto manufacturing. A package had been placed on the roof and he eagerly grabbed it, holding it by the pale light of the moon in a vain attempt to see its contents. Ah, but no matter; it smelled of home-cooked chicken sandwiches and creamy potato with cabbage, and if he was lucky, there'd be a cookie still soft and delectable. God bless Brigit, he thought as he crossed hisself. She always looked out for him, she did, and wanted nothin' more than to be a good Catholic woman. She knew, for sure, that he didn't earn enough to keep a monkey alive, much less a man, and what's she to do with the food the house threw out each day when the guests didn't eat it all?

He opened the tin can door and tossed the bag to the console before climbing in behind it. With a final glance at the second floor window, he started the engine and made his way down the winding drive toward home. He'd be back in the morn, bright and early, he would, and maybe he'd catch a glimpse of her again.

~~

Vicki watched as Dylan finished off his glass of champagne before setting the flute on the nightstand. He was sitting up, his back against the tufted headboard, with her curled up beside him, her head resting against his shoulder. The fire had died down somewhat, the embers casting faint warm flickers around the room, but the heat was dissipating quickly. Dylan did not seem to be affected by it, but she pulled the duvet above her naked breasts and snuggled more deeply against his warm body.

"I need to tell you something," she said, breaking the silence.

He peered down at her under heavy lids. He appeared tired, which wasn't surprising; they'd had a long and eventful day and she was ready for a good night's sleep herself. "Aye?" he prompted.

"You remember the man at the restaurant?"

His eyes grew slightly wider as if he'd awakened more fully. "I do."

"He spoke like he was Irish."

"Not w' any accent I'd ever heard."

"Oh?"

"But go on."

"He wasn't Irish, Dylan. He was Russian."

He sat up so straight that he nearly toppled her. As she pulled herself to a seated position beside him, their eyes locked. His were unblinking and his brows were knit, casting a shadow across his face. "What?"

"His name is Alexei Volkov. He's the scientist I told you about, the one stationed in Siberia. His specialty is anti-electro-magnetic design."

"But," he said, "wouldn't it have been more prudent for him to pass off the package to someone else within Siberia? Say, his handler?"

"That's exactly what I've been thinking. It's too risky for him to have traveled from Russia to Ireland. How could he have left undetected?"

"*Why* would he have left?" He combed his hair with his fingers but a lock fell stubbornly across his brow.

"Well, his note did say he wanted to defect."

"Still… Why not ask that of his handler, I wonder? Why ask you and I, unknowns to him?"

"Unless…"

They stared at one another. "You don't think—?"

"His handler is a double-agent?" Vicki finished.

"No."

Dylan rose. He crossed the room in silence, grabbed the bottle of champagne from the table and returned to the nightstand, where he poured them each a fresh glass. Handing one to Vicki, he was still shaking his head.

"But what if his handler *is* a double-agent?" she pressed.

He sat on the edge of the bed and took a swig before he replied. "What would his handler have known?"

"He might have known about my mission."

"*Might* have?"

"It's hard to say; the CIA can keep things so compartmentalized that no operative really knows the full story."

He took another swallow. "We have to assume his handler knew everythin'."

Vicki sipped the champagne. It sent a warmth trickling down her throat but she still felt herself shiver. Bundling back under the covers with only one hand poking out with the glass, she nodded. "That would mean his handler knew about my mission—and also knew about yours."

"Perhaps. Or—perhaps he was supposed to hand over the microchip to his handler and he disappeared instead."

"Then," she added, "There's the matter of the man seized in Donegal. Who was he?"

He shook his head. "There are too many questions, to be sure. First, who was he supposed to turn the microchip over to? Second, if he wasn't the one expected in Donegal, how did he know about the rendezvous? You said yourself the CIA keeps things compartmentalized. If his mission was to give the chip to his handler, he couldn't have known about the hand-off in the restaurant—or about my hand-off to the other gent."

"Unless—maybe his handler isn't the double-agent. Maybe he was captured and tortured for the information."

"That would make Volkov the double-agent."

"Which would make this whole thing a set-up."

Dylan finished off the glass, set it back on the nightstand and crawled back into bed, drawing Vicki against him. As she settled in, he took her glass and set it beside his. "There's only one way to figure this out. We need to reach Sam. We need to find out who was supposed to meet us in the restaurant."

A moment of silence ensued. Then Vicki asked quietly, "Are you going to call Sam?"

"I was just debating that. He said he'd be in touch; I'll give him until the morn and if I haven't heard from him by then, I'll phone." He leaned over to kiss her, his lips lingering on hers. "But for the rest of this night, let's focus on our honeymoon, shall we?"

11

There was something magical about watching the sun rise at 8:30 in the morning. The skies had been black as coal as Vicki and Dylan had showered and made their way downstairs for breakfast, and it had remained so until they were finishing a meal of rashers and eggs, soda bread and jam. By that time, the thinnest streak of pink peered over the horizon and within minutes, the sun's rays had cut through the darkness like dozens of threads and then a few dozen more, until the light had begun to fuse one to the other.

They'd been quiet during breakfast with an odd combination of emotions, from enjoying the pure happiness of their honeymoon to concerns about their CIA missions. One didn't go with the other and it left a strange fluttering in Vicki's stomach, one that even her Peppermint Patty—hot peppermint tea with chocolate creamer—couldn't settle.

"And would you be needin' anythin' else now?"

The melodic sound of the young woman's voice interrupted her thoughts. She turned to the smiling server, a lithe girl in her teens with straight black hair and large green eyes.

"No, thank you. I'm fine."

"So, you're honeymooners, I hear?" she asked.

Vicki felt the color rise in her cheeks as if by admitting it, the young woman would know precisely what they had been doing all the night long. "Yes. We are."

"I'm Aislinn. I'll be cleanin' your room and servin' your meals, so if there's anythin' at'al that you'd be needin', please be lettin' me know."

"We will," Dylan said as he finished off the soda bread. "School is out now, 'ey?"

"Aye, until after Epiphany."

"Well, then."

"My family owns this property," she continued, nodding toward a slender woman who was clearing a nearby table. "That's m' mum, Brigit."

"You look like you two could be sisters."

"She may as well be," she answered with a smile. "She's m' best friend, she is."

"The horses," Dylan interrupted, nodding his head at the window, "would they be available to ride?"

"Oh, yes, indeed," Aislinn answered.

"And would that be your da out there?"

"Oh, no," she laughed as if the mere thought of it was farcical. "That's Jack, the groom. He takes care o' the horses and also takes visitors on horseback tours—like y'self."

"I'd love to ride again," Vicki said, reaching for Dylan's hand. "I haven't been on a horse since the last time we were in Ireland."

"Jack would enjoy it, I'm sure, takin' you around and about."

"Could you call down to him?"

"Call—no, he doesn't carry a mobile, I don't believe. Just have a walk down and he'll be there. There are no other guests about, on account o' the holidays, you know."

Before they could answer, she brushed past them, rushing to help her mother with her kitchen chores.

"I haven't heard from Sam," Dylan said, glancing at his watch.

"It's what—four a.m. in North Carolina now?"

"I should've phoned last evenin'. I don't know what I was thinkin'." A slow smile crept across his face. "No; I take that back, I do. I knew exactly what I was thinkin' and Sam was the furthest thin' from it."

Vicki giggled. "If you don't need me to stick around, I can go to the stables and arrange a couple of horses for us."

"You do that, darlin'. And I'll be joinin' you directly."

With that, they both rose. As Dylan made his way to a quiet parlor at the front of the mansion, Vicki returned to her room to gather her hooded coat and scarf. It was going to be a beautiful day, she thought, but one thing she'd learned already about Ireland was to expect the sun and prepare for the rain and anticipate them both within a few minutes of one another.

~~

She could smell the stables long before she reached them. It was odd, she thought; though she hadn't grown up around horses, she found the mixture of sweat and hay and manure familiar somehow. She spotted half a dozen horses in the fenced yard beyond the stone building but instead followed the sound of whistling coming from within.

It took a moment for her eyes to adjust to the gloom. When they did, she realized she was standing in a building made completely of stone; even the floor was cobblestone. The center aisle was wide enough to drive a bus through, and except for bits of hay between some of the stones, it was pristine—perhaps not unsullied enough for a house, but certainly much cleaner than she would have expected in a stable.

At both her left and right sides were a row of stalls, each with a horse eagerly chomping on hay held in feeder dishes attached to their doors. At the far end was the man she'd heard whistling; he sounded as if he might break out in song as he swept the floor clean of debris.

He was dressed in faded, threadbare jeans that looked as if they'd definitely seen better times—and at some time in the far distant past. He didn't wear a jacket but a red and black plaid shirt that seemed substantial enough for another layer to be underneath. His shirt sleeves were rolled up to the elbows, revealing muscular forearms. His back was broad but his shoulders stooped, and between the slight curve in his posture and the gray hair intermingling with the black, he looked as if he might be in his late 60's. When he turned around, however, she realized he was probably much younger.

"Ah!" he exclaimed as he noticed her, staring at her wide-eyed as if he recognized her.

Vicki stepped forward. "Have we met before?"

He appeared startled by her question, taking half a step back before responding. "No, no, I'm quite certain I would recall it if we had." He leaned against the tattered broom handle. "And what would be bringin' your fine self to paradise this morn?"

She laughed. "Paradise? I like that."

"Ah, but it is, wouldn't you know." Still leaning against the broom, he nodded his head toward the horses. "Sweetest coworkers I ever had. Always up for a nuzzle and a carrot or two, and the best company a man could want… Other than…"

"Other than?" she prompted when his voice faded.

"No matter." He took a deeper breath and suddenly jerked as he grabbed for his throat.

"Are you alright?"

"Quite. Quite. Just me throat's buggered, is all. Shouldn't have taken me such a breath, caused the cold to champ it."

She wasn't quite sure what he'd just said so she stood there for a moment, thinking through an appropriate response. But she needn't have worried because in the next instant, he was talking again.

"So, and did you come for a ride now?"

"Yes." She glanced at the horses. "My husband and I were thinking of riding a bit this morning; that is, if it's alright."

"Sure and of course it is. It's what we're all about here, you know?" He narrowed his eyes as if sizing her up. "Would you be skilled at riding?"

"Not at all. I've only ridden a couple of times."

"Then I have just the gal for you." He laid the broom against the wall and strolled to one of the stalls where a beautiful palomino with a blond mane eyed him. "This one's an old gal but herself's a sweetheart and she wouldn't do more than trot even if you wanted her to."

Vicki giggled. "Then she'd be perfect for me."

"And your husband? Is he the same?"

"Oh, no. He can ride very well."

He led the palomino out of her stall while nodding toward another horse on the opposite side. "Then he might like one with a bit more spirit like Dougal there."

"Dougal?"

"The black one there. He's a young one and quite the stallion." He chuckled.

"And what's this horse's name?" She stepped forward

to run her fingers across her muzzle. Her eyes were large and her lashes so long they looked almost false.

"Fennore."

"Fennore," she repeated.

"American, 'ey?" he asked as he led the horse into the soft sunshine.

"Yes."

"Husband too, I presume?"

"No. He's from here."

"Here?"

"Well, a couple of hours from here."

He grew silent as he gathered a saddle and pad while Vicki eyed the area beyond the stables. The ground sloped upward in hills interspersed with grass, moss and rock. The winds were biting and she gathered her thick scarf further up her neck.

~~

Dylan observed Vicki from the tall windows of a sun porch that extended beyond the main house. It was obvious that she was trying to remain close to the stables, sheltered from the winds that blew across the island. As close to the ocean as they were, there was nothing to slow the airstream until it reached the mountains. The horse's back looked as tall as she was and he smiled at her gumption.

"Did you hear me?" Sam's voice sounded preoccupied.

"I did. We're to return to the restaurant this afternoon precisely at one o'clock."

"His code name is Arctic Fox. We have to assume if he wants asylum, he won't go far from where he passed the package to you."

He ran a hand through his hair. "Beggin' your pardon, Sam, but there are other factors to consider here."

"Such as?"

"For instance, did he observe the other fellow bein' pulled off the street before the transfer could take place?"

"I have a team en route to investigate that operative's disappearance."

"Well, I suppose I should be thankin' you for not interruptin' my honeymoon to hunt that one down."

"Yeah, well."

"Sam, are you supposin' the same group who abducted the first man may also have abducted Arctic Fox by now?"

"We don't have any evidence of that."

"And how precisely would you be gettin' that evidence?"

Sam chuckled. "Watch it, Dylan. Before long, you'll be as cynical as me." His voice grew solemn. "You're our eyes and ears on the ground at the moment. Needless to say, you're to report back to me when you have the answers."

"Right. Which means I'm hangin' in the wind here, 'ey."

"Not quite. We have a team monitoring chatter. There's been nothing about the Russian." After a pause, Sam continued, "His handler went missing the day he was to receive the package from him."

"Care to fill me in on that?"

"His handler works at the American Embassy. Arctic Fox was scheduled to attend a scientific conference in Moscow; he took the train from Novosibirsk, Siberia several days before; it's a long journey."

"I can only imagine."

"Two thousand, fifty-two miles, to be precise. Roughly 46 hours travel time. Our operatives confirmed his departure and also his arrival in Moscow."

"So the plan then was for him to turn over the package to his handler while he was in Moscow?"

"That's correct. His handler left the Embassy for the rendezvous at Filevsky Park. One of the staff members was at an upper floor window and observed his departure; shortly after he left, it appeared as though another man began to follow him."

"Would that not have raised suspicion?"

"Not at all. It's always a cat-and-mouse game, every time anyone leaves the Embassy. We have to assume they are being followed, that their homes are bugged, that every meeting is observed."

"Then why schedule the meeting there?"

"It really wasn't a meeting… Our people are trained on losing their tails. He might have doubled back, hopped a trolleybus or a marshrutka, got lost in a crowd or traffic…"

"But you said it wasn't a meeting?"

"It was meant to be a pick-up. Arctic Fox was instructed to drop the package; there's a monument just off Nevsky Prospekt in honor of Catherine the Great. He was to leave the package behind the foot of Ekaterina Dashkova, one of the figures at the pedestal under Catherine the Great's figure. It should have been in a watertight bag no larger than the chip itself. Arctic Fox should have then left, his handler—Verrucosa—would have come in behind him, stopped for mere seconds at the monument, picked up the package and kept walking. But obviously, that didn't happen."

"Obviously." The horse was saddled and the hostler disappeared inside the stable. Dylan watched as Vicki stroked the horse's long muzzle. "Could Arctic Fox have witnessed Verrucosa gettin' snatched off the streets of Moscow?"

"One of the questions we'll have to ask him. Once you have him in your custody, we'll arrange to get him transferred back to the U.S. for questioning."

"Sam, I know you've thought o' this… If Verrucosa was snatched and also the operative I was to pass the package to, doesn't that mean our plans have been compromised?"

"We're working on that angle."

"You'll have to do better than that, I'll tell you right now." He moved closer to the window as the hostler led a spirited black horse outside the stable. Watching the two horses together, he came to the quick conclusion that his would be prepared to leave the other in the dust once they hit the trail. This was going to be interesting.

"We're looking into the possibility that our messages have been intercepted," Sam was saying. "That the Russians have broken our code. Or..."

"Or?"

"Or we have a mole."

"Oh, now isn't that just fine and dandy? You know, we've been down this road before, Sam."

"I know," Sam sighed. "It's one of the constant battles waged in the intelligence community."

"You'd think your operatives would be loyal to their country, wouldn't you now?"

"You'd think."

Dylan ran his hand through his hair. "And how do I know that Vicki and I wouldn't be walkin' straightaway into a trap, goin' back to Donegal as we're directed?"

There was silence on the other end.

"Sam? I'm talkin' to you here."

"Yeah. I'm still here."

"Did you hear what I'm sayin' to you?"

"We're working on it."

Dylan exhaled sharply. "As I said, you'll have to do better than that." After a moment, he added, "Sam, are you distracted?"

"Maybe I am." He sighed heavily. "I've got fungus growing on some of these fish eggs."

"You're in the angelfish house now?"

"You told me to take care of them."

"Good Lord. The stakes are high here, Sam, and I've an instinct they'll be gettin' higher. Do you think you could stop for a moment and pay attention?"

He heard the sound of footsteps and envisioned Sam walking across the hard tile floor.

"Okay," Sam said as a door creaked open, "You've got my full attention."

"Oh, that's a comfort."

"I'm working on getting surveillance satellites in place. We won't be able to keep an eye on things inside the restaurant, obviously, but once you're in the open, we'll be able to track you. When the time comes, I'll want an open line to you. I want to hear everything that's going on and be able to relay information to you in real time."

"A phone line? Or something more secure?"

"This line will do it. It's completely secure."

"You're certain about that, are you?"

"Absolutely." He hesitated. "And I'm working the angle of a mole. I have to make certain your mission is kept off the books—for now. At least until we get Arctic Fox to a secure location inside the U.S. and we also have that package… I'm also working to get someone to Ireland to retrieve it. I want to separate the information from our asset."

"Well, you might want to hurry things up a bit."

"I'm waiting on a phone call now that the operative you'll be passing it off to is on the way from the U.S. to Ireland."

"Then it might happen tonight?"

"That's the plan."

"Just when were you plannin' on lettin' me in on all this?"

"You'll have to trust me, Dylan. Sometimes bits and pieces are doled out for a reason."

Dylan had a brief flashback to his training at the CIA before consciously attempting to dismiss the images. He had been subjected to torture—presumably so he would understand the physical and psychological attacks that would be expected if he was captured. The experience had been pure hell and yet he knew the agency had stopped short in their training. Enemy captors would be far more merciless.

"So," Dylan said, "about the fungus on the fish eggs. How many tanks?"

"Just one."

"What are the parents doin'?"

"They're both at the other end of the tank with their backs to the eggs."

"Oh."

"That's all you're going to say?"

"Well, they've determined there's somethin' wrong with the clutch—the eggs. So they're not carin' for 'em so's they'll die. I wouldn't be surprised if they ate them."

"Great. What am I supposed to do? Stand back and watch the sushi bar?"

Dylan chuckled wryly. "Remove the eggs. Toss 'em. They'll lay more in another week or two. But check the water temperature and conditions, okay? And keep an eye on the others and let me know if this happens again?"

"You got it."

"Okay, Sam, I've got to go. Vicki is waitin' on me."

"1:00."

"I'll be there. You just make certain I've got backup—even if it's remote."

~~

The black horse was saddled and ready by the time that Vicki spotted Dylan leaving the manor house. While Fennore stood regally in the open, free to roam but preferring to remain still, Dougal champed at the bit, raising his forelegs into the air, and seemed to fight the leather that kept him restrained to the fence post.

"So, as I was sayin'," Jack said, "you've your pick of the trails, depending on how long you'd like to be gone. If you're planning to stay out more than a couple of hours, I'll have Brigit prepare you some sandwiches…"

"I think we'll be back by then," Vicki said, waving to Dylan as he drew near. "Is there anything else we should know?"

Dylan returned his mobile phone to his pocket. "It's a fine day for lettin' a horse have 'is legs," he called out as he zipped his jacket. "Perhaps we can wander down the cliffs to the water's edge. I imagine it's quite beautiful there."

"Is that safe?"

"Well, we won't do it if it isn't. I wouldn't be endangerin' you, you know."

"Did you talk to Sam?"

He glanced at his watch. "We'll have just about enough time for an hour's ride. We're to return to Donegal."

"Oh?"

"Aye, and I'll be hopin' all goes accordin' to plan. I'll be damned if we're to be expected to drive there every day of our honeymoon. There are other thin's I'd like to be doin'."

"Oh, Dylan," Vicki exclaimed. "I forgot. I'd like for you to meet—I didn't catch your full name—" She turned but the man was gone. "Well, that's odd," she murmured.

"So which horse would you be takin'?" Dylan asked with a mischievous smile.

"Oh, you. You know I wouldn't last a minute on that black one—his name is Dougal, by the way."

"Very imaginative."

"What do you mean?"

"The horse's name. It means 'black'."

"Oh. Well, his trainer didn't tell me that—and he seems to have just disappeared." She peered into the stables. "Excuse me?" she called.

She was met only with the whinnying of horses.

"I don't understand that," she said, returning to the palomino. "He was here. We were having a conversation just as you were walking up. I don't know where he could have gone to…"

"Well, I wouldn't worry about it at'al, if I were you," Dylan said as he guided Fennore to a nearby stump. "You think you can handle this one?"

"You might have to rescue me."

He helped her atop the stump. "It would be my pleasure. Put your foot in the stirrup here, and I'll help you onto her."

12

The water was sapphire blue and so calm that it appeared frozen in time. Vicki found herself in a cove with pristine white sand that seemed oddly out of place against the backdrop of steep, formidable cliffs on either side of them. They'd managed to find the only trail that led downward to the ocean, a meandering footpath in which she felt like she could plunge right over her horse's head and down the embankment with a simple wrong step. But Fennore held true as she followed behind Dougal, hugging the way and taking her time, until they had descended to the shore.

Dylan pulled Dougal alongside her. "Beautiful, isn't it now?"

"It's stunning."

"Do you see that rock out there?"

Vicki peered in the direction he pointed. Some distance from the cove was an outcropping of rocks that appeared to be alive, like a very busy ant farm. "What is that?"

"They're seals. From the looks o' things, I'd say there might be hundreds of 'em."

"Seals?"

"The gray seal. What you're seein' out there are the cows with their pups."

"Their babies? Really?"

He nodded, his eyes riveted to the scene before them.

"Can we go there?"

"What, to see them?"

Vicki nodded.

"Oh, darlin', I would love to accommodate you, I would. But I'd advise against it. Only half o' the pups will likely live, and in these parts we like to leave them alone. Too much stress can have a negative effect on the herd, you know."

"I wouldn't want to upset the pups."

"Or their mothers."

She shaded her eyes in an effort to see past them. "What's that, over there?"

He followed her gaze to a set of cliffs that jutted out from the mainland. Perhaps a hundred feet high was a precarious link from one cliff to another. "A rope bridge."

"That's a bridge?"

"They're fairly common along the shores. Fishermen often string them up."

"Why?"

He laughed. "To get to the other side, o' course."

She guided Fennore to the opposite side of the cove, where Dylan joined them.

"For centuries, the salmon fishermen have strung rope bridges to the outlying isles. I hear there's not too many salmon left—the Japanese harvest them before they reach Irish waters these days—so either that one was abandoned some years ago or…" He shrugged. "Who knows for sure?"

"Would you walk a bridge like that?" she asked.

"I don't see why not. You'd be able to tell, for sure, if it's been maintained."

A gust of wind caught her square in the face, chilling her skin and turning her nose and cheeks red. The rope bridge dangled precariously like an empty hammock.

"Would you?" he asked.

"I seriously doubt it."

He laughed. "Not afraid o' heights, are you now?"

"Not usually. But it doesn't seem safe, you know?"

"Tell you what we'll do. We're supposed to be on our honeymoon, 'ey?"

"Supposed to be?"

He smiled. "We'll do a bit o' the tourist thing, why don't we? There's a well-maintained suspension bridge called Carrick-a-Rede—"

"Carr-a-what?"

"Carrick-a-Rede Rope Bridge. It's actually in Northern Ireland, a few hours from here. A sight to be seen, for sure. And we'll walk the bridge together. It won't be crowded this time o' year."

She chuckled. "You'll have to hold onto me, if it swings like that one."

"I wouldn't let you fall, darlin'." He glanced at his mobile.

"Text?"

He read silently for a moment. "Sam."

"I figured as much. You mentioned going back to Donegal. What does he want us to do now?"

He studied their surroundings for a moment before answering, as if to make certain they were alone. Despite the fact that they were isolated, he moved Dougal closer to Vicki and her horse. "We're to return to the restaurant."

"Why?"

"Sam thinks Alexei—Arctic Fox—will attempt to go there again, hopin' we'll have read his note and we're ready to bring him in."

"What are we supposed to do with him?"

"According to the text I just received, we're to take him to Galway."

"What's in Galway?"

"You mean 'who', don't you?" He reached down to stroke his horse's mane. "We're to take him to the Promenade outside the Galway Atlantaquaria. Sam is sendin' someone from London to receive him."

"And the microchip?"

"I assume that as well. Though I could've sworn he said someone was arrivin' from the States. No matter. I'm sure we'll receive additional instructions."

She nodded. "I'll bring it in my purse... Unless you have other plans."

He chuckled. "I think considerin' where you hid it, it would be less likely to raise suspicion with you than with me."

Vicki laughed. "I have a large tote; I'll bring it in that—package and all."

He peered upward at the cliffs above them. "We'd best be turnin' around now. We'll have enough time to climb back up and skirt the cliffs before returnin' the horses to the stables."

"Perfect. Then we'll dash back to the room where I can freshen up and grab the chip, and we'll be on our way."

He waved his arm in an elaborate gesture. "After you, m' darlin'."

~~

Jack chewed the mouthpiece on his pipe as he watched the couple appear over the crest of the cliffs. He'd been that way countless times, he had; the trail could be a dodgy one, even on the back of the best horse. He was surprised the girl took it; he'd expected them to stop at the edge, perhaps point as tourists do, before winding along through the flat meadow instead. A nice, easy stroll, it would have been. The girl had more spunk than he'd given her credit for.

She was a looker, too. It was just a shame—

"Ah, and there you'd be."

He glanced at Brigit out of the corner of his eye. Ah, and she was a looker herself, wouldn't you know, and when she was younger, there was none fairer. She was but a wisp of a woman but with a spine of steel; he'd seen her green eyes flashing in anger though never at him and he aimed to keep it that way. Now her salt-and-peppered hair seemed intent on unraveling from the loose bun at the nape of her neck. He remembered when it was as ebony as a piano's keys and glossy as a spit-shined coin. Ach and Life had a way o' macing the years.

"Keepin' a spyin' eye on our guests, are you now?" she asked.

"That I am. Its part o' what you'd be paying me for, is it not?"

She handed him a doubled piece of paper before she folded her arms in front of her breasts. She turned her attention to the horses as they meandered through the meadow while Jack opened it.

"After I take care of them?" he asked, nodding toward the couple.

She shook her head. "Won't be necessary. You're expected in Donegal."

He nodded, carefully folding the paper before placing it in his pocket.

"Take my vehicle," she said, without taking her eyes off Vicki and Dylan.

Without another word, he turned and left. He'd find her keys hanging from the visor, where she always kept them. It would be a long drive to Donegal. He patted his pocket. And he'd best be taking care of business.

When he glanced behind him, she was still standing there in the shadows, as he had been; her arms still crossed, her chin jutted upward, carefully observing the couple in the distance.

13

Jack placed the packages in the back seat of Brigit's Honda runabout, but as he leaned across the seat, his eyes were focused some distance away. His hackles were up for sure and they had been ever since arriving in Donegal. He'd parked near the center of his errands, which required him to go back and forth from the vehicle to one shop or another, piling packages in the boot as he went. As he collected Brigit's sewing machine from the repair shop, he'd noticed the man standing on the corner just across the way; bristled blond hair and steely eyes, he had, and no way was he an Irishman. That had gotten him going and the more he looked, the more he saw.

There were at least six of them spread out and every now and again their mouths would move ever so slightly, always at the same time as their eyes flitted about. Oh, they were conniving to make the jump on somebody; that much was obvious, at least to him.

So he'd begun to inquire. "Whatsup w' the dodgy one lightin' up?" he asked at the butcher shop. "Sos, what's the gent doin' cleanin' your walk?" he'd asked at the fruit market. "Hey and what's that wanker doin' down the way there?" he'd asked at the laundry.

He knew their reactions like he knew his own mother. Sharp eyes roamed to the windows; lips closed and set. Provos, the lot of 'em, and each one knew there was trouble about.

On his latest trip to the vehicle, he'd met the eyes of a burly man with black hair and stubble down his neck. "Soft auld day, 'ey?" he'd said cheerfully.

The man nodded. "Right you are."

Right I am, my arse, Jack thought as he continued without missing a step. Anyone who'd spent a day in Eire knew that meant it was misting but it was dry as a bone, for sure. What's more, with three words, he knew the man wasn't Irish; he wasn't British or Scottish and he wasn't American. He was from the former Eastern Bloc, yeah, perhaps even Russian.

Now as he made a show of arranging things proper-like in the back seat, he noted their eyes on the local pub. If it was going down, it was going down there. The question would be whether he'd stand back and watch it happen. As his eyes scoured the surrounding area, he noted the butcher had come outside as if to inspect a wicked blade in the scant sunlight; the market manager was rearranging the bins on the sidewalk; the postal clerk was taking his time with the mail, though he should have moved on five minutes earlier… One by one, each was out. And each was ready.

Jack slammed the door shut and locked it before holding up his list as if to read the next errand. His instincts were high and keen. In a flash, he'd stuffed the note in his pocket and had begun a brisk walk toward the pub. Sinead would be there as she always was, and it was nigh in the afternoon when it would be quiet inside with perhaps few or no patrons. As he walked, he noted surrounding activity as if everything was unfolding in slow motion: Patrick finished stuffing the mail into his vehicle, closed the door and turned toward the pub; Sean set down the last bin of fruit and picked up a two-by-four; Declin began striding toward the pub, the blade in full view.

He was half a block from the pub when the door opened. From this angle, Jack couldn't see inside but he noticed with an increasingly heightened alertness that the men he'd been watching were also making their way toward the same building. Five, six, then seven men, some with hands stuffed in their pockets, others peering this way and that, as if to size up their surroundings; and then a dark van started up down the street, slipping into gear almost before the engine had turned herself over.

His gait quickened.

Shops that had appeared nearly asleep on an otherwise lazy afternoon sprung to life as merchants poured out.

Jaysus, but things were about to get wicked.

A man stepped out of the pub and stopped momentarily on the stoop. Tall, black hair, broad shoulders. He felt his cheeks grow hot though the air was frigid.

A moment later, a woman emerged.

Jaysus, Jack thought again.

Just before a third person came into view, he was upon them, pushing them back into the pub. "Arthurs on the house!" Jack bellowed in his most jovial voice.

"Hey—" The tall one blocked his way. "I don't know—"

"I know him." It was the woman, the American, who spoke in a rapid, hushed voice.

The man cut his eyes to her, a look of surprise skimming his face before it grew dark.

"They're ill set on ya," Jack said. "Get inside and quick."

~~

Before Vicki could process the man's words, they were pushed back into the bar. The man from the stables swung around, slamming the door and ramming the bolt through it in one swift movement.

"You'll have to trust me," Jack continued as he hurried past them toward the bar. "They've been lyin' in wait for yous."

As Vicki's eyes followed him, she realized that Sinead had rushed behind the bar. Just a moment earlier, the wall had been neatly stacked with bottles of alcohol, arranged on shelves in front of a mirror that spanned the entire length of the bar. Now one section was pulled away from the wall a mere twelve inches and Sinead was standing back as the stable man made a rush for the opening.

A man's voice called out and instinctively, she spun her head toward the front windows. Men were converging with all manner of weapons, from hammers to heavy wrenches to clubs.

"Follow me," Jack was saying, gesturing into the opening.

Dylan grabbed Alexei by the shoulder and pushed him toward the bar. "Who are y'?" he demanded as the mysterious man disappeared into the blackness.

"Name's Jack," a voice returned. "Get in quick."

Dylan thrust Vicki inside, quickly followed by Alexei. With one parting glance toward the front of the restaurant, he stepped in behind them.

They found themselves in an alcove that was so dark they could barely see one another. As Dylan turned back toward the opening, the wall closed on them with a solid thud, surrounding them in an inky blackness.

"What about her?" Dylan asked. "Will she be alright?"

"Aye," Jack said. "She's done it before, countless times." Vicki felt him brush past her and as her eyes adjusted to the darkness, she could see him leaning against the wall they'd just moved past as if listening. "It's yous they wanted."

"Who are you?" Dylan demanded.

"He's the man from the stables," Vicki said.

"Where we're stayin'?"

"Yes."

"Do you work for Sam then?"

"Shh." Jack held up a hand. The sound of muffled voices reached them. "Don't move," he cautioned.

Their four bodies were touching and in the confined space, Vicki could hear the others breathing and her own heartbeat thudding in her chest. She couldn't make out the words of the men though Sinead's came through loud and clear. "They went out the back."

There was silence then; not even the sound of footsteps broke the stillness. She realized she was holding her breath, afraid to breathe. The others appeared like statues as if they, too, were reluctant to move an inch.

After a moment that felt too long and too oppressive as if the air was turning thicker, Jack turned toward them. "You won't be goin' out the way y' came in." He pointed past Vicki. "Follow me."

As he started to brush past them, Dylan stopped him. "Who do you work for?" His voice was low and deep but unmistakable in its tenacity.

"I work for Brigit at the manor house," he answered impatiently. "Not that it should mean a handful o' bollocks to you."

"And no one else?" Dylan pressed.

Jack stopped to stare at him in the murky darkness. Though they were just inches apart, Vicki couldn't make out the features on either man. Dylan stood a few inches taller than Jack; otherwise, she would have had difficulty telling them apart.

When Jack didn't respond, Dylan added, "Why are you helpin' us?"

Jack took half a step back. "I've seen men the likes o' them before. They were comin' after y' like a pack o' wolves. If they'd 'ave handed y' yer arses on the street y' would've gotten off easy. No; they were out to snatch you, all o' yous."

"How do you know this?"

"Let's just say I've been at the receivin' end a time or two." His arm brushed against Vicki's as he punched a finger in the air. "Now I can rap on that wall there and y' can go back the way you came and take yer own chances. Or y' can shut your trap and follow me to safety. The choice is yours but make it soon because I've just about run out o' the little bit o' patience I have left."

She could feel the tension building in the enclosed area. Alexei had remained perfectly silent but now in the darkness she could feel his adrenaline surging, just as it had when she had walked him through his Siberian mission.

After a brief moment, Dylan said, "Lead on."

Jack pushed past her, stopping a few feet in front of them. After a few seconds, a flashlight switched on, illuminating narrow steps that led downward into what appeared to be a black hole.

"I'm not going in there," Vicki whispered.

Dylan moved beyond her, coming to stand beside Jack. They remained at the top of the stairs as the smaller man rolled the light over the walls and to the floor deep below.

"Vicki," Dylan said, motioning for her.

"Dylan—"

"You'll be alright."

Jack began the descent and Vicki reluctantly stepped onto the first stair. It was made of wood and as she slowly made her way down, she quickly came to the conclusion that both the steps and the railing were made from scrap.

"Will it hold all of us?" she whispered hoarsely as Alexei began his descent.

Jack chuckled. "It's held more than the lot o' us."

The railing shook as Alexei grabbed onto it and as Dylan stepped downward, it felt as though it was teetering. She could no longer see the floor beyond Jack's broad shoulders and though the light seemed to lead him, it did nothing for those who were following close behind. The air grew stale and putrid, the deeper they went; soon the tang of humid soil began to permeate her nostrils.

When she finally moved off the last step, she turned to peer upward. She could hear Alexei and Dylan on the creaking stairs but it was as if she was staring into an endless abyss. Had she not known the stairs were there and the alcove was somewhere above her, she would have sworn she was in an underground dead end.

"This way."

Jack's voice propelled her onward, her feet unsteady on an uneven earthen floor, her hands held in front of her lest she bump into something in the black void. The light appeared frenetically as Jack's body blocked most of it from view; it weaved and bobbed along one wall and then another as they made their way deeper into a tunnel that grew increasingly narrower.

On an impulse, she thrust her hand forward until her fingers locked onto Jack's shirt. She felt his muscle tense beneath her touch before relaxing again, and his profile appeared grainy in the gloom. "That's right," he said, his voice softening. "Just you hold onto me, darlin' and I'll get you out o' this nasty bit o' conundrum."

A few minutes later, he stopped abruptly. Turning to face her, he cast the flashlight behind them to reveal Alexei's legs and then Dylan's.

"Are you alright then?" he called.

"How much farther?" Dylan asked.

"Oh, we're almost there for sure." He turned back around to shine the light on a ladder that looked to be centuries old. "We'll have to go up one at a time, for obvious reasons."

"Where will we be?" Dylan pressed.

"The church." He shone the light at the top of the ladder where it appeared to disappear against a solid floor. "I'll have to go first and get the door open. Who will be comin' up last?"

"Me." Dylan's voice was firm.

"Then take the light. I can go up in the darkness; I've done it afore, countless times—"

"Why?"

"The less y' know, the better off y'll be." He thrust the flashlight into Dylan's hand. "But you'll need to shine it for your lady here, and..." his voice faded as he glanced toward Alexei. Then he turned abruptly and began his ascent.

They gathered around the base of the ladder as he climbed ever higher. When he reached the top, he slipped his hand into a recess that would have gone unnoticed had Dylan's light not been shining harshly on it. Something told Vicki that the man would have found it in the dark. It appeared to hold a key of some sort; it was very large, possibly five inches long, and even from this distance she knew it was ancient.

Jack slid it into a hole in the wood, turning it with a click, before sliding it back into the recess. Then he pressed his shoulder against the floor above him and inched it upward. Apparently satisfying himself that it was safe to emerge, he crept the trap door back until it revealed a small square hole barely large enough for a man and in the next instant, he was gone.

"Vicki." Dylan's mouth was pursed as he guided her to the ladder.

The rungs were rounded, causing her feet to roll forward with each movement and as she climbed ever higher, she began to fight against vertigo. She knew not to look down but she made the mistake of peering upward, instantly regretting her action. It was much farther than she imagined, appearing almost out of reach. And the ladder seemed woefully inept. The rungs were crudely inserted through irregular holes in each of the vertical supports, which meant they could not only roll but also work their way out. Jack had made it seem so easy as he'd scurried up the ladder, and in contrast, she felt as though her own climb was taking forever.

When at last her head popped through the opening, she was surprised to find herself in a confessional. She had to straddle the hole as she carefully unlatched the door. Making her way unsteadily into the thankfully-unoccupied sanctuary, she sank into the first pew and struggled to get her heartbeat under control.

Only after her breath had returned to normal and Alexei and then Dylan had emerged, did she realize that Jack was gone.

14

Dylan leaned against the door jamb, absent-mindedly gazing at the pasture as he listened intently to Sam's voice on his mobile. Behind him a horse whinnied while another made an ungodly ruckus trying to get comfortable in his stall. Darkness was not far off, judging from the disappearing sun; but it was always difficult to tell in the winter months, as the sun never truly made a solid appearance until the weather warmed in the spring.

A dozen horses lazily snacked on winter grasses while a few ducks waddled close to the pasture on their way to a pond that rippled with the incessant wind. There was a crispness to the air, a freshness borne of the winds that traveled across the Atlantic; winds that wouldn't rest in the hills and valleys of Ireland but which would pass right through on their journey to the rest of Europe and beyond.

"Aye," Dylan said now, "once we poked about the church, we found we were not too far from the vehicle.

We'd walked close to a mile underground, as it turns out." His voice carried a touch of awe in it.

"No one saw you in the church?"

"Well, the priest came upon us. And he looked at us and we looked at him and he cut his eyes to the confessional where we'd crawled out of and none of us blinked."

"And?"

"And then he walked away like it was the most normal thin' in the world. And we got our bums out o' there straightaway."

"Then what?"

"Well, as I said, we discovered we were on the other side of the square and not too far from the vehicle. We were able to reach it without further incident and we drove straight to the manor house."

"And you're positive you weren't followed?"

"No doubt about it at'al. I took the back way, well off the beaten path, along a road that was barely wider than a cow path. And," he added, "I had a clear view ahead and behind."

"Where's Arctic Fox now?"

"At the manor house with us. I left him in the dinin' facility; the man acted as though he hadn't eaten a bite since departin' Siberia. And I checked him into the room next door to us—under an assumed name, o' course."

"What name?"

"Frank Sinatra."

"What?"

"It was the only name I could think of at the time. I was under a wee bit o' stress."

"Christ." Dylan thought he heard Sam stifle a chuckle. "And the proprietor wasn't suspicious?"

"If she was, she didn't let on about it, I can tell y' that. As a matter o' fact," Dylan continued, "she kept her eyes down like she was quite accustomed to people poppin' up that she didn't care to know."

"That sounds suspicious in itself."

"I wouldn't be knowin' that it is."

"What do you mean?"

"Well, without goin' into a history lesson, which I'm sure you wouldn't fancy, thin's kind of go on in Ireland… Let's just say there are different factions, especially the farther north you get."

"Oh, I get it. Protestants and Catholics."

"Mm. More like the native Irish and everybody else. And you learn what you don't want to become involved in fairly quickly."

There was silence on the other end of the line. A flock of geese were headed north, which never ceased to amaze him, though he'd seen the unusual migration each winter. As the season became colder and the days shorter, the geese began to move northward instead of south as one might expect. They made quite a din about it and he pressed the phone closer to his ear in an attempt to drown them out.

"They knew Arctic Fox was there," Dylan stated.

"Do you think they anticipated you and Vicki?"

"I do."

"And this guy who helped you—Tell me again who he is?"

"Vicki met him only this morn and I've not had an occasion to see him in the light. He works in the stables here at the manor house. I barely caught a glance at the back o' his head; everythin' happened so quickly. And when we reached the church, he just disappeared."

"Could he be a spy?"

He shrugged as if Sam could see him. "I cannot imagine that he would be. If he's a spy for the Russians, why would he 'ave helped us, I wonder? And if he was one o' ours, you would've known… Wouldn't you now?"

"You'd think. I'll do some inquiries here, just in case."

"I can't believe he would be," Dylan repeated. "It would be too much of a coincidence."

"Then why did he help you? A hidden door, an underground tunnel? I mean—"

"It's not all that unusual, Sam. It really isn't. You see, history lesson or no, many o' the structures around these parts—businesses and homes alike—are centuries old. The restaurant and pub might've been built around the time o' Henry VIII. When the king left the Catholic Church and began the Church of England, he established the Church of Ireland here. Catholics were persecuted, captured, tortured, killed…"

"So they built those escape routes?"

"Aye. Chances are likely it was meant for those in the church to escape to the pub and not the other way around."

"Did it look like it hadn't been used in centuries?"

"Oh, no. It's been used to date. And this fella Jack knew it quite well. I suspect he's Catholic and might've used it durin' the time o' The Troubles."

"The Troubles," Sam repeated.

"Ach, you're makin' me into a history professor whether I like it or not, aren't you now?" Without waiting for an answer, he continued, "The Troubles were a thirty-year period in which the Catholics and Protestants were attemptin' to annihilate one another."

"I remember it. Bill Clinton brokered a peace deal back in, what, 1998 or thereabouts?"

"Officially, yes. But there's still an uneasiness in Northern Ireland, dependin' on where you go."

"But you're in Ireland; the Republic."

"Aye, but you have to remember, there's no real border between the two, not since the EU. Things spill over."

"Hhmm." Then, "Did you pat him down?"

"Arctic Fox? Oh, aye. For sure. And I took his mobile and destroyed it."

"How?"

"Crushed it. Then tossed it down a well as we drove through the countryside."

"Good. He have just the one?"

"Aye." Dylan moved away from the doorway, venturing around the corner of the stables. There was still no sign of the man and that alone was worrisome. He didn't care for a man who appeared and disappeared like a phantom. "So, what's it to be?"

"We'll have to change our plan."

"You think now?"

"We have to assume there's a mole—whether there is one or not."

"Could they be listenin' to us now?"

There was a slight hesitation. "Not a chance," Sam said at last. "Not with the technology we have."

"I think you're gonna have to trust me to get him back to the States, Sam."

"You mean on your own?"

"That's what I'd be thinking. Have you a better idea?"

"Hhmm."

"I mean, think about it for just a moment, will you? The fewer people who know of his whereabouts and our plans with him, the less likely we are to get blindsided again."

"It will mean cutting your honeymoon short."

"Not a chance, I'll tell you that. He can lay low for the time I'm enjoyin' my lovely new wife."

"How's Vicki doing?"

Dylan hesitated. "Holdin' up well, all thin's considered. Ireland is good for her, I think."

"I'm glad to hear it. Just don't make it too good. I need her back here."

"Alright then."

"But I don't like the sound of him laying low. The longer he's there, the more likely he is to be found. And I have fewer resources there than I have here."

Dylan took a deep breath. He wanted to suggest that Sam get him himself; certainly he could arrange an impromptu agency flight, pick him up and be over the Atlantic before anyone was the wiser. "Tell me," he said, "when you flew Vicki and I here for the first time, the military plane landed in the northwestern section of the island; it was pretty remote as I recall."

"Yeah, I remember."

"So you have a runway."

"A place we can use, yes."

"Can you make arrangements to get a plane there?"

"When do you want it?"

"The sooner the better if you're wantin' him out o' the country straightaway."

There was a pause. "I can have it there overnight," Sam said thoughtfully. "It'll take a few hours for the clearances and about five hours to cross the Atlantic. I'll have to figure out who I can trust."

"Make it you, Sam."

"I can't, Dylan. I'm made—my identity is known."

"You won't have to get off the plane. I'll see to that. You tell me when to be there and I'll be waitin' with him. I'll put him on the plane m'self. Refuel and turn the plane right around."

"It won't be me, but you have a good plan. I can put in the paperwork for Germany or London and divert it over the Atlantic."

"Do that, Sam."

"Take care of Vicki for me."

"Oh, I will. You can count on it." He clicked off the mobile. He stood for a long moment staring across the pasture. Damn but he was ragin' frustrated that he couldn't find that blasted stable man.

~~

"I should remain here." Vicki was waiting at the front of the manor house; Dylan had barely cleared the bottom step before she began speaking. "I can be your eyes and ears."

"Now just why would you be thinkin' I'd be headed anywhere?"

She chuckled but there was no mirth in her voice. "I don't have to be psychic to know. I know Sam. And I know *he* can't stay here indefinitely."

They both turned their eyes upward as if they could see through the floor above to their charge.

"Sure, and you'd be right about that one."

"He's eaten, by the way, and he's in his room—showering or taking a nap, I suppose. So," Vicki said, crossing her arms, "tell me the plan."

Dylan motioned toward a table and chairs on the veranda. He had no doubt that in the warmer months the house would be teaming with guests, but with the shorter days and cold weather settling in, the veranda was deserted. He peered through the window closest to their chairs but saw no one. After a careful perusal of their surroundings, he explained their strategy.

"So all you have to do is drive from here to this—runway—and deliver Alexei?"

"I wouldn't be sayin' it like it's a simple thing. Or did I neglect to mention the tiny detail o' a half dozen men or more tryin' to find us?"

She tapped her fingers on the table, deep in thought.

"Or," he continued, "the fact that I'm quite certain they have weapons and I do not?"

"Okay. First, the men. We'll go upstairs and I'll try a remote viewer session. I'll see if I can determine where they are and what their plans would be."

"Ah, bein' married to a psychic spy has its advantages for sure."

"It *is* my specialty," she grinned. "But what about the microchip?"

"Sam didn't mention it. We were too busy boggled w' this latest wrinkle." He rubbed his chin. "I have to be prepared to hand it over at the same time, wouldn't you think now? The faster I get it out o' my fist and into his, the better we'll be."

She nodded. "We need to make a backup of it somehow. Just in case," she added with a furtive look.

"And I need weapons. Not clubs or crowbars but real, honest-to-God guns. Those guys have fire power; I know it. I've got to be ready to meet 'em with our own."

"Where will you find guns in this country?"

He shook his head. "It isn't like America w' gun shops on every corner. Even ammunition here is rationed, and that's only for hunters and those with livestock to protect."

They grew quiet as they watched a bright yellow car make its way down the narrow road toward the manor house. Even from a distance, they could spot the garish logo on the side door even if they couldn't read the single word they knew was there: *Taxi*.

"The Russians wouldn't come here in a taxi," Vicki mused.

Slowly, Dylan began to rise. "You wouldn't think so, now would you? Or maybe so because it would be the last thing we'd suspect."

Vicki stood.

"Go upstairs. Get Alexei. Bring him to our room. Best keep the two o' you together. Don't open the door unless I'm the one on the other side o' it."

She nodded and started toward the wide double doors before stopping abruptly. The taxi was pulling into the drive. The driver appeared to have a single passenger beside him.

"What are you waitin' for?" Dylan hissed. "Go!"

"No," she said suddenly.

His eyes widened and his brow grew dark.

"Look!"

The car stopped a few yards from them at the base of the steps. Before it had come to a complete stop, a slender woman with a mountain of copper hair thrust open the passenger door. As she exited the vehicle, she rested her forearms across the window frame. "Well, hello there, Irish," she announced in a husky voice. "Aren't you a sight for sore eyes? Makes that little trip across the pond all worthwhile, seeing you standing there like that." She took a deep breath. "I can smell the testosterone from here."

"Brenda!" Vicki was down the steps in a flash. "What are you doing here? You didn't break out of prison—?"

Brenda Carnegie cut her eyes toward the taxi driver, who had stopped in his tracks and was staring at her. "Just a little joke between my sister and me," she said smoothly. She closed the door just as Vicki reached her. "Hey, Sis."

Vicki wrapped her arms around her. "God, it's good to see you."

Dylan accepted Brenda's suitcases from the driver and paid him while the sisters continued their greetings.

"Oh, and Keagan, dear," she said, gliding to the driver, "I *so* enjoyed our little drive out here."

Keagan's cheeks turned deep red and he seemed frozen in place while his eyes locked onto hers.

She kissed her fingers and then pressed them to his lips. "So much I'd love to do to you," she purred, "and so very little time."

"I can come back," he managed to whisper hoarsely.

Dylan took hold of her arm. "Come back in about three days' time," he said to the driver. "And if I haven't killed 'er by then, she's all yours."

"Oh, Irish, darling," she said, turning her attention to him, "here I am, officially your sister-in-law now, and you treat me like that." She turned her mouth into a seductive pout. "And I didn't even get to see the wedding."

"Upstairs," Dylan ordered. "Both o' yous. Don't stop at the desk, don't stop anywhere. Go straightaway to our room."

"You're no fun at all."

"Are you understandin' me, woman?"

Without answering, she took Vicki's arm in hers. "Come on, Sis. We've got a lot to talk about."

15

"You broke out o' prison!" Dylan exclaimed before he'd barely crossed the threshold into his room. In an instant, his mind registered his sister-in-law stretched across the bed on her stomach, her hair fanning across the linens like a river of copper. Vicki was perched against the headboard and pillows, her legs crossed under her. "As if I didn't have enough goin' on without the likes o' you addin' to my misfortune."

"I did not." Brenda arched her brow.

"Sam sent her," Vicki added.

"I just got off the phone with Sam not an hour ago and he didn't mention a blasted thin' about you."

"Why would he?" Brenda purred.

"Why *wouldn't* he?" he retorted.

She shrugged. "Well, I suppose it's because everything is so hush-hush. You would think I was here to pick up the atomic bomb or something."

Dylan stole a glance at Vicki.

"I didn't tell her anything," Vicki said.

"She didn't have to," Brenda added.

"Is Alexei still in his room?" Dylan asked, his eyes quickly surveying the room.

Vicki nodded. "We checked in on him when we came upstairs. He said he was going to get some sleep."

He nodded and pulled a chair beside the bed. "I wouldn't be havin' all the time in the world just now. I'm just a wee bit busy. So what's the story?"

"I should be offended by your lack of concern for me, seeing that I traveled all day to get here." She made a pout with full lips.

"I'll make a note to meself to show concern for you later."

Brenda grew solemn as she looked from one to the other. "I'll cut to the chase. Sam tells me you have a microchip."

"Go on."

"I'm to get the data off it, encrypt it and send it to them electronically."

"Is that safe?" Vicki asked. "You using the Internet?"

"It's why Sam wanted me to do it. He knew I could encrypt the data so no one else could intercept it—or read it, if they did. That way their analysts would have the information immediately. Apparently," she added, "it's urgent. And of great national importance. Imagine," she continued, pouting again, "He couldn't get me out of prison to go to your wedding, but he was able to get me out for this."

"Imagine that," Dylan said. "The CIA and the FBI putting national security above our wedding." He placed his hands on his knees while he stared at her. "I still wouldn't be understandin' why Sam didn't mention this little turn o' events here."

"Do I need to spell it out to you, Irish?"

"Apparently you do."

"Sam has been trying to get me released into his custody from the day I arrived in prison. Apparently, he believes that the country can benefit from my... expertise."

"He never said anything," Vicki said.

"There are a lot of people in very high places who would rather see me put away for life—and a short life would serve their needs, if you get my drift. I knew he was working back channels but I also knew he had to tread very carefully. I had the impression that it wouldn't be known to more than a few that I'd been released until Sam was ready."

"I don't understand," Vicki said.

"I believe I do," Dylan interjected before Brenda could respond. "You were sneaked out o' prison, weren't you now?"

"I always knew you weren't just a pretty face, Irish."

"And even though Sam had everythin' in place," he continued, "he didn't know for certain you'd actually be on that plane."

"It was en route to a military installation in Germany. I was put on as a *hop* at the last minute. Given a passport under an assumed name. My code name is Dragonfly, by the way. I kind of like that."

Dylan rolled his hand as if to prompt her to continue.

"So the plane touched down just north of here just long enough for me to disembark. It was back in the sky before I had reached the rental car waiting for me."

"But you arrived here by taxi."

"Score another one for you, Irish. I was on my own. And I knew then," she paused to look from one to the other, "just as I know now, if I'm captured, nobody knows I was here. No white knight will be sent to rescue me."

"So you ditched the rental."

"I drove it to Belfast and left it at the airport rental lot. Took the shuttle back to the airport terminal and grabbed a taxi."

"And came here."

"Not directly here. Let's just say I took a couple of detours."

"So where do you go from here?" Vicki asked, her brows furrowing.

"I'll find out when my mission is done. So, where's the microchip?"

Vicki looked at Dylan. "I'm ready to do this."

He nodded, and she rose and retreated into the bathroom. A moment later, she emerged with a toiletry bag. "Brenda, I'm needin' for you to pay close attention," Dylan said while Vicki rifled through it, "we have a lot o' balls in the air at the present. Vicki needs to do a remote viewin' mission as quickly as possible. And I have a defector I need to be escortin' to a rendezvous site."

"Alexei," she whispered. "Yes, I met him briefly. What a hunk."

"My meanin' is, all o' this—your mission, my mission, Vicki's mission—it all has to take place within the next few hours. Yours and Vicki's as soon as we can get it done. And I need to be out that door within the hour. Are you understandin' me?"

Brenda swung her legs over the side of the bed. "More than you know."

Vicki recovered the box of tampons and sat beside her sister as she went through the process of finding the right one.

"What the hell—?" Brenda asked with a devious grin.

Vicki opened the selected tampon and popped the microchip into Brenda's palm.

"Aren't you the crafty one?" she said in obvious admiration.

Dylan rose. "You have it, Brenda. Now get to work. Vicki, you've a mission to do."

16

Vicki didn't remember a time when she was unable to reach the trance-like state required for remote viewing. After her parents' death when she was only twelve years old, Sam had adopted her, moving her not into his home but into CIA facilities at Langley instead, effectively separating her from her siblings. It was there that her natural psychic abilities were honed and sharpened by the best of the best—the founders of the earliest remote viewing programs for the CIA and Department of Defense, master psychics in their own right. Nearing retirement, they had been eager to turn over the program to a new generation of psychic spies. Now it came to her as instinctively as breathing.

She lay on the bed, the drapes drawn and the room darkened. Somewhere in the back of her mind, she knew that Brenda was sitting at the table across the room, her laptop open and her fingers flying across the keyboard, dedicated to completing her own mission. But as she closed her eyes and concentrated on her breathing, the clacking of nails on the keyboard faded into the background and then was gone.

Dylan was silent as he watched her. On a subliminal level, she knew he was recording the session with his mobile phone. At some point, it would be transmitted to CIA analysts in Washington who would review every frame. Her sessions were normally performed with a handler—most often, Sam—who would guide the mission and prompt her with questions that would help to ensure that necessary intel was being gathered. This time she was on her own. But there was no need for anyone to guide her now. She knew what was expected, and she knew the stakes.

As the room dropped away from her, she felt her mind separate. It was as familiar to her now as eating or sleeping. It began with a tingling sensation in her skin, somewhere between the numb feeling of a limb falling asleep and the perception that a chill wind was sweeping over her flesh. Seconds later, she had the sense that she was flying. It was as though she had become an eagle that soared ever higher above the manor house, peering down at the surrounding terrain. She caught sight of Jack bringing the horses in from the distant pen, the stable doors flapping in a growing and ever-present wind. She knew she was witnessing his actions with the same unquestioning faith she might have had if she'd been watching from a window. She knew the difference now between mere dreams and astral travel; she knew it from years of training and hundreds of missions.

She felt the same breeze that slammed the barn door shut behind Jack as if it was sweeping her into its current, ruffling her feathers. Inwardly, she smiled. It was always much easier to envision herself as a powerful eagle; it prevented the sudden realization that she was a human attempting the impossible and thus avoided an abrupt crash to terra firma. The wind caught her now under her imagined wings, lifting her ever higher. The cold north winds that could chill her to the bone when her feet were firmly planted on the ground held no dominion over her now as the bird's powerful metabolic rate kept her warm.

In the distance, a farmer and his border collies were marching cattle down a country road from a picked-over pasture to one with fresh cool weather grass and a bale of hay. The incessant cackle of chickens reached her ears from yet another farm with a giant coop surrounded by dozens of free-roaming chickens.

Ducks rested atop a nearby lake; like her, oblivious to the cold, while a lone car puttered along a narrow road toward a stone house set near steep granite cliffs and the majestic canvass of the North Atlantic.

She turned her thoughts inward to her subconscious. Astral travel and the art and science of psychic spying were based on the principle that everything is connected. It meant that she could locate someone with the same instinct and effortlessness as one locates their finger or their toe. Space means nothing in astral travel; the object of her mission could be located a few feet away or halfway around the world and she could be there in equal time.

The terrain beneath her disappeared in the blink of an eye, replaced by a quaint village. She searched for the name of the locale on business doors but finding none, she focused her eyes on a bed and breakfast. It was set in the middle of a long block of three-story, adjoining structures comprised of businesses on the ground floor and residences above them. It glowed now; to an untrained eye, it would have been easy to miss but to her expert eyes, the glimmer was faint but unmistakable, an aura that beamed like a beacon to let her know that what she sought would be found within.

In another instant, she was inside. She hesitated as she gathered her bearings, describing the room to Dylan in a quiet whisper as she circled it. It was an entire floor of the bed and breakfast; a convention or party room, she realized as she took in a dozen or more round tables, each set with eight chairs. The tables were scuffed, but she knew intuitively that white cloths would cover them. One long table near the front of the room had a row of chairs behind it, as if for the featured speakers—or a bride and groom. The rectangular table was also scuffed and old, but a stack of white cloths lay atop it, ready to dress them.

As she became accustomed to the room, she realized she was not alone. Though most of the chairs remained empty, several men crowded around a table in the far corner. Their voices rose as a heated discussion ensued.

As she eavesdropped, she relayed their conversation to Dylan. He remained silent beside her, grunting quietly in acknowledgement. The importance of her words would be captured by his mobile. She only knew a few words of Russian and was tamping down frustration when another man joined the group.

He was on the petite side, especially for a grown man; he might have been around five feet, six inches tall and perhaps all of a hundred and thirty pounds. But no sooner had he crossed the threshold than the other seven men rose in respect, their conversation quieted until he entered the discussion.

"Where are they?" he asked. His voice seemed too robust for his stature, and he spoke in English rather than Russian, though his accent was thick. He tilted his sharp chin upward. One thin brow rose as he stared down each man in turn with his steely gray eyes.

"They escaped." A brawny man with a thick beard and bushy black brows met his gaze. She tried to place his accent. Brooklyn?

She pulled herself back to the conversation as the smaller man asked, "How could you allow that to happen?"

"IRA got involved. We had no choice but to back off."

"They were coming at us like a gang," offered another, a younger man with pale blue eyes. "Out of the woodwork. If we'd have stayed, we'd have had a public commotion."

"You think I'm concerned about a 'public commotion'?" The small man's voice became ice cold.

"It seemed like the whole town was coming after us. Somebody tipped them off to us." This time the voice came from the other side of the table, where a strapping man leaned back in his seat with a fluid ease. "We would have had a bloodbath in the middle of town." He glanced around the table. "I have no doubt who the victors would have been, but it wasn't the time or the place."

"And where are they now?" The leader's lips set in a thin line as he spoke. "When is our next opportunity, Sasha?"

"Soon. The operative's wife—Vicki Maguire—came through GNIB at the airport. We'll soon know what address she listed while in the country."

Vicki felt the scene before her swim precariously as her mind instinctively whirled to the moment they left the commercial flight and made their way through the airport. While Dylan was an Irish citizen, she was not, requiring her to pass through the Garda National Immigration Bureau. The image of the innocuous white card she completed on the plane now loomed large in her mind, along with the tiny box that requested an address where she would be staying while in Ireland.

Shock resonated through her system. She was accustomed to being a fly on the wall, an anonymous set of eyes and ears. It was disconcerting to hear her own name spoken, and her married name at that. Though she had a growing sense of Dylan seated beside her, he remained perfectly silent. She was aware that Brenda's fingers had stilled. This was a game changer.

"Stay focused, Vicki." Dylan's voice was calm. It cut through the clutter gathering in her mind and her training reemerged, sending her mind back to the men.

"Are you saying you didn't have them tailed?" The man's voice was steely and without emotion. His unruffled composure was almost stifling in its coolness, causing a chill to run up Vicki's spine.

"We couldn't. We didn't see where they went."

"They just disappeared."

"Look, Iakov. They came out of the restaurant and were within a few steps of the abduction point. Then some Irish guy—I suspect someone with the IRA—tipped them off to us. They moved inside the restaurant and we were surrounded on the street. We had no other recourse but to back off."

"No other recourse," the leader, Iakov, repeated. His thin lips began to sneer as he rose slowly from his chair. He turned his back on the others, walking around the table to stare out a window.

"I left Boris to keep an eye on the restaurant—they hadn't seen him; he was some distance behind us—"

Iakov turned abruptly to a large man with prematurely white hair. "And what did you observe, Boris?"

"They never came out. A few minutes later, after everything had died down, I went inside. Nobody was there; just a serving wench. She said they'd gone out the back door."

"Gone out the back door." Iakov returned to the table, walking behind Sasha. "Something this important and you don't even cover the back door." One hand slipped into his jacket pocket so smoothly that it was almost imperceptible.

"We had no indication that—"

Before he could finish his sentence, Iakov pulled a knife from his pocket. In one fluid movement, he grabbed the man by his hair while the knife sliced through the jugular, spraying those seated nearest him.

The man remained seated as though in shock, his eyes widened. Then with a monstrous gurgle that seemed to come from both his bloody lips and his gaping throat, he teetered to the side briefly before his lifeless body collapsed to the floor.

The men around the table gasped collectively and Vicki jolted with the unexpectedness and brutality of the attack. In the aftermath, all the men remained perfectly silent as though their gasps were the last breath each of them had taken. Those with blood spattered upon them did not make a move to wipe themselves clean, as if any movement would bring unwanted—deadly—attention.

"Kolya," Iakov said, turning to a strapping man with a wide, pale face and bald pate, "do not allow them to get away again. The Kremlin wants all three—Alexei Volkav, Dylan Maguire and Victoria Maguire—delivered within twenty-four hours." He wiped the knife blade on the dead man's shirt before returning it to his pocket. "Failure will not be tolerated."

~~

"We don't have any time to waste," Dylan said as he rose from his chair. "We must leave immediately."

"I won't be finished," Brenda said.

"You'll have to be."

"It's one file, Dylan. It'll take an hour to encrypt and transmit. This thing is huge. Do you know what's in here?"

"Aye. I do." He crossed the room to the door. "I'm

going to alert Alexei. Vicki, pack our bags. Good thing we traveled light."

"Wait," Vicki said. She rose groggily to a seated position. There was always a period of time after a psychic mission in which she felt as though she'd been drugged. It was disconcerting at the least and life-threatening at its worst. Under perfect circumstances, she would sleep off the effects of astral travel but now she was acutely aware of the urgency of their situation.

Dylan turned back to her.

"I didn't give them this address. I didn't know it."

"What—?"

"I gave them the address to the cottage—the one where we spent our wedding night."

"I have to alert Thomas."

"That buys us a bit of time," Brenda said.

"I'll call Father Thomas," Vicki offered. "Dylan, they knew my name. Your name. They had to have known we were married just two days ago. But how—?"

"I don't know." Dylan hesitated, his hand on the door knob. "After I speak with Alexei, I'm going in search of that stable man again—"

"Jack," Vicki offered.

"Aye. I need to know who the men were in Donegal and why they helped us."

"Does it matter?" Brenda asked.

"The Russians said they were IRA," Vicki said.

"It might matter indeed," Dylan answered Brenda. "And they might very well be IRA. And I might need their services again." Without waiting for their replies, he opened the door. A moment later, it was closed behind him as his footsteps echoed down the hallway.

17

Dylan found his way to the stables by a gentle tentacle of light that streamed from the manor house. Fast-moving clouds had formed overhead, effectively shrouding the stars in their smoke-colored haze. A car sat along the dirt path to the stables, a brown grocery bag atop the hood.

"Jack!" he called as he neared the stable doors.

There was no response and he hesitated briefly as his eyes became adjusted to the darkness inside. A single bulb burned overhead, which served only to create claw-like shadows that bobbed and flickered. The horses moved restlessly in their stalls.

An ethereal figure appeared in his path. It was as if it materialized out of thin air. Dylan narrowed his eyes as if he could bring it into focus. It was solid; solid as a bear on all fours or a Tibetan mastiff. The only things he was certain of were two glowing blue eyes appearing like orbs through the darkness.

Another shadow crossed the floor at the opposite end of the stables. "It would be fine, Toby."

The dog did not move.

Dylan forced himself to look beyond the dog. "Are you Jack?" he asked.

"I would be."

"I'm—"

"I know who you are."

Soft footsteps sounded behind him. He knew even before he cut his eyes toward her that it was Vicki. She moved behind him in the darkness, hugging her neck with the cowl of a heavy wool cardigan. He wanted to ask what she was doing there but the words remained unspoken.

She shook her head slightly as she joined him. Then she peered into the murky depths. "Jack?"

"What is it you're wantin'?"

Dylan cleared his throat. "We wanted to thank you," he said, taking another step into the stable, "for what you did this afternoon."

"No need." He stood a few yards behind the dog, his hands in his pockets. Though they couldn't see his face, Dylan had the impression that he was looking at them impassively, neither hurried nor hesitant.

"Just who would you be workin' for?" Dylan asked.

There was a moment's pause. "I work for the manor house, the very one you'd be stayin' in."

"And no one else?"

"And just who else did y' think?"

"What were you doing in Donegal? Did you follow us?"

He chuckled. "I can assure you, I have far better things to do w' me time than to follow our guests about. I'd say that what you do is your own business... But somehow it's become mine, hasn't it now?"

Vicki slipped her arm through Dylan's.

"Wouldn't it be me who should be askin' who are the likes o' you?" Jack asked.

"Just a couple on their honeymoon."

"Oh, is that so? And every couple on their honeymoon goes into town to fetch a Russian, wouldn't you say now?"

"How did you know?" Vicki blurted. Dylan's arm tensed.

"I live in Europe," he answered, bemused. "You don't think I can recognize a Russian when I see one?"

"Then why did you help us?" Dylan asked. His voice had softened but his muscles remained taut.

"Isn't it enough that I did?"

There was a moment of silence as they stared at one another. As his eyes became adjusted to the darkness, Dylan could see the man's outline, standing with both hands in his pockets, his feet set wide apart. Vicki continued clutching Dylan's arm as the two of them peered at him while the hulking dog remained midway between them, his head down, his eyes up and his ears alert.

"I came to ask for your help," Dylan said finally.

"Oh, so first you question my help and then you want it, 'ey?"

"That's about it, I suppose."

Jack exhaled. "You want to ferry that Russian away without detection, I take it."

"How did you—" Vicki began again.

"Vicki." Dylan's voice was firm.

Jack chuckled again but it held no mirth. "I wouldn't be thinkin' you'd like the extra company on your 'honeymoon', now would ya?"

"That's right," Dylan said. "I have a—friend—coming to pick him up."

"Coming here?" He moved then, as if surprised.

"No."

"I see."

He opened his mouth to speak again, but Jack cut him off. "Are you into somethin' illegal here? Drugs perhaps?"

"No," they both said in unison.

"Weapons? Gun runnin'?"

Dylan spoke before he could catch himself. "I'd say we have a lot more weapons in America than you have here."

"Ha. You've got yourself a point there."

Vicki moved gingerly toward the dog. She reached out her hand tentatively to stroke Toby's head. "We're the good guys."

Jack snickered. "Is there such a thin' now?"

"Yes," Dylan said, joining her. "I give you my word that what we're doin' is not illegal."

He nodded in the shadows. "Then what would you be needin' me for?"

"My friend is flyin' a plane into the far end o' the island—Ballypóg."

"Bally—" He stopped. "When?"

"Tonight."

Jack scratched his chin. "If you wouldn't be mules, then you'd be with the government."

"No—" Vicki started.

"Aye," Dylan interrupted. "Our friend is. And he's takin' the Russian with him."

"Back to America?"

"I don't know. And I don't care to know."

"On his own accord?"

"Aye. You can ask him yourself."

"I don't take kindly to grabbin' a man off the streets and ferretin' him away now. How do I know I didn't fight the wrong ones back in Donegal? Maybe you're the ones he needed savin' from." He lit a match and for the briefest of moments, Dylan caught an indistinct glance of his profile as he lit a pipe. Then the match was snuffed out and all that remained was the faint red-orange glow of the tobacco.

"As I said," Dylan replied, "you can ask him yourself."

"Ah-ha. And what precisely would you be needin' me for?"

"To get there." Dylan's words had been measured but now they rolled across his tongue rapidly. "We have to avoid the main roads. You strike me as a man who knows the backroads—"

"Aye. That I do." He stepped closer to them, coming to rest his hand upon the dog's head alongside Vicki's.

"Those men you saw in Donegal today—they'll be comin' after him. We need to leave right away if we're to keep him safe."

Dylan took a step forward so they were standing almost face to face. As his eyes grew more accustomed to the inky darkness, he saw Jack's features clearly for the first time. He was older; much older. His face was lined and his hair was veined with silver. His eyes were narrow, wise and somehow foolish at the same time, a man prone to a quick temper and set ways, a gentle man whose large hands could soothe a young child—

Dylan felt his breath freeze in his throat. Time stood still. New York, a crumbling apartment building with no running water; a loud, friendly voice as the door opened and a beefy palm offered a lollipop. A beer popping open, the scent of a meager stew wafting from the oven, his mother doting on this man—*this man*—

His fist flew through the air, catching Jack on the chin and catapulting him backward. Toby bounded straight up but Vicki's head was between Dylan and the dog. Suddenly the air was filled with her surprised cry.

"Don't hurt the dog!" Jack screamed, his arms outstretched.

"You feckin' sono'abitch!" Dylan shouted.

"Don't hurt the dog," he implored.

Dylan tore his eyes away to find Vicki on her knees, her arms around Toby.

"He didn't mean to hurt me," she said, "I was in the way—"

"Are you alright?"

"I'm fine."

"Call the dog off her."

"Toby," Jack called. As the dog joined him, he came to stand in front of Dylan. "What the hell did you do that for?"

Vicki scrambled to her feet as she tried to stop her lip from bleeding.

Dylan didn't answer but stood almost nose-to-nose with him. Jack's eyes widened as he stared at him.

"No. It can't be—" Jack's voice was hushed.

"You thought you'd never see the likes o' me again, now didn't y'?" Dylan spat.

"You know each other?" Vicki's voice sounded small and incredulous.

"She—she called y' Dylan."

"Did y' forget my first name, you wicked bastard?"

"Mick Maguire. I'll be damned."

"You will be damned, you sorry good-for-nothin'"

"Stop it." Vicki moved in between them.

Dylan noticed her lip for the first time. "Did the dog bite y'?"

"No. I was in the way. When he leapt up, he busted my lip." She wiped the blood. "I'll be fine. He didn't mean it."

"Mick," Jack whispered hoarsely.

"Get the hell away from me," Dylan snarled as he grabbed Vicki's arm. He half-dragged her as he strode out of the stable.

She wrenched her arm free. "Stop it," she said, digging in her heels. As Dylan whirled around to face her, she said, "We need him, Dylan. I don't know what's going on between you two, but—"

He glared back at the stable as Jack came to stand outside. "There's nothin' between us but blood." He pointed his finger at Jack accusingly. "That sorry bag o' wank is my father!"

~~

They had almost reached the manor house before Dylan heard Jack coming up behind them. He spun around, his hands drawing instinctively into fists.

"She's right," Jack said, spreading his hands wide. "You do need me. And whether you're into somethin' illegal or no, I owe you every bit o' help I can muster."

"Forget it," Dylan spat.

"I won't forget it," Jack pressed, rushing toward them. "Any more than I could forget the only child I'll ever have and the best woman I could ever have hoped for! Don't you think the image o' both o' yous has haunted me every day o' my wretched life?"

"Then why the hell did you leave us?"

Jack stopped; his eyes wide and his mouth open. "I didn't leave you."

"Oohh," Dylan said, his fists growing tighter.

"They took me off the streets," he continued breathlessly.

"Who?"

"The Brits."

"You lyin'—"

"I'm not lyin'. I swear on my own mother's grave. I was runnin' weapons for the Provos, and I didn't think they'd catch me clear on the other side o' the world but they did. They snatched my sorry arse right off the street and brought me back to Eire. I didn't even have a trial, Mickey. I couldn't contact the two o' you's—they slammed me into prison and there I'd be now, but for the grace o' God." He began to cough uncontrollably and though he tried to continue speaking, he was forced to wrap his hands about his throat as tears welled from the pain.

18

The drapes were drawn, the room cast into semi-gloom. Six people were gathered around the small table, their heads bent over an electronic tablet, their eyes riveted on a map of the island.

"Can you divert the plane to Innisbarracar?" Jack was asking, pointing at the far northwest corner of the island.

Dylan leaned forward to study it. In terms of distance, it wasn't much further than Ballypóg as the crow flies. It was in a more remote area with the Croaghgorms, or The Blue Stack Mountains, serving as a barrier between Innisbarracar and the rest of Ireland.

"Why?" he asked. He tried to tamp down the animosity that threatened to overcome his senses. There would be time enough for that later, he reminded himself. Now everyone's lives depended on him remaining logical and free of emotion. But afterward, he told himself, afterward he would give the man nearly thirty years of thrashin's due.

"There's but one road through the mountains," Jack said, indicating on the map where it was located. "But there are scores o' cattle paths."

"But that won't help us."

"Oh, but it will." Jack looked from one person to another: Dylan, Vicki, Brenda, Alexei and Brigit. "The best way to deliver this gent 'ere is not by automobile. Those headlights would call attention to us for miles around. No, the best way is on horseback. We can move quickly, silently."

Dylan rubbed his chin.

"Y' see," Jack continued, "we can be off the beaten path w'in minutes o' leavin' the stables. We take this direction 'ere. There'd be nothin' for miles around but the northern lights to guide our way."

"How long will it take?"

"Three, maybe four hours. We get to Innisbarracar and there might be ten people livin' in the whole village. They don't take kindly to strangers. But they know me."

Dylan studied the map. The route Jack proposed offered very little risk, assuming that there were few natural dangers. Could he trust the man who had walked out on them thirty years ago? He looked up to find everyone watching him, waiting for his response. "Can y' ride, Alexei?"

"I can," Alexei answered in a heavy accent.

"Then we all leave as quickly as we can."

"Ooh, hold up a minute now," Jack said. "Would you all be leavin' Eire along with him?"

Dylan met Vicki's eyes and then Brigit's. "I don't know."

"May I make a suggestion then?" Without waiting for their reply, he continued, "The men in Donegal were after this man, were they not? Then just the three o' us go to Innisbarracar—Mick, me and him."

Dylan's eyes met Vicki's. "No. I can't leave Vicki. She stays w' me."

"I go where Vicki goes," Brenda said.

"Dylan, I know what you're thinking," Vicki said. Her eyes locked onto his. She couldn't speak freely in front of the others but her mission was fresh on her mind, along with the realization that the Russian government wanted them both captured along with Alexei. "We'll be okay staying here," she offered. "Remember the address. Those men will be looking for us near Croghan Hill."

"Croghan Hill?" Jack exclaimed. "County Offaly? Why on earth would they be searchin' for you in the bogs?"

Dylan shook his head.

"They'd be goin' to Ballytullmac," Jack said in a hushed voice. "To your mam's village."

"I called Thomas," Vicki said. "When you went to the stables to find Jack, I—"

"Thomas?" Jack interrupted.

"Thomas Rowan," Dylan offered.

"Thomas Rowan? The auburn-haired babe that almost didn't make it, on account o' he was born two months earlier than expected? *That* Thomas Rowan?"

"*That* Thomas Rowan is *Father* Rowan now, and he's not a man you'd be triflin' with." You'd have known that, had you stuck around, he wanted to add but the unspoken words were left hanging in the air.

"Well, the world is a strange place indeed," Jack said. Then, "How would you be knowin' where those men are headed?"

Dylan and Vicki avoided his eyes.

"Ah," Jack said, a broad, sly smile spreading across his face. "She's fey, isn't she?" He pointed his thumb toward Vicki.

"I'm what?" Vicki asked.

"Don't you go denyin' it," he said, placing his face close to Dylan's. "Your mother was fey and your mam was fey and you don't think I'd be knowin' a fey lady when I see one?"

"The important thin' for now," Dylan said firmly, "is we know they're expected to head south while we head north. But I don't mind tellin' you, I'm concerned about leavin' the ladies here alone in the event they change course and we haven't yet made it back."

"Oh, we needn't be alone," Brigit offered. "I've just to make the call and we'll have all the men we need. If the foreigners show up here, they'll be met with someone they wouldn't be expectin'."

"She's right," Jack said. "They'll be safe here. And—no offense intended, but we can travel faster without them."

"I like that idea," Brenda offered. She'd been silent for most of the conversation. Her laptop continued to whir in the background, the light coming on intermittingly as the file was uploaded. She'd kept an eye on it even as she'd joined the group, peering at the map and listening to Jack's recommendation with keen interest. "Three horses can move faster than five and if you encounter any problems, we won't distract you."

Dylan turned to Brenda. "Tell me you brought weapons with you."

"I didn't," she answered, a blush rising in her cheeks. "Not this time. They kind of whisked me from—well, I didn't have an opportunity to arm myself."

"You say y' need a weapon?" Jack asked.

"Guns," Dylan said, almost apologetically. "I know they're not permitted here, it's just—"

"So it's guns that you need?" Jack's face brightened. "Aye, and I can help you with that one, too."

19

The winds whistled and swirled in the frosty night like a chorus of apparitions dancing and bobbing, leaving soft whispers against Dylan's ear, enticing, cajoling, flirtatious and deadly. Ah, but they could drive a man insane on a night like this, he thought, pulling his collar tighter about his ears. He wore an Irish tweed cap and still the winds licked at his hair like fingers running through it, soothing, insistent and treacherous.

The horse's mane was grasped as well by the same invisible force, the long strands stretched as though they were being combed by an otherworldly creature that would not let go. They were nervous tonight and he imagined given their heads, they would turn about and leave the eerie foothills of the Blue Stack Mountains. He kept a firm hold on Dougal's reigns as the horse snorted, the sound unnaturally shrill.

He could read a horse like he could read a man's face, and tonight it didn't bode well. Dougal's ears were stiff and pitched forward, a sign of unease for sure, and every now and again they twitched and trembled as his haunches dipped low. Dylan peered through the shadows at the other horses, both as spirited as his; and yet their tails were clamped low, their voices constant.

In contrast, the men were hushed as they had been since leaving the manor house, the silence broken only intermittently as Jack announced a change in direction or a distant landmark for which he was aiming. Even then, his statements were terse as if he was reluctant to speak in the eerie terrain.

The ground beneath the horses' hooves was uneven and unpredictable. As the night sky began to brighten with the first vestiges of the aurora borealis, he began to see why their progress had slowed since entering the mountain range; the horses had to pick their way around craggy rocks, the tall grasses obscuring whether the land was firm or soft until their hooves either landed on solid ground or they felt the disconcerting descent into boggy earth.

He inched the horse forward until it was nearly even with Jack. He rode a silver mare with a jet black mane and tail, a beautiful animal to be sure and under the stars her coat was mesmerizing as if it was aglow.

"Are you certain this is the way to Innisbarracar?" Dylan asked.

Jack glanced in Alexei's direction before shifting his attention to Dylan. "You said you needed weapons, did you not?"

"Aye."

"Then we'd be taking a bit of a diversion." He pointed at the mountain's highest peak. "Innisbarracar would be on the other side through the pass. We'll be headin' in that direction—" he pointed slightly to the left of the mountain "—where we'll be arming ourselves first."

"Ah."

They rode for a few minutes in silence before Dylan asked, "And what type of weapons would you be havin' there?"

Jack looked at him out of the corner of his eye. "Whatever kind you'd be needin'." With that, he urged his horse forward.

They found themselves on a course that was hardly wide enough to be considered a path. Forced to ride single file, Jack took the lead as Dylan urged Alexei into the middle and he took up the uneasy position of rear guard. The Russian was proving himself to be quite an accomplished rider; his appaloosa was a spirited stallion that was rearing his head in a clear signal that he wanted to take the lead. Alexei was constantly pulling back on his reigns to keep him in check.

As they climbed ever higher, the mountains loomed large on either side of them, nearly obscuring everything else on their periphery. It was a fine place to be ambushed, he thought. He wasn't certain the horses would even have the breadth to turn about if needed. He wondered how much further they would be forced to travel on this dangerous route but Jack was too far in front of them and he dared not call out.

In the distance he heard a chorus of owls; each one individually might have gone unnoticed but together their voices were eerie, ethereal; both soft and surrounding so that he couldn't tell from which direction they came. He told himself it was nothing but the long-eared owl, or Ceann cait, a species widespread in Eire; and on a cold night such as this one, they were as likely to huddle in groups of a dozen or more as not. But his gut told him their nesting had been disturbed, setting off a chain reaction of calls.

His eyes shifted skyward, seeking the outline of the mountains that rose above them. The ridgeline appeared to be set afire from the dance of the Northern Lights.

Flashes of red, purple and green pranced and undulated, the colors becoming more vivid as they climbed ever higher. Here in the rural, largely uninhabited Blue Stack Mountains, the skies were spectacular. There had to be thousands of stars, he surmised, and for the briefest of moments he wondered if there were life forms on any of those distant white dots and whether somewhere, someone was looking back at this blue planet and wondering the same.

They came to an opening and Jack held up his hand briefly, stopping his horse while he surveyed the landscape before him. Then he looked back to Alexei and Dylan, nodded, and began a descent.

As Dylan cleared the last of the rocky mountainside that had impeded his view, he found himself on a crest overlooking a valley that was sufficiently wide enough for the aurora borealis and starry skies to illuminate it. Tall grass still stubbornly green was covered in hoarfrost, the winds causing the tall reeds to ripple as if shivering. He stopped Dougal for a moment while he drank in his surroundings. He noted Jack well out in front, covering the ground more rapidly now, with Alexei's stallion directly behind and gaining ground. He scoured the area for Jack's intended destination, eventually coming to rest on an outcropping of vegetation that might otherwise have gone unnoticed. He spurred his horse forward.

~~

The vegetation turned out to be a mass of overgrown wildflowers now gone to seed, the stalks that stubbornly remained brown and twisted and larger than any had a right to be. They blended almost seamlessly with ancient, mangled hawthorn, misshapen limbs nearly naked but for a scattering of red berries here and there, the best long ago eaten by the stalwart birds that remained for the winter.

As they drew ever closer, he discovered the plants hid a structure beneath their tapestry. An image rose in his mind of a vibrant cottage built perhaps four hundred years in the past, the walls of the same stone that littered the ground even now, the shades of brown and beige blending seamlessly with its surroundings. Underneath the gnarled shelter of limbs was a sheath of thatch; no doubt a thick layer in days gone by, it was now worn thin and weathered with time but was remarkably still intact.

Jack reached the front of the structure and dismounted and as Alexei and Dylan joined him, Dylan realized the back of the house was cut into the mountain itself, obscuring it completely from two sides. A door was deep set, its muted and peeling red paint a reminder that it had been someone's home in days long past.

He dismounted his horse and joined the others at the entrance. Metal plates had been added on one side, nails painstakingly driven into the stone itself, now encrusted with rust. The plates joined others set into the door, married with a thickset chain. Jack fumbled with a lock, blowing on his hands as if to unfreeze fingers from the bitter chill that had permeated them all. Finally, the key clicked in the lock and the chain fell away, landing with a clatter on the rock beneath their feet.

"I'll be getting a light on directly," he said, brushing into the room.

Alexei stepped to the doorway and Dylan remained just outside. There was one window on this side of the house, the glass rippled and imperfect but unbroken. He caught a glimpse of light within and he turned back to follow Alexei through the door.

He found himself in a room of perhaps twenty feet wide and fifteen feet deep. Underneath the window he had just been studying was a thick table of simple, utilitarian lines. Atop it was the oil lantern Jack had just sprung to life. As the flame caught and grew, the rest of the room leapt into clearer focus. All four walls were stone but two were interspersed with earth from the mountainside they were cut into. Only one other window existed; it was set into one side wall. From Dylan's vantage point at the door, he could see another structure through the mottled glass; it appeared to be built like the first one but much smaller. Beyond that was a heap of thatch from years gone by that might have once reached six feet high but was now compressed through years of harsh Irish weather.

Jack picked up the lantern and moved to the opposite wall, illuminating two long, narrow tables. They had been placed against the earthen wall and held stacks of rifles, pistols and ammunition.

Jack glanced at Dylan and smiled. Then, like a small boy eager to show off his toys, he moved to the head of the first table.

"These would serve our purpose well," he said, his voice gaining enthusiasm as he continued. "Have you ever seen the Armalite AR-18?"

"Can't say I have," Dylan answered.

"No," Alexei said, joining them.

"They're old, I won't be denying that, but I'd wager they're as good as the day they were purchased."

Alexei picked one up and studied it in the lantern's light. "American?"

"Aye," Jack replied proudly. "It's lightweight and you'll notice the shortness of it. The stock folds so it's easily hidden." He eyed Dylan's long leather jacket. "You can easily carry it under your jacket there, and we can place an extra in each of the horse satchels. We've plenty of ammunition—" he waved toward a separate stack of boxes "—as you can see." To demonstrate, he picked up one of the rifles, folded the stock, held it up to show its shortened length, and then extended it once again. He popped a magazine in front of the trigger. "Forty rounds," he announced. "That should do us, wouldn't you think? Load our pockets with extra magazines and we'll be ready for anything."

"Aye," Dylan said quietly, picking up an AR-18 and inspecting it.

"These are Russian made," Alexei said. He had replaced the AR-18 he'd been holding and was now admiring another.

"Ah, that would be the Kalashnikov AK-47," Jack said. "But then, you would have known that, wouldn't you?"

Alexei's voice was hushed. "How did you get these?"

"Those? Oh, those likely came from Libya, you know. We got our weapons from all o'er the world."

"We?" Dylan asked.

"Aye. *We*."

"How many would be knowin' about all this?" Dylan asked, motioning toward the long tables.

"Oh, I see the wheels turnin' now, I do. Don't you be worryin' about anyone happenin' across these and turning 'em on us." Without waiting for Dylan's response, he pointed to another area of the table. "Pistols o'er there, if you prefer them, and might not be such a bad idea after all to line our pockets with 'em. Whate'er you fancy, we're likely to have it as not—Browning, Beretta, Taurus—I'd wager a Glock or two. Even a Webley, if you prefer."

Dylan wandered down the table's length. In one way, he felt as if he was at a modern-day gun show. In another way, he sensed he had stepped into the past. His mind began to calculate his age when the weapons were likely to have been amassed. He had an uneasy feeling that continued to grow as the realization of what was stored here began to sink in. By the time he had reached the end of the table, perspiration had broken out across his brow, despite the fact that the cottage was frigid. "What are these?" he asked. But before Jack had answered, he knew exactly what he was staring at.

"Those?" Jack said excitedly. "Those are rocket launchers. RPG-7's, they are. They'll penetrate tanks, they will. And those o'er there—those are SAM's."

"SAM's?" Alexei asked, joining them.

"Surface-to-air missiles."

"Enough for an army," Dylan said quietly.

"Aye," Jack said. He looked him square in the eye. "Enough for an army."

20

A blast of frigid air grabbed the thick wood door from Dylan's grasp, slamming it against the stone wall within. He stepped quickly inside and wrestled against the winds, finally managing to close and latch the door.

"How are the horses?" Alexei asked. He was sitting at the table under the window, seemingly oblivious of the dank chill.

Well, he is from Siberia, Dylan reminded himself. This is most likely a balmy summer's day to him. He gestured toward the window with a view of the smaller structure. "Turns out, that's a stable and though it sounds improbable, the hay inside was not too old at'al." He glanced at Jack. "But I'm supposin' you knew that already."

Jack set some containers on the table. "Have a seat," he said, gesturing to an empty chair.

"I'll stand."

"Suit yourself but you'll be standin' awhile, I'd wager. The horses need a rest. The next part o' the ride is a bit more challengin' than the last." He slid one of the packages toward Alexei and the other toward Dylan.

"What is this?" Alexei asked as he inspected the box.

"Ration packs," Jack answered, tearing the top off his.

As the two men dove into the food, Dylan pulled up a chair and reluctantly opened his. Truth be told, he wasn't a bit hungry. But, grudgingly, he had to admit that Jack did have a point. The plane was somewhere over the Atlantic and if they showed up too early at the rendezvous point, they'd be left to cool their heels—quite literally—in the open air.

Surprised he had decent mobile reception, he had texted Sam from outside the stable. It had only been two words: *Divert Innisbarracar*. Less than a minute later, he'd received a reply: *Acknowledged*. Ah, but technology could be grand.

Now he glanced toward the fireplace but even before Jack spoke, he knew that lighting a fire would be improbable.

"Unsafe to light it," Jack said as if reading his mind. "Smoke could give away the location." He motioned toward the weapons and ammunition. "Quite obviously, we wouldn't want the wrong gents pokin' about our business now would we. Besides," he added, "since the hawthorn has formed a labyrinth over the chimney, we'd be runnin' the risk of settin' the whole place on fire."

"Hm," Dylan responded.

"Besides," Jack continued, "now that we have a few minutes to spare, I want to tell you what happened."

"I don't need to know," Dylan said curtly.

"Ah, but you do. I don't want to go to my grave thinking you believe I ran out on you."

"It doesn't matter."

"I beg to differ with you. It does matter. It matters a lot."

Dylan looked at Alexei, but the Russian kept his head down, his eyes on his food.

"You wouldn't mind me weavin' a wee bit o' a story now would you, Russki?" Jack asked.

Alexei glanced up, found the two men looking at him, and returned to his food. "I'm just grateful to be where I am," he said. "I'm not a field operative. I'm a scientist. I'm not used to any of this, and I won't breathe easy until I'm heading farther west. So, yes, a story might help to calm my nerves."

Dylan snorted. "It would have to be a hell o' a story to calm mine."

There was a moment of silence before Jack shoved his meal an arm's length away. "So," he said, "I'm certain you're wonderin' what all o' this is about." He waved a hand toward the weapons.

Without waiting for a reply, he continued, "I was born not far from here in a place that rightly couldn't even be called a village. More like a crossroads. Sheep on one side, cattle on the other. Nine children in my family; seven boys and two girls."

"I'm sure that Alexei doesn't care—"

"A Catholic family," Jack continued. "Do you know what it means to be Catholic in Northern Ireland? I won't bother borin' the likes o' you with details of the Irish Confederate Wars or the Williamite War, and never you mind they took place four hundred years ago and counting. The island that has been my family's home dating to the 6th century and before was snatched away from us by the bloody English." His final words were spat as if the invasion had only just occurred.

"And I won't be boring you with how Ireland fought for her independence and how the Protestants whose land was stolen from the rightful Irish owners voted to keep Ulster part of the United Kingdom. Or how their vote ensured that this tiny island was divided into two separate countries when it should have always remained one." His voice had become raspy and he paused long enough to rise, cross the room to a wooden pallet and withdraw three bottled Guinness. Returning to the table, he passed one to each man and popped open his own.

Dylan opened his beer as well and allowed the cold liquid to slip down his throat. Truth be told, Guinness was far better when it was poured into a glass and allowed to settle but his nerves were getting the best of him. Maybe he did want to know why the man had left him and his mother alone in America and set his life on a path he would never have chosen for himself. But he most decidedly didn't want to hear a rehashing of Ireland's problems. He glanced at his watch. They should be leaving soon, and he'd feel the better for it even if it meant jumping from one foot to the other to stay warm while waiting for Sam's plane to arrive.

"Ah," Jack said once his throat was sufficiently coated. "Let's see, where was I?"

"It doesn't matter," Dylan said.

"You were saying Ireland should have remained united," Alexei said.

Dylan shrugged his shoulders and motioned at Jack to continue.

"You'll find weapons and ammunition," Jack said, nodding toward the back table, "dating to World War II if not before. The truth is, there's been a movement underfoot to unite Ireland since it was broken apart in 1922. Bad blood between us, for sure; the Protestants are largely Unionists—those who want Northern Ireland to remain united with the United Kingdom—and Nationalists, primarily native Catholics, who want a united Republic of Ireland."

He waved a finger. "And to be born in Northern Ireland is to be born part o' one group or the other. There is no neutral ground."

Dylan rose. "It's time we should be leavin'."

"Ah, sit yourself back down," Jack said. "Five more minutes and then I'm done, I swear to you."

"An Irishman tellin' a story in five minutes?" Dylan scoffed. "This, I have to see." But he sat once again with a deep sigh.

"I'll go straight to my involvement." He began to cough again and paused while he fought the pain in his throat. "It was the time o' The Troubles—a time when the passions and the hatred had reached a boilin' point. I became a man along with my brothers at a time when it wasn't safe to be a Catholic in our own land. We couldn't find work because the jobs were goin' to the Protestants. Elections were gerrymandered so we would always remain the minority. The police force was almost entirely Protestant and could pick us up at will and keep us for as long as they wanted. And," he continued, gathering steam, "it was durin' the time o' The Troubles that three of my six brothers were killed in police custody. There were no warrants, no charges brought, no trials. One day you were on the street and the next, rotting in some English prison."

Jack locked his eyes onto Dylan's. "You most likely have no idea what it took for me to raise enough money to get me and your mother to America. I knew she was pregnant and I'd be damned if any child o' mine would be raised under the murderous flag o' Iron Maggie."

"We really have to go," Dylan said. This time, he rose and adjusted his cap for the cold that he knew would assault him as soon as he opened the door.

"I was runnin' weapons for the Provo's." Jack's statement was said with force.

"The Provo's?" Alexei had come to his feet as well, and now he glanced from one man to the other.

Dylan pulled his collar closer to his neck and placed his hand on the door latch.

"The Provisional arm of the Irish Republican Army. Aye, what you see here is not but a fraction o' the arms we gathered. And the truth is, I was on the streets o' New York with a new wife and a babe at her tit, arrangin' a shipment—funded entirely, I might add, by Irish-Americans sympathetic to our cause—when they snatched me right out o' the Bronx. I couldn't believe it." His eyes grew wide. "I'd made it to America, wouldn't you know. I was a free man. And the next thin' I know, I've two black eyes and a broken nose and I'm being hauled back across the blasted ocean!"

Dylan froze with his hand on the latch. The room grew so silent that he could hear the beating of his own heart. He turned his head in Jack's direction but did not meet his eyes. "You swear to God that you did not leave of your own accord?" he asked.

Jack rose. "I wouldn't have left that gorgeous angel and my only child if Satan himself had come for me." He gathered the trash left from their meals into a paper bag. "Only thing is, the Devil did come for me, and I found I had nothin' to say about it!"

"But—" Dylan started but Jack had dissolved into another coughing spell. He watched his father wrapping his hands about his neck in a vain attempt to stop the pain. When he finally calmed and wiped his mouth with the back of his hand, Dylan cleared his own throat and said, "We'll be late if we wait another minute. Help me get the horses ready and the weapons loaded and let's get us the hell out o' here."

21

Vicki was almost finished with her phone call to Father Thomas when someone rapped softly at their door. She looked first at the clock on the mantel before turning to Brenda. It was approaching midnight but it seemed much later since the skies had turned dark shortly after four in the afternoon. Now she exchanged a furtive glance with her sister, who had remained at the table with her laptop all evening.

"It's Aislinn," came a voice muffled by the door. "I've brought you tea and scones."

"I'll get it," Brenda said, rising.

"I took a gamble you'd still be awake," Aislinn said as she stepped inside with a wide tray. "We couldn't sleep either, and we've busied ourselves in the kitchen, though we're preparin' to retire..."

Noting that Brenda was clearing a space for the tray at the table, Vicki turned toward the window in an attempt to focus more fully on Thomas' voice.

"I'm in the bell tower at present," he was saying. "I've a clear view of the area and nothin's yet occurred that is outside the ordinary."

"You've alerted the people in the village?"

"Aye; tis the first thing I did. I've men at the cottage where you like to stay and others in the village and surrounding area. It's quite peaceful, actually. Though m' teeth are chattering."

Vicki smiled despite the gravity of the situation as she envisioned the priest in the bell tower atop the church. In her mind's eye, she imagined the rolling hills in three directions and the village proper in the fourth. The village lights, especially along the main road, would be lit for another two hours or so; at least until the pubs closed. The rest of the terrain… She paused in her thinking. The skies were alive tonight; perhaps the stars and the aurora borealis would keep the hills from becoming too shadowy. Shadows and darkness were enemies on a night such as this. Thomas made a sound as though he was freezing and her mind settled on the bell tower once more, where the bitter winds could reach right through to a man's bones. "How long will you remain up there?" she asked.

"Oh, a couple more hours at the least. M' mam will be bringing me a pot o' tea to warm m' fingers," he added in an obvious attempt to allay her concerns. "And Wills, the village butcher, will be takin' m' place long before dawn."

"You'll let me know if anything happens?" The murmuring behind her grew more animated and she half-turned to watch Brenda and young Aislinn chatting. The teenager's black hair was pulled into a loose bun and Vicki noticed she was wearing a thick fleece robe. Her eyes swept downward to fur-lined house slippers.

"Absolutely," Thomas was saying. "Soon after we set them on their merry way, that is."

"Stay safe, Father. And we'll talk later," Vicki said before adding her good-byes. Then turning fully toward the room, she said, "That smells wonderful. What is it?"

"Oh, its orange spice tea, it is," Aislinn said. "And scones fresh from the oven made with cinnamon and raisins. It's my mother's secret recipe. You won't be findin' anythin' w' the likes o' this anywhere else in Ireland."

"Aislinn was just telling me that she and Brigit will be retiring to their rooms," Brenda said. She reached for a scone as she peered over the shorter girl's head, her eyes filled with an unspoken message.

"Oh?" Vicki asked.

"Aye. I'm also to tell you there are three men with a watch on the house."

"Just three?" Vicki smiled nervously.

"How many would you be needin'?"

"What will they do if they notice anything?" Brenda asked.

"Oh, they'll know what to do, for sure."

Vicki reached for the teapot. Her hand hesitated above it as she noticed a tiny piece of paper tucked beside the plate. Glancing up, she caught Aislinn's eye.

"That would be my mother's mobile number," she offered. "She said to phone if you're worried or hear somethin'; she doesn't intend to get much sleep tonight."

"Is your father one of the men on watch?" Brenda asked.

"My father? Oh, no." She hesitated. "My da's been gone a long time, he has."

"Traveling?" Vicki pressed.

Aislinn moved toward the door. "No, I'm afraid he met His Maker when I was just a babe."

"I'm sorry," Vicki offered.

"I never knew him, really. He was caught up in The Troubles, you know." She paused, her hand on the door.

"It's how he met Jack, actually. How we all met him."

Before either could respond, she was through the threshold, closing the door gently behind her.

"What was that look you gave me all about?" Vicki asked.

"The file's uploaded," Brenda said, moving to her laptop to check the screen. "I'm waiting now for confirmation of receipt." She took a bite of the scone but frowned as she stared at the computer. "I should have received it by now."

"Something's not right, Brenda. I can feel it."

"What do you mean?"

"I just got off the phone with Father Thomas. Nobody has been at the village."

Their eyes met. "It's early still."

"No it isn't. Those men could easily have made the drive by now." Forgetting about the tea, Vicki moved back to the window where she peered outside. It was as still a night as she'd ever experienced. Too still, she thought.

"We don't know that. And we need to avoid making assumptions." She held up her hand to prevent Vicki's protestations. "The village is off the beaten path, you know that. And the other village you saw—the one where the men were—might also be well away from the motorways. And don't assume they left immediately."

Vicki shook her head. "Something's wrong."

"Well, you're right about that."

She turned around to find Brenda leaning over the laptop.

"What's up?"

"This isn't the message I expected to see."

Vicki made her way to the table to stand beside her sister. A popup box had appeared atop the screen Brenda had been working on. It contained a single row of odd characters. "What is that?"

Brenda pulled up a chair and sat down heavily in front of the computer. "It's Russian. Translated, it means Packet Received."

22

They reached the rendezvous point at precisely midnight. The last hour had been the most challenging part of their journey, a trek that involved dismounting at times in order to navigate the steep rocks that almost completely surrounded Innisbarracar. They came from the southeast, descending from the Blue Stack Mountains under the constant waltz of the Northern Lights, which illuminated their paths. It was a blessing as well as a curse for Dylan could clearly view their precipitous position along ridges, the rock made smooth and slippery by the damp night air, and the vertical drop along the cliff face should they lose their balance.

Just as they had descended from the mountain range, they were faced with an uphill climb that eventually skirted the outer edge of Innisbarracar. Just as it began to feel as if they were on the back side of the moon, they came across the clearing where the plane was expected to land. It was the only appropriate landing spot, Dylan thought, but he felt uneasy just the same. It felt too much like the pilot would be expected to find a needle in a haystack.

Now Dylan lay on his belly with Alexei on one side and Jack on the other. They'd left the horses tied to a hawthorn about fifty feet below and behind them before climbing the final rock on foot. Once at the top, he could clearly view the landing site. There was nothing but rock here; a conglomeration of odd outcroppings. Some claimed they were the remnants of ancient volcanic activity while others swore they were placed there by a giant race long since disappeared from the face of the earth. Three sides of the landing site were bordered with higher ledges while the fourth tapered off to the ocean. As his eyes followed the smaller ones, they almost appeared to be pillars, stepping stones only a giant could traverse, that led to a lighthouse some distance away.

"She's kickin' up her heels tonight, she is," Jack said in a low voice, nodding at the waves that lashed against the lighthouse, the white froth beating against the ancient stone structure. With each surge, the waves grew higher like a child in a swing, determined to reach the top no matter the danger.

Dylan wished he had the forethought to bring a pair of binoculars, but he supposed it was no matter now and where would he have found some anyway? He certainly could not go back and get some and with any luck at all, Alexei would be on board and the plane would be back out over the ocean in short order. His eyes traveled from the base of the lighthouse to its top. Along the way were scattered narrow windows, more at the top than the base, where brutal waves could more easily crash through glass. He had been in many lighthouses over the years; it was, perhaps, a rite of passage for one living on an island. He knew that somewhere along its height, there would be the Head

Keeper's living quarters, usually consisting of a living area on one floor and a bedroom on another. Both rooms would be round with views in all directions and connected with the same spiral staircase that wound its way from base to gallery. At the top of this particular structure were two galleries—a walkway completely around the lighthouse with a railing around it. The keeper could easily stand inside the gallery and peer through the glass or brave the cold and the wind along the walkway.

He supposed that lighthouse—like most around Ireland—had been there for hundreds of years. An untold number of keepers would have lived in its cold and dank rooms, shining their lanterns and later their lights to keep ships from coming too near to shore and crashing their hulls on the sharp rocks that lie in wait just below the surface.

He thought he caught a glint of metal in the gallery. Narrowing his eyes in an attempt to focus, he said, "Is there a keeper in the lighthouse now?"

"A keeper? Oh, no. Not in this one, I wouldn't believe. It's been abandoned for quite some time. There's a newer one farther from shore on account o' boats with deeper hulls, you know, than what they once were. Why would you be asking?"

Dylan shook his head. "I thought I saw something."

"Tis the Northern Lights playin' tricks on your eyes, boy."

"I suppose." He stared for a bit at the gallery and the lantern pane before realizing that there was no light atop the lighthouse. It would make perfect sense, he thought, to avoid the cost and maintenance of this one if a newer one had been built farther out.

"Ah," Alexei said. "Is that the plane?"

Dylan's eyes followed Alexei's. In the distance was a light, nearly imperceptible against the brilliance of the

Northern Lights, but as it drew closer the landing lights were switched on. "Aye, that would be it, I'm sure."

"It would have to be for sure," Jack agreed. "I wouldn't be thinkin' it would have its landin' lights on if it was headed to Belfast and it would be too far north for Shannon."

Dylan began to rise and then quickly held out his hand for the others to remain where they were. Something else had caught his eye and this time it was unmistakable. He motioned for them to follow his line of sight to a glow along the western border of the landing site.

"What is that?" Dylan whispered hoarsely.

"Is it a pipe? A cigar?"

It would have gone unnoticed in the daylight and if other ground lights had been visible, it might have blended in seamlessly. But as he trained his eyes at the ground level, it stood out against the starkness of the land. It moved slightly before gradually descending below the rock.

"Someone is out there," Dylan stated the obvious. "They're hidin' on the other side of the rock."

Jack pulled his AR-18 forward and trained it on the rock where the light had been.

"Not yet," Dylan said, though he also readied his weapon. "I don't want to harm an innocent bystander."

"If they're out here, they're neither innocent nor a bystander," Jack answered.

The plane appeared to turn further southeast so it was flying directly toward them.

"We'll have to move quickly," Dylan said. "As soon as it touches down, get ready to run. Don't even wait for the stairs to touch the earth before you're clamberin' up them, Alexei." He nodded at Jack. "You'll remain here. Cover us. As soon as I get the signal from the pilot—or whoever our contact is—I'll be rejoinin' you."

"Aye."

The plane was growing larger, the engine sounding loud and rude in an otherwise silent night. It was then that Dylan realized that not even the sound of wildlife, of gulls or distant whales, had pierced the calm. It was as if there was no life on the ground at all except the three of them—and the mysterious stranger a hundred feet away.

The plane was closer to the lighthouse now. It would most likely fly directly over it as the pilot trained his sites on the makeshift landing strip.

"If you have to fire," Dylan whispered, "make certain you don't hit the plane."

Before Jack could respond, an explosion erupted across the night sky, the red and orange appearing like fireworks that blended with the aurora borealis. Had it not been for the sound of the blast, Dylan might have thought it had all been a trick on his eyes. But as he stared, wide-eyed and open-mouthed while the fuselage scattered in all directions, his brain tried to wrap itself around the realization that the unthinkable had happened.

"Mary, Mother o' God," Jack breathed.

Alexei appeared as stunned as Dylan.

"It came from the lighthouse," Jack said, scrambling to his feet.

"Wait." Dylan held out his arm to stop him. "Stay low. We've got to get the hell out o' here. Go back to the horses."

23

Brenda hurriedly zipped the laptop case. "We've got to get out of here," she said.

Vicki was already slipping on her boots. "The microchip."

Her sister crossed the room and held out her hand. In her palm was the minuscule microchip containing some of the most secretive data in the world. "Hide it where you did the last time." Her voice was strained. "If they could intercept my encrypted transmission, we have to assume they know exactly where we are."

Vicki disappeared into the bathroom, emerging a moment later.

Brenda grabbed her jacket and slipped the laptop strap over her shoulder. "Where—?" she started to ask.

"Don't worry about where it is," Vicki replied. "Let's get to Brigit and Aislinn."

With a final glance back at the room, Brenda opened the door and the two slipped into the hallway. The manor house was three stories tall, a gray stone fortress that had served as the home of the wealthy and elite landowners in centuries past. Everything appeared oversized, including the wide and winding hallways. Though much of the home had been modernized, there were telltale signs of renovating limitations. As Vicki's eyes adjusted to the darkness, she took in the antique sconces, still powered by oil, centuries of soot coloring the stone so that the original hue was buried somewhere beneath. The dimmest light emanated from them and she wondered briefly about their purpose, as they did nothing to illuminate their path.

"I saw back stairs leading into the dining room," Brenda whispered.

Vicki nodded. "They must be that way." She signaled toward a black void at the far end of the hallway.

It was odd how darkness changed everything, she thought. In the light of day she had traversed that hallway a dozen times without giving it a moment's thought. But in the gloom of the night, every step felt challenging. The stone floor that had felt so smooth only hours earlier now held bumps and jagged edges that threatened to trip her at any moment. Keeping her eyes on the course ahead, she could see where the sconces were beginning to disappear around the curved hallway. Her heartrate increased and her breathing grew shallow. It was so cold that she shivered despite her layers of clothing, her fingertips frigid from touching the stone wall as she made her way toward the back staircase.

When it came into view, it was not like the sweeping staircase in the expansive front hall but it appeared to drop into oblivion. Here, the sconces stopped abruptly, leaving them staring into a narrow stairwell the color of pitch.

"I'll go first," Brenda offered.

Stepping to the side, Vicki allowed her sister to move into the stairwell. "I won't argue with you."

"It's steep," Brenda whispered. "And it's spiral. Stay to the outside, where the steps are wider." Her voice faded as she descended.

Vicki moved forward. Somewhere behind her, a door closed, the unmistakable clicking of the lockset in the door frame causing a chill to slither up her spine. She hesitated, her toes extending over the first step. It seemed as if someone was shuffling behind them but the curvature of the hallway hid them from view. Aislinn? She thought before quickly abandoning the idea. The young woman would not have returned.

She stepped into the stairwell. Somewhere below her she heard Brenda's faint footsteps, cautionary and measured.

A glacial draft hit her full in the face as if the stairs led directly to the wintry outdoors. Her shivers grew as she descended, her toes searching for the widest portion of the narrow steps. In a home so vast and opulent, this was clearly a servant's staircase designed for utilitarian use. There were no rails and the steps were irregular, the stones uneven and slick as if they might have been covered in dew—or mildew.

She began to feel as if someone was breathing down her neck and she hesitated, turning back to peer behind her. She saw nothing but darkness; the stairwell wound too tightly and the ceiling was so low she could reach up and touch the slimy surface. She dared not speak and tried telepathically to caution Brenda, afraid she would call out in the darkness and reveal their location. She could no longer hear her sister's footsteps and she hurried as much as possible into the black abyss.

When the Baltic cold struck her, a sliver of colored lights revealed a door opening onto the lawn. She wavered in the doorway, unsure of whether to continue into the darkness or step out into the glow of the Northern Lights. When Brenda's head popped into view, she was so startled she almost cried out.

Brenda opened her mouth to speak but Vicki quickly held her finger to her lips, shaking her head and nodding upward to the stairs behind her.

Brenda nodded. She had been outside and now she stepped back into the stairwell and closed the door gently behind her. Then the footsteps continued into a blackness made even more ominous in comparison with the light from the heavens that had just been snuffed out.

Vicki finally found herself emerging from the stairwell. The two sisters stood in a tiny hallway. Glancing in one direction, Vicki recognized the tables in the dining room. The windows, she remembered, sported draperies that were held apart by iron tiebacks. The light dancing across the nearest table was a kaleidoscope of green, red and blue.

Brenda had moved in the opposite direction and now beckoned for Vicki. As she began to follow her sister, she stopped abruptly, her eyes riveted on the dining room. A whiter light had appeared along with the rainbow of colors, but this light did not sweep gently across the tabletop; instead, it waved back and forth like a lantern searching in the night.

24

They scrambled down the face of the rock, their bodies low to the ground, hugging their weapons as they went. Dylan pushed Alexei ahead of them, hoarsely whispering for him to hurry though his instructions were not necessary. Dylan was close on his heels, glancing backward just long enough to spot Jack behind them, his body moving like a crab as he fought to keep his head down.

He could feel his blood pounding in his head, his breathing rapid. Every second felt like a full minute as they clambered away from the landing site, and with every one that passed, Dylan was certain they were only a moment away from a shootout or a capture.

The sounds of men shouting reached his ears but it was difficult to tell how many there were. From the distance their voices traveled, he realized they had been spread out and quite possibly had them surrounded, though it was impossible to know whether they had yet detected their presence.

The horses had been spooked by the explosion and were fighting against their constraints, ready to bolt.

"Cover their heads!" Jack whispered as he joined Alexei and Dylan. "It'll calm 'em if their heads are covered."

Dylan's fingers felt too thick and icy as he untied Dougal. He had nothing but his jacket with which to cover the stallion's head. Though it felt as if he was wasting precious time, he slipped out of the jacket and tossed it over the horse's head, grabbing it underneath to keep it taut. Alexei was already out in front with his appaloosa, Tiernan, and Jack was coming up beside him with Ciara.

"Stop at the clearing," Jack said in an urgent whisper.

The clearing was another thirty feet away from them and they each slipped and slid as they traversed the ridge to reach it.

"We can't stop," Dylan whispered tersely.

"We must. We can't go back the way we came."

As they struggled to reach the clearing before they were detected, Dylan tried to focus on their surroundings. He needed a plan but he had none. Now the chatter was rising in his head as instinct tried to combat the fear.

The clearing could not have been more than twenty feet in diameter. A ridgeline of barely six inches in width joined the southern tip. A wider path led past thickets to the east toward Innisbarracar. It appeared the most likely route because they could traverse it more quickly, especially with the horses. For a fleeting moment, he considered releasing his hold on Dougal, allowing the beast his freedom, but he knew they would never make it back on foot without the aid of their horses. The animals could travel much faster and with less rest. What mattered now was putting as much distance as possible between them and the men behind them.

The shouting was increasing but their foreign language prevented him from understanding their words. The men were gaining on them. He could only assume that they had discovered where they had been hiding and they would soon be upon them.

A third option was southeast, a mere footpath that forked away from the clearing.

Or they could make their stand in the clearing itself. They would have to use the horses as barricades as there was no place to hide. The thought of placing the horses in the line of fire sickened him.

"Go to the right," Jack whispered hoarsely.

Alexei's head jerked toward the right before he swung around to face Jack, wide-eyed.

Dylan understood the man's thoughts. To the right—the west—was nothing but nearly sheer cliff. They would tumble upon the craggy rocks below and meet their deaths.

"Let me go first," Jack said.

"I can't let you do that," Dylan said.

"We've no time to argue."

"It's suicide!"

"I've been this way before. Trust me." His eyes locked with Dylan's. "Trust me."

Dylan stood to the side.

With Alexei in front of him and Dylan behind him, Jack grabbed his jacket around Ciara's head with an iron fist. He jerked the horse's head downward until the mare's nose was touching the ground. As he moved in front of her, her neck stretched forward until she was crouching.

"Follow my lead," Jack said.

The men's voices grew louder. They were shouting in Russian and although Dylan could not understand their language, Alexei's face grew as white as death. He knew their meaning by looking at the man's face. They were on their trail and there was no escape.

The cliff was a forty-five degree angle and impossible to see past the first ten feet, as brambles obscured the precipitous fall. Jack quickly slipped down the slippery stone, his hand still so tight at the horse's muzzle that she followed. Immediately realizing that she was sliding, her back legs began to kick as if to back up, but it was too late. Gravity created the momentum, propelling them both downward.

A mere second later, Jack called up. "Hurry!"

His voice was oddly only a few feet away.

"Go!" Dylan ordered, helping to grab Tiernan and guide him into position. Alexei was down the cliff face before he had a decent hold on his horse and the jacket slipped out of Dylan's hand. The horse made an unearthly sound, and then Jack's voice rose again.

"I've got him! Hurry, Mick!"

He could hear the footsteps now and in a few more seconds, they would make the clearing. Dylan didn't wait to move Dougal into position. Jerking downward, he grabbed onto the horse with both hands and jumped. Once the horse's front legs were over the precipice, they were both freefalling.

He knew the horse would land atop him and crush him underneath, yet there was nothing he could do to slow their progress. The men burst into the clearing just as Dougal's hind pasterns cleared the rock.

They landed with a thud just twenty feet below the surface on a ledge that could not have been more than six feet wide. Dylan realized in horror that had the ledge not stopped their momentum, they would have plummeted another two hundred feet to the ocean below.

Jack grabbed Dylan, shoving him behind him before he pulled the jacket from Dougal's head long enough for the horse to come to his feet. Every second counted and with every second that passed, Dylan was certain the men would peer over the cliff's edge and find them below.

Then in the next instant, he found himself under a ledge from which an outcropping of tangled brambles barely hid them from view.

The footsteps stopped above them as the voices continued, seemingly so close that he felt as though he could almost reach out and touch them. They pressed their horses and their bodies as close to the ancient stone as possible. Jack was busily moving his jacket to Ciara's muzzle and Alexei and Dylan quickly followed suit. He knew instinctively that the leather would mask any noise the horses were tempted to make, and Dylan tightened his fist against the muzzle so only the nostrils were visible.

He glanced to his side to see Alexei with a similarly firm hand on his horse. Jack had one hand on Ciara and with the other hand, he was busily stuffing a handkerchief down his own throat. Dylan watched in revulsion as his father appeared to be gagging himself but he dared not speak. As he watched Jack's throat convulsing, he understood. He was on the verge of another coughing spell, one that without doubt would give away their position. The gag would keep him silent.

He could barely make out his eyes in the shadows. They were watering so badly that tears were flowing down his cheeks. He shoved his face against Ciara's long neck, his knuckles growing whiter as he held onto her.

Then the voices began to move farther away.

Dylan cocked his head. They didn't take the narrow ridgeline to the south; had they done so, they would have remained directly overhead and eventually within view. He strained to hear them. Their voices were moving away too quickly. They were taking the wide path toward Innisbarracar, the path that would have been easiest for the horses.

Dylan started to move forward but Alexei grabbed him. He shook his head silently, rolling his eyes above their heads.

They froze in place for what seemed an eternity. With each excruciating moment that passed, Dylan prayed the horses would not make a sound and give them away. Jack seemed on the verge of silently choking. He had to move. He had to do whatever he could to expel that gag from his father and yet somehow keep him mute.

"Privet!" a voice yelled directly above them.

Dylan jerked his eyes toward Alexei, who shook his head vehemently.

"Zdes! Zdes!" another voice answered some distance away.

After another long moment, Alexei raised his finger to his lips and stepped to the edge of the rock. Unable to see, he handed his horse's reigns to Dylan and moved silently along the ledge, sometimes so close to the brink that he appeared a half a step away from plunging over it. He stopped about twenty feet away and watched silently. Then he made his way back to the men.

"They're gone," he said.

Dylan grabbed Jack, but he waved him back. Slowly, he began pulling the handkerchief from his throat. It seemed much longer than it had going in and was obviously paining the man as he attempted to extract it.

"There are four of them," Alexei whispered. "Three were together. The fourth must have been in the lighthouse. I heard them debating which way to go, and they mentioned the last man by name—Viktor."

"Did you recognize any of the voices?"

He shook his head. "None."

Dylan turned to Jack. "How do we get out of here?"

Jack wiped the tears from his face. "We follow this ledge. The horses will be fine. They've been this way before."

"Where will it take us?"

"Farther west."

"How far out of our way?"

"Oh, a bit for sure." Jack rubbed his throat. "We'd best hurry before they double back."

They donned their jackets once more and it was only then that Dylan realized he had been shaking from the extreme cold—or perhaps it was from the adrenaline, he thought. Either way, he was ready to put this place behind him. He had a lot of thinking to do and a lot of planning, to boot. He needed to reach Sam but he was apprehensive about it as well. He couldn't help but ponder who else had known about their mission, and which of them had tipped off the Russians.

The horses were surefooted as they made their way along the ledge. Eventually, the path led upward so their heads were above the ridgeline. Alexei was in front. Though he remained in shadow, Dylan could sense him peering over the ridgeline in the direction the men had gone. When Dylan came to that same point, he too scrutinized the distant terrain in the direction of Innisbarracar.

As Jack came up behind them, Alexei held up his hand.

In the silence of the night, they could hear the men shouting. They could no longer see them, but from the sound of their voices, they were a good distance from them. Perhaps closer to Innisbarracar, Dylan thought. They why—?

He followed Alexei's signals.

There in the distance was a faint glow.

He narrowed his eyes. A lantern, perhaps?

"Zdes! Zdes!" the voices seemed to be saying, their shouts growing louder and more urgent.

Jack came to stand between Dylan and Alexei.

"What are they saying?" Dylan asked.

"Over here! Over here!" Alexei interpreted.

"They're following the lantern," Jack breathed. His voice sounded strange and Dylan turned to look at him. His face had gone completely ashen.

"Are you okay, Jack?" Dylan asked.

"It's Nettie O'Connelly," he answered in a revered whisper.

"She's in danger then," Dylan said, his words coming fast.

"Oh, no. It's not Nettie O'Connelly who would be in danger, son. It's anyone who would follow her."

The voice grew louder and more insistent and the sound of gunfire rang out. The three men stood riveted to the scene unfolding in front of them. The lantern bobbed, appearing in one place and then another so rapidly that the woman was clearly running. They could not see the men behind her; they could only hear their voices as they tried to follow.

"They think it's us," Alexei said. "They think they're firing at us."

"They'll kill her," Dylan said, starting forward.

Jack held him in place. "They can't kill her. Nettie O'Connelly is already dead."

25

They huddled in the corner of the kitchen, a room so large that two tables stretched across its length, tables that no doubt had been the workspace of many a cook charged with feeding a mansion's inhabitants. Narrow windows nearly twelve feet high allowed slivers of light to find their way in. The Northern Lights had turned red, causing the light to appear like flames licking their way across the tables and floor toward them.

"The back door had been jimmied open," Brenda whispered. "The strike was bent."

"They're here," Vicki said, her own voice hoarse and dry.

Their eyes met, widened, speaking volumes that their lips could not. Three men should have been guarding the manor house in the night; three men surrounding the vast stone walls. There were too many alcoves, Vicki realized, too many places in which a man could get lost amid the shadows. Too many areas in which the mists that grew and morphed in the night could conceal a man determined to remain shrouded in its embrace.

"Someone was upstairs," Vicki whispered. Her eyes darted around the room. They were standing in the only shadows, a corner far removed from the windows. The kitchen had been renovated over the years; counters lined one wall, broken only by a cast iron stove more than double the width of any she had ever seen before. On the opposite wall were floor to ceiling cabinets and drawers, none large enough to hide two women. And at the opposite end from where they stood was a commercially-sized refrigerator, the bold stainless appearing out of place in the otherwise old-world setting. "There," she pointed.

Without waiting for her sister, she moved quickly toward the small door set beside the refrigerator. It was barely four feet tall and had her nerves not been so acutely aware of her surroundings, she might have missed it. It had no frame but seemed to be cut directly into the stone, the gray paint causing it to blend in. Only a hasp kept it from gaping open and now she slipped it open and poked her head inside.

Brenda was on her heels. "They're stairs."

"I'm going in."

Without hesitation, Vicki bent low to move through the doorway.

"Hurry!"

Her hands clutched a rickety wood rail that threatened to give way under her grasp, but there were no walls to help maintain her balance. Turning around to face Brenda, she began to descend backward, keeping her palms on the wood steps in an awkward attempt to stabilize herself. Before she disappeared from view, she caught a glimpse of the white light shifting from one side to the other as though moving through the short hallway toward the kitchen.

Then Brenda was climbing in after her, pulling the doorway to and plunging them into complete blackness once again.

26

The witching hour was still upon them when they found themselves on the western edge of the mountain range. The voices and the gunfire had stopped only a few minutes earlier, the shouts of the men morphing into horrific screams that carried on the wind.

The three men halted in their tracks. They kept their attention focused on the east where the last sounds had resonated but they were met only by the howling wind.

"It was indeed Nettie O'Connelly," Jack said at last, breaking the silence.

"Who the hell is Nettie O'Connelly?" Dylan asked.

He nodded toward a small clearing. "We can take a rest o'er there," he said. "We'll be sheltered from the wind and the cold and I'll tell you the story o' Nettie O'Connelly."

"We can't take the time—" Dylan objected.

"But we must. We've gone off course and the horses have far to go. We'll just take a few minutes and we'll be thankful we did."

"I can't run the risk of getting caught," Alexei said. "I can't."

"Oh, I'll wager you've seen the last o' them, at least those four." Jack walked his horse into a sheltered area, tied her loosely to the branch of a tree, and sat down heavily on a fallen log. Reaching into his shirt pocket, he retrieved a flask. As the others joined him, he took a swig of whiskey before offering it to the others.

"Nettie O'Connelly," he began, "was the mother o' nine children and a widow to boot. She lived in west Belfast within a stone's throw o' The Falls Road and within full view o' the Divis Tower. It would have been the early 1970's, so it would." Jack shook his head. "There was violence every blasted day and night. The Catholics lived on one side o' the road—divided by the Protestants by what is now known as the Peace Wall."

He fell silent for a moment as he collected his thoughts. "Divis Tower was manned by British soldiers. Not much was done about violence against the Catholics—" he snorted for effect "—but violence against the Protestants, even in retribution or defense, was dealt a heavy hand. A heavy hand indeed."

Dylan took a long drink and allowed the whiskey to warm his throat before passing it back to Jack. Alexei had had his fill, at least for now. As Jack continued to speak, Dylan turned his attention to the east, where he continued to strain his ears for sounds of the men.

"So it didn't go unnoticed when one o' the British soldiers stood at Divis Tower and looked down at Nettie's home. Not once, mind ya; not twice. Every blasted day. She spent time each day washin' and hangin' her clothes in the yard—nine children can dirty a lot. She was still attractive, children or no; hair the color of a sunset and eyes snappin' green. Petite thing she was."

He slipped the flask into his shirt pocket and zipped up his jacket, pulling the collar against his neck for warmth. "Then things started to go wrong. We'd get a shipment o' weapons in and the Brits would intercept them. Or a Catholic lad would be hidin' out and the Brits would make a beeline direct for his hidin' place. It was one thing after another and it left us all scratchin' our heads, not knowin' what to make of it."

A gust of wind howled through the night, sounding like a woman's protracted moan. Ciara began to paw the ground and Dougal snorted.

"We began to suspect a spy in our midst. Oh, it was a bad time, to be sure. Neighbors watchin' neighbors. No trust, even for brothers. The slightest thing could set off the neighborhood like a powder keg just waitin' to blow. There were brawls a'plenty. Boys gone missing overnight. Anyone suspected of cavortin' with the Brits was dealt with severely."

He rose and stepped to Ciara, stroking her mane in a gentle effort to calm her. "Then the ladies along the block began to notice a correlation between the colors o' the clothes Nettie washed and hung and what happened afterward… When she washed her whites, she always seemed to leave her home at a particular time and always went a round-about ways. No one knew where she went. It wasn't to the neighborhood butcher or grocer or any of the usual places a woman would go. Then one day she was spotted in the center of Belfast—an area declared to be accessible to both Catholics and Protestants, unionists and loyalists, which was laughable indeed."

Dylan and Alexei waited for Jack to continue. He looked into the distance where they had heard the men's screams. After a moment, he continued. "She was speakin' with the soldier, the very one that watched her home every day."

"So Nettie O'Connelly was a spy?" Alexei asked.

"We'll never know, boy. That very night she was hauled from her home, right in front of her nine children.

And never seen again." Just as they thought the story was over, he continued. "My brothers were there. They told me about it afterward, I think as a warnin' to keep my own mouth shut and my head down. They drove Nettie O'Connelly to the very spot where we were to meet the plane. Three carloads o' men, at the least, and Nettie beggin' for her life and for her children's safety. A woman could scream till her throat grew bloody and not a soul would hear her out at the old lighthouse. And so it went on for hour after hour."

Jack looked at the skies. "It would have been just about this time o' year, I'd wager. The skies grew black around four or five o'clock and the sun wouldn't make its appearance until nigh on ten o'clock the next morn. Long nights, they were. They said that Nettie was tortured until the witching hour approached, but she never confessed, never admitted to giving any one of us up. Not even when her children's lives were threatened. She always maintained her innocence." His voice grew quiet and then stopped.

After a long moment, Alexei asked, "What became of her?"

"They thought she was dead. Her body was laid out on a flat rock whilst the men debated what to do with her. Some wanted her buried, others brought out to sea. It wasn't a night like this one, you see. There were no Northern Lights that night. No stars, not even a moon. Just a thick fog that rolled in from the sea, uncanny it was. It was so murky that the men carried a lantern from the cars to the water's edge; otherwise, they wouldn't have been able to find their way. My brothers said they set the lantern beside Nettie's body while they huddled just a few feet away. They realized everythin' had gone black around them and when they looked back, she and the lantern were gone."

Dylan rose and stomped his feet in an attempt to rid them of the chill that had so pervaded him that it had seeped into his boots.

Jack inspected Ciara's bridle for a moment before continuing. "It was easy to see which direction she'd gone; the lantern was bobbin' along one o' the paths, around the brambles and the rocks and along the ridgeline. They followed it for a bit, shoutin' as those men did—" he nodded his head toward the east "—and then the lantern was snuffed out."

He wiped his nose. "They continued searchin' for her but it was too dark. Black as pitch, it was. They left sentinels along the main roads to Belfast and left others in charge o' watchin' her home and her children. It wasn't until summer that they found her at the base o' a cliff, her neck broken. It's said they brought her body—ravaged by time and the elements—into the ocean some three hours out and dropped her overboard."

Alexei joined the two men. "And that was the end of the story?"

"Oh, no," Jack chuckled but his eyes held no mirth. "That was only the beginning. For it's said that Nettie O'Connelly still haunts these parts after all these years, carryin' her lantern at the witchin' hour, lurin' men to their deaths."

"I should've known it was a ghost story," Dylan said. Truth be told, he was trying to brush it off in an attempt to stave off the goosebumps that were stubbornly gnawing at his skin.

"Aye, that's what I thought, too," Jack said, his eyes narrowing. "Until they began to find men in the very spot where Nettie O'Connelly had been found, their necks broken by a fall from the very same cliffs."

"Are you saying," Alexei pressed, "that you think she lured those men to their deaths just now?"

"That's exactly what I'm sayin' indeed. You saw the light a-bobbin'; it was Nettie O'Connelly herself who was carryin' it. And you heard the screams as they tumbled to their deaths. And you haven't heard them since, now have you?"

The men mounted the horses.

"And I'd wager if you return to that exact spot tomorrow in the light o' day, you'll find four men at the base o' the cliffs, their necks broken."

27

The scent of damp earth pervaded Vicki's nostrils. They had descended down steep wood stairs too wobbly to be considered a staircase. As their eyes had grown accustomed to the gloom, she could only assume they were in a cellar of sorts. Her first thought was that they had reached a room with no other outlet save the one they had entered through, cutting off their chances to flee. They both remained silent as they roamed the room as quietly as possible, shuffling their feet across what she surmised to be a dirt floor.

As her eyes became more adjusted, she was able to pick out long open shelves. They were filled with all manner of objects, from glasses to bottles to small appliances that appeared to be decades old, all covered in a thick layer of dust.

Brenda was quickly moving down the length of one table, her fingers hovering just beyond the items as she went. Vicki took the next aisle, traveling alongside her sister with only the open shelves between them.

Abruptly, Brenda stopped. Vicki froze in place, her eyes darting nervously in the direction of the cellar door which was now completely bathed in darkness.

"Here," Brenda whispered, shoving something at her.

Vicki reached out to grab her sister's clenched fist, discovering the handle of a knife within her grasp. She could barely see the glint of the butcher's blade as she accepted the weapon. She heard rather than saw Brenda pulling another from a butcher's block. Her sister bent briefly as if reaching for her ankles before becoming upright again. She shifted the laptop strap on her shoulder. "That way."

They shadowed one another's movements, discovering that the room that she had originally assumed to be a square or rectangle was actually more complex as it followed the curvature of the tower at the corner of the manor house. The floor also appeared to slope ever so slightly, a condition Vicki confirmed when she glanced behind her to find the shelves gradually rising to her rear.

As they rounded a bend, the appearance of light caught them both off-guard and they stopped dead in their tracks. Her heart was beating so wildly that she could feel it throbbing in her temple.

The light was dim, seeming to dance in shades of lime and jade, an odd mixture that made it appear as though it was a living serpent trying to find its way in. It crawled along one side of the wall before turning abruptly toward the ceiling and then back again.

"A door," they both whispered at once.

They hurried as quickly as they dared on the uneven dirt before hesitating as they reached it. Silently, they assumed opposite sides of the doorway. Their eyes met, only the whites of their eyes revealing themselves through the murk.

Then Brenda took a deep breath and pushed the door open slightly. They both peered out from their respective positions but their vision was blocked by tall ramparts. Slowly, she pushed the door open further until they were peering onto a path overgrown with moss.

Vicki stepped outside, glancing backward as her sister joined her. Before the door was closed, she caught a glimpse of the tunnel they had just walked through. The stone walls were damp and covered in moss that glistened in the ethereal glow of the Northern Lights.

She shivered involuntarily in the frigid winter air. On either side of the path on which she found herself were earthworks perhaps eight feet tall, above which trees stretched toward the sky. Without further hesitation, they made their way down the path, stumbling across ancient roots. The path, like the tunnel and the hallway, was curved. It continued to slope downward, often at an angle so steep that they struggled against the urge to begin running. As Vicki glanced skyward, she caught a slice of the manor house rising above them, the three stories now appearing twice that tall, foreboding and surly, the windows frosty as they reflected the green and red glow of the Northern Lights.

Then the path ended so brusquely that they almost stumbled over one another in their efforts to stop.

They found themselves at the river's edge. Ice encrusted the shoreline, extending over the banks until a fast-moving current dispelled it, sending shards downriver. The chill from the water plunged her into uncontrollable shaking as if she had been shoved into a freezer. In an instant, she realized what they had traversed: in ancient days, the servants would have traveled through the cellar to remain out of sight from the wealthy landowner and his family. The trail that led to the river was the path they had most likely taken to fill buckets of water to return to the kitchen, a journey that would have been uphill carrying heavy pails. Maneuvering through the winding tunnel, they would have emerged eventually at the base of the wood steps, where they would have climbed them with their pails, slipping them through the tiny doorway into the kitchen. It was a journey they undoubtedly would have taken each and every day and possibly several times in the course of each day. It would have been backbreaking; considered women's work, she could envision a slight young woman or a stooped elder making the trip in the dead of winter.

Brenda had been peering in one direction and now she took a few steps down an opposing path to examine the opposite terrain. As Vicki followed her gaze, she noted there were no lights from neighboring homes. Her first inclination was to run to a neighbor and phone the authorities about an intruder, but now she couldn't remember seeing another home for miles around on their excursions to Donegal. The only neighbors she had spotted had been during her psychic mission and now she struggled to remember which direction they had been in.

"Well, we can't cross the river," Brenda whispered. Her voice shook with the cold, her breath appearing like a fog around her face.

"The trees are closer in that direction," Vicki said. "We need cover."

Brenda looked back toward the house. "Where did Aislinn say they would be?"

"Their rooms, I think."

"Do you have any idea where they would be?"

Vicki shook her head. "None."

"We can't leave them in there."

"We can't go back after them. Our best bet is to get help—"

"We can't leave them. *I* can't leave them."

"Are you suggesting—?"

"I'm suggesting that you get to the cover of those trees. Try to get to the stables, if you can. Do you think you can mount a horse on your own?"

She nodded. "If I need to, I will."

"Ride bareback. I doubt you could saddle a horse properly."

"I—"

"Once you're on horseback, head back into the woods. Stick to the shadows and find your way to somebody's home. There has to be someone else living out here somewhere."

"What about the men who were guarding the house?"

Brenda shook her head. "Do you see them anywhere?"

Vicki swallowed. "What about you?"

"I'm going to make my way around the manor. See if I can spot any lights. Then I'll find a way back in."

"You can't—"

"I can." Brenda clutched the knife she'd found in the cellar. In the light from the stars and the aurora borealis, Vicki could plainly see it was a hefty butcher knife. She had forgotten her own knife as she'd held it within the grasp of her frozen fingers.

"Keep that knife close to you. And don't hesitate to use it."

Before Vicki could respond, Brenda was disappearing in the opposite direction, her copper hair catching the starlight before she vanished into the shadows.

28

Dylan knew his growing apprehension was not reasonable but then fear was often irrational, was it not? It often had no face and no voice but for the inner utterances in the mind; the nagging suspicion that something was gravely amiss. It was that feeling that someone was breathing down his neck when there was no one there; someone was watching from the shadows of the forest, moving stealthily alongside them though it would have to be entirely illogical. It was the tautness in his belly, the prickling of his skin, the whispers on the wind…

He took a deep breath and for the umpteenth time, glanced behind him. Of course there was no one there. There was nothing but the gloom, the distant outline of mountains growing lower with each step of the horses' hooves and the huddle of trees that bent and swayed with the North Sea winds.

They were traveling southwest now but he had no idea where they were in relation to the manor house. His mind had been swirling with the memory of the explosion, the people who might have known about the mission, the defector still in his custody and most of all, the options available and the options now closed.

For the umpteenth time, he pulled his mobile phone from his pocket and checked the signal. He had tried repeatedly to call Vicki but in this remote area of Ireland, there were insufficient towers to allow him to connect.

Jack pulled his horse alongside him as they entered a broader expanse. Alexei appeared on his opposite side so they could hear one another.

"We've a bit to discuss," Jack announced. His voice was raspy and he pressed his hand against his throat as he spoke as if trying to tamp down the chronic pain.

"Aye," Dylan said, returning his phone to his pocket.

"First off is that phone o' yours."

"What of it?"

"It's a trackin' device; you should know that."

Dylan peered at him out of the corner of his eye. "What are y' sayin'?"

"I'm sayin' that phone o' yours, whether signal or no, contains GPS that is most likely still functionin'."

The chill grew stronger about his neck. "Aye."

"And I'm sayin' you'd be best to rid y'self of it."

Dylan's eyes met his father's. "You shouldn't be concerned about my phone."

"And why is that, do you suppose? Could it be because your government issued it to you?"

"Why would you say that, I wonder?"

"No need to wonder. I'll tell you. I'm not the smartest can o' peas but it's quite glaringly obvious that you work for somebody's government and I would wager it isn't the Russians."

Dylan nodded.

"And if you're in the line o' work that I'm thinkin' you are, then your phone might be encrypted, 'ey?"

"It's a secure line. Let's leave it at that."

"Oh, but I can't."

"Yes, you can. It isn't your problem."

"Oh, but it is. It is my problem. It became my problem the moment the three o' us left the manor house. It became my problem when I supplied y' with weapons. When I showed y' the stash. When I took y' to the landin' site. And most especially, when I found m'self runnin' for my life with armed men on m' arse. Aye, I'd say it's my problem alright."

"I'm sorry about all that," Dylan said quietly. He pulled his phone out again. Still no signal and the battery was running low.

"And it's my business now because y' can't be tellin' me that there's no one lookin' for us now, that they're just goin' to say, 'Oh, we buggered the mission and couldn't catch them and we'll just pack up our toys and go home to Moscow.' No; I'd wager they're gatherin' reinforcements and they're usin' technology to find us and complete whatever it is they plan to do."

"He's right," Alexei said. His voice was level but persuasive. "They're not going to stop until they've captured me. I'm a liability to you both. Maybe—"

"Don't say it," Dylan said, holding up one hand as if to stop his words. "I am not about to separate from you. I was told to bring you in, and by God, I will."

"And how do you propose to do that?" Jack pressed.

"I haven't decided yet."

There was silence for a long moment. They each watched the terrain in front of them, a topography that loomed dark and enigmatic, shifting with the winds and unseen forces.

"Lose the phone, son."

Dylan didn't respond immediately. He felt the phone grow increasingly heavy in his pocket. He thought of Vicki and the remoteness of the manor house, a state of affairs that could work in their favor or doom them. "I use this phone to communicate on a secure line with the man who directs my missions."

"And would that be the same secure line used to set up the last one?"

Dylan peered at him without replying.

"You know," Jack said, "we think o' governments as these big, faceless entities. Of concrete structures and endless hallways and countless offices. Yet if there's one thing I've learned in this wretched lifetime o' mine, it's that governments are made up o' people, people the same as you and I."

"What are you gettin' at, precisely?"

"People are individuals and they often have differin' opinions, separate agendas... Their loyalties may lie with the obvious or no. They look no different than you or I but their hearts are turned in a different direction. And each o' us believes we're in the right, that the gods support us and what we do, that ideology is accurate in our minds but not in those whose opinions differ from ours... And I'm sayin' that y' can't trust anybody. So the man who gave you the mission—your boss, I presume—told you to get this gent here to safe shores. So that's what y' do but you don't trust anybody in the chain. Are y' understandin' me now?"

"You would have made a good operative," Dylan stated flatly.

"Don't go thinkin' I've never been one."

Dylan met his eyes before turning back to the path in front of them.

"So who are y' workin' for, exactly?" Jack asked.

"The United States."

Jack let out a whistle before succumbing to a wicked cough that strafed his throat. He wrapped his hand around the front of his neck, squeezing to stop the pain.

"What is it with your cough?" Dylan asked when he had settled down.

Jack dabbed at tears. " 'Tis nothin'."

"Is it cancer?" The question seemed too rude, too blunt, in the silence of the darkness.

Jack almost chuckled but held back lest his throat get the best of him. "No."

"Then what it is, then? Have you seen a physician about it?"

"You really want to know?"

"I'd be supposin' we have a long road ahead o' us," Dylan said. "And remainin' off the beaten path, we can't move much faster than this, at least till the break o' dawn. So it's appearin' as if I have the time to listen and you have the time to talk."

"Aye," Jack said, smiling. Then he grew somber as he began to speak once more. "When they snatched me off the streets o' New York, they brought me back to Northern Ireland and then straightaway to England. It isn't as if they wanted a quick chat w' me, you know. And they didn't release me after a few days o' interrogation."

He looked to the stars and then turned his horse further westward. The others followed suit.

"The reason you didn't hear from me, boy, is that I was incarcerated for nigh on fifteen years."

"Are you serious?" Dylan breathed.

"I'd be there still, I'm quite certain, had it not been for the Good Friday Agreement—the so-called Peace Agreement between Northern Ireland and the UK."

"So I was a teenager when they released you."

"Aye. And I found you, I did. It wasn't hard. I returned to the village; had a visit with Bonnie O'Sullivan."

"Mam?"

He nodded. "I didn't know you were there. I thought she would be able to tell me where y' were in the States; I assumed you and your mother had remained there. But she told me how she'd brought the two o' you back home and how you'd come to live with her."

"She never told me. And I never saw you."

"That's because she threatened what shameful life I had left if I didn't disappear and never come back. She thought my presence in your life would be too disruptive. Too destructive. I was a felon, you see. Never convicted but that didn't matter. What's more, I'd been branded a terrorist."

Dylan nodded. It had been impossible to grow up in Ireland and not see the stories on the telly news about the IRA and the bombings. At one time a hotel in Belfast had the dubious distinction of being the most bombed building in the world before the moniker was moved to a hotel in Baghdad. Adjoining the hotel was the largest bus terminal in all of Belfast, thousands of people coming and going, but it was the political importance of the hotel's guests that kept it as one of the IRA's prime targets. And though that was Northern Ireland and a world removed from the village where Dylan had grown up, the violence had been reported every day for decades. Now his mind wandered to how many times his father might have been involved in the bloodshed.

"Granted," Jack said, as if reading his mind, "I was never directly involved in any bombin's, mind you. But they'd caught me red-handed runnin' weapons and that was just as wicked."

"So, your throat—"

"Ah. My throat. I'd digressed a bit, 'ey?" Without waiting for a response, he continued, "I can speak o' it now and perhaps it won't be so bad, but for the longest time I couldn't talk o' it without feelin' the anger all o'er again... You see, every now and again, we had hunger strikes. We felt—and still do—that we were not terrorists; we were political prisoners. Ah, I could fill your ears about the history o' Ireland and how it ne'er rightly belonged to the British, how even after the period of Colonialization ended and they gave each country autonomous rule, they refused to give up Northern Ireland. But what's the point of it now? Suffice it to say, the treatment we received in prison was worse than a serial killer's. Fact was, they branded all o' us as serial killers, whether warranted or no. And, mind y', I was never convicted in a court o' law."

He glanced behind him and then took another peek at the skies before guiding his horse back toward the south. "So all we had to protest our treatment was our bodies. We thought the world would take notice if we went on a hunger strike. It was a collective agreement, and I don't mind tellin' y' there was considerable pressure to participate. To break ranks was to leave a man in a no-man's land, not a unionist and not a loyalist."

He brought his hand to his throat as if remembering. "So as we were wastin' away, there was significant effort to prevent another incident like 1981, when ten strikers died o' starvation. So if we were determined not to eat on our own accord, they would force-feed us." He bit his lip. "And don't go thinkin' that they sat us down in a chair and fed us with a teaspoon and wiped our lips like a babe. Oh, no. There were at least four o' them, sometimes six, dependin' on their mood and how much o' a fight we put up. They came into my cell. They strapped me to my bed, sometimes after a whippin'. My arms tight to my side, a strap across my chest; legs so tight sometimes they'd have my ankles crossed with a strap there as well. My head would be off the bed, droppin' back, my neck stretched out."

He swallowed. "Then they'd ram the hose down my throat. These were not physicians, boy. Not medical personnel at'al. They were prison guards with no knowledge o' the human body or the damage they could cause. They'd ram that hose all the way down my insides until it poked into my stomach and then they'd pour the food in."

"Jaysus."

"Oh, I called his name sure enough, first with my voice and then with my mind. I can't begin to tell you the horror o' it. Three times a day, breakfast, lunch and dinner. When it wasn't happenin' to me, I heard it happenin' to the others, heard their screams… I covered my ears, closed my eyes, prayed that God would take me right then and there, but o' course, He never did… Sometimes the cruelest punishment is to remain alive."

Jack shifted in his saddle. "And that's the story behind m' coughin', boy. My throat was so bloodied and raw that the scars never healed. The cold irritates it. The wet irritates it. The winds and the winter. Takin' a deep breath. Takin' a shallow one. Talkin' too much… Truth be told, Life itself irritates it."

29

At first, Vicki assumed that she had stumbled upon protruding tree roots as she made her way through the heavy woods that ran along the southeastern edge of the manor house. But as she grasped for the nearest trunk to stop her fall, she realized with horror that she had tripped over a man's legs.

Hurriedly, she bent over him. It was difficult to see his face in the shadows. She felt along his body, expecting the stickiness of blood to confirm her suspicions but there was none. It was only when she reached for the vein alongside his neck to feel his pulse that she realized he had been strangled. She hastily pulled the twisted material from around his throat and searched for a pulse but found none. He would have been killed silently, she thought, without raising the suspicions of the other men.

She looked up to take stock of her surroundings. The Northern Lights were waning as clouds moved in. That could work both as a friend and a foe, she thought, shielding her from enemy eyes but preventing her from seeing all that she should.

The manor house was perhaps fifty feet from where she crouched. It seemed monstrously large from this angle. There were no lights in any of the windows, causing each set to appear like sunken eyes that watched her and waited patiently, ominously, for her to slip up. Yet somewhere in its bowels were two women who might be asleep in their beds, wrapped with a false sense of security. And perhaps somewhere else within its confines, her sister was wandering the halls searching for them while trying to avoid capture herself.

She stepped over the dead man and continued treading softly and silently through the woods until she could go no farther. She was now perhaps thirty feet from the front corner. Now she could peer upward to the second floor and spot the bedroom where she had been earlier; it seemed like hours ago. The warm glow from the lights left on beckoned to her with the promise of a snug bed and cozy fireplace. A cloak of weariness swept over her and she began again to tremble with the cold.

Her eyes swept over the front of the house. No other lights were lit except a faint one marking the front entrance.

In the opposite direction and the farthest corner from where she stood were the stables. The double doors were closed tight against the wind and the cold. In the relative quiet of the night, she could plainly hear a dog howling from the stables and somewhere in the distance others answered. Jack had locked Toby inside but now she wished the huge dog had been left free. Perhaps the man in the woods would still be alive if he had.

She calculated her movements. She would be forced to leave the shadows and risk being discovered by anyone peeking out the windows. Each set continued to appear like pairs of eyes that had followed her movements, and now they all seemed to be staring at her, watching her, taunting her.

She had no choice. To get to the stables, she would have to get back to the house. She would move alongside its stone walls, ducking under the windows on the first floor, rushing past the main front doors as well as another set at the far end. Once at the opposite corner, she would have to sprint to the stables. One bright light loomed in the darkness: the light over the stable doors.

She pictured herself beneath that light, struggling to open the huge barn door, remembering she would have to leave it open wide enough for the horse to exit. It was an impossible task. She had no idea how many men were inside the house or how many might be posted outdoors, watching and waiting. Perhaps one was watching her now.

But Brenda was counting on her. And whether Aislinn and Brigit knew it, their lives might be dependent upon her as well. She had to reach safety—and help.

She took a deep breath and then rushed across the front lawn to what she hoped and prayed was the safety of stone walls that would now become her fortress.

~~

There was a time in which Brenda had been only a programmer. Her world consisted of four walls and a computer screen that served as her window onto the world. She didn't quite know how it happened, but one day circumstances presented themselves and then others followed close behind. And before she knew it, she had crossed a line. She had moved into the dark web and found that she loved it, relished it, craved it.

The risks had been high, the danger intense. And the deeper the peril, the more she felt her spirit come alive. Perhaps it was the adrenaline rush. Perhaps it was the power that came with knowing powerful men's deepest, darkest secrets. Perhaps it was the cat-and-mouse game that she coveted.

And now as she crouched in the reeds beside the river's banks, she felt the knife's handle cold beneath her fingers, the blade hidden in the shadows of the night.

She had seen him when she and Vicki had been at the edge of the path leading from the manor house. And he had been her reason for sending her sister to the opposite side and hopefully to safety. They were opposites, she and Vicki; they had grown up separately, victims of lost parents and a dysfunctional social welfare system. While Vicki had been sheltered by a clandestine government agency, Brenda had been raised on a rural farm. The experience of her upbringing had served to combine her intellectual savvy with a high tolerance for risk and a higher tolerance for pain.

But regardless of her penchant for living on the wrong side of the law, there were times in which she could not tolerate harm to others. Animal cruelty, for example, sent her over the edge, and so did putting innocent people in the path of harm—or death.

But there was more to her decision to go back into the house after Brigit and Aislinn. She would save the two or give her life trying. And, she thought as she watched the man stride into the woods, she knew she was ready to kill the intruders. Never one for organized religion, even vehemently rebelling against it, she nonetheless breathed an internal prayer for protection.

He was a tall man; medium frame, she wagered. She might have missed him if he had not been lighting a cigarette; it had been the flame from the lighter that had first alerted her to his presence. And now as she watched him wander through a tiny clearing nestled among the trees, his fur cap was easy to spot in the moonlight.

Who wears a fur hat in Ireland? She mused. The Irish wore distinctive caps that were flatter on top, where his was obviously taller and shaped very differently. And she didn't recall ever seeing an Irishman with fur on his cap.

No, he was Russian. He had to be.

He was moving away from her, wandering farther into the woods. She tracked his movements, remaining close to the rushes until she could dash into the tree line, where she pressed her body against a wide trunk. She closed her eyes for the briefest of moments while she calmed her breath. Silence was absolutely necessary.

Peering around the tree, she spotted him about ten yards from her. He had stopped, his arms fumbling in front of him. Amazing, she thought. The guy was taking a piss.

She felt the knife's handle in her grasp as though it was an extension of her arm. Quickly, stealthily, she moved through the woods. An owl hooted in the distance and his face instinctively turned upward.

Twigs beneath her feet snapped and his head began to jerk toward her, but he was too late. She was upon him in a split second, her wrist around his throat, the knife slicing through his jugular. The blood spurted from him and their eyes met. His were wide and incredulous and then they were angry.

She dropped away from him. She watched him sway slightly, one hand moving toward her as if to grab her, but then his knees were collapsing beneath him. He seemed to hang there for a long moment, the blood gushing onto the forest floor, turning the leaves crimson. He gurgled but whether he was attempting to talk or it was the sound of his breath escaping through the hole in his throat, she couldn't tell.

She waited until he lost his balance and he buckled over, his head landing unnaturally onto the leaves, his eyes still staring at her. She stepped forward, swiftly dipping her hand into one pocket and then another until her fingers wrapped around the gun. She extracted it and took a moment to look at it. A Makarov. Twelve rounds. She grappled through his pockets until she found extra ammunition.

Brenda placed the extra bullets in one pocket and the pistol in the other and then wiped the knife across her pants before sticking it inside her boot, wedging it in place with her thick sock. Then she turned toward the house.

The door off the hallway was in plain view, hanging ajar as it had been when she and Vicki had been making their way down the back staircase toward the kitchen. She made a dash for it across the open expanse of lawn, the clouds parting so the moonlight found her like a beacon cutting through the darkness, following her until she had slipped inside.

She had the strangest feeling that someone was still out there and she stopped just on the other side of the threshold to look back. Her eyes scoured the tree line. She could no longer see the dying Russian; he was hidden now by the shadows. She narrowed her eyes. There was no movement. No one was there. But as she turned back to the cavernous manor house, she couldn't shake the feeling that she was still being watched.

30

The skies were the color of tar, the Northern Lights only a distant memory as the three men neared a plateau overlooking a sleepy village below. Nothing about it appeared familiar to Dylan and he searched his memory as he tried to connect it to the manor house. Finally, he turned in his saddle to face Jack.

"Did you get us lost?"

"Ha!" Jack retorted. "Blindfold me and set me on the saddle arse backwards and I'll still be able to navigate you to anyplace on the isle."

Dylan pulled his horse to a stop. "Then do you mind tellin' me whereabouts we'd be?"

"We'd be right here."

Alexei laughed.

"Don't encourage him."

Jack nodded toward the village center. "That would be our destination, at least until we can reach the ladies and make certain it's safe to go back to the manor house."

"You took us in a different direction altogether? Do you think you might have shared that wee fact with us?"

"Oh, it wouldn't be a different direction. Just a roundabout one. We're not far from the manor house; perhaps another hour—" he pointed to the south "—due south."

As the other horses came to a stop beside his, Dylan pulled out his mobile phone once more. "Ah. Finally." Just as he was about to dial Vicki, headlights appeared over the next rise. He hesitated, watching the lights along the meandering road. They had remained off the roads for much of their journey and were now situated perhaps a quarter of a mile from the street leading into the village.

"Best we get off the ridge and into the shadows," Jack said, motioning toward a tree line. "We can move into the village once we've reached the other side. And by then, we'll know where that auto is headed as well."

"Seems awfully late to be out driving," Alexei said as the men turned their horses away from the approaching vehicle and moved stealthily down the hill toward the deepening shadows.

Jack peered behind them. "Might just be a fella coming from a neighborin' village pub. But we'd best be safe about it."

Dylan slipped the phone back into his pocket. He didn't want to run the risk of his smartphone's light gaining the attention of the driver, even if the light was fairly dim. There would be time enough, and they were only an hour away if Jack's calculations were correct.

"How did you figure on reaching the ladies from the village?" he asked.

"Not from that GPS target o' yours, I can assure you," Jack said, nodding toward Dylan's pocket. "There's a landline we can use in the village. We'll phone Brigit and Vicki, we will."

Dylan didn't reply. He'd fought a persistent feeling that they were being watched and followed ever since they'd left the landing site. In the hours of silence along narrow, rugged trails that were often no wider than a cow's breadth, he'd dissected the rendezvous point yard by yard. Now he went through it once more.

The men had followed them toward the mountain range by foot, and yet if they had taken the briefest of moments to study the clearing they would have most certainly known that Dylan, Jack and Alexei had traveled there on horseback. They didn't mount their own horses, Dylan thought for the umpteenth time, because the Russians had not arrived on horseback. They had most likely come by automobile.

"Aye," Jack said in a hoarse whisper, "I've felt the warmth of eyes boring into my back as well."

Surprised, Dylan turned toward him. The horses continued into the safety of the trees, picking their way between them. "Why didn't you say anything?"

"And just what might I have said?" Jack shrugged. "I did what I thought was best. I diverted us to a place they would not likely be looking."

Despite the fact that a ghost story told within the backdrop of the Irish mists gave him fierce angst, Dylan said, "You said when the men brought Nettie O'Connelly there, they drove her."

"Aye."

"So there had to have been a road?"

"Aye." Jack chewed his lip for a moment. "The three of us were facing almost due north as we looked at the lighthouse, 'eh?"

Dylan nodded, though he doubted the man could see his movement in the shadows.

"The plane approached from the west, then turned south toward us. The road would have been off to our east, it would; it ended, oh, say a quarter of a mile away, between where we lay and Innisbarracar."

"So in the off-chance there were more men—say, some stayed in the vehicle—or if all the men didn't follow..."

"Didn't follow Nettie O'Connelly off the cliffs?"

Dylan half-waved in a vain attempt to dismiss the thought of her apparition. "Could they have followed us somehow by automobile, y' think?"

"I'm not seeing how they could, don't y' know. We remained well off the beaten trail where there was no parallel road. And they could not have known in which direction we would go. We zigged and we zagged..." Jack's doubt-filled voice faded.

"But you felt it, too? The eyes on us?"

"I felt it, too," Alexei offered before Jack could respond. "I thought it was just me being paranoid."

"Well if you were, I'd say we all are in unison," Jack said. He pulled up his horse and motioned for the others to stop. They were on the southern tip of the village now, ninety degrees from where they had been just a few moments earlier. They watched the car's headlights as it snaked around the hill. "She's going awfully slow, she is."

"As if they're looking for someone," Dylan finished. They watched in silence for a few moments as it drew closer to the village. Dougal pawed at the ground in impatience. "And just where would you have us heading?"

Jack pointed to a gray stone church with a soaring spire. It rested at one edge of the village but four streets converged into a roundabout at its base, making it appear like the hub of a wheel and the center of the community. "Church of Ireland."

Dylan stared at him. "Protestants?"

"Don't you go worrying now. They won't be skewering us."

After a moment, Dylan turned back toward the village. The car was continuing to slow, the only movement in a tiny community that seemed to be sound asleep. Occasional lamps mounted outside the doors shone dimly, their yellow haze amplified through the mists but having no influence on their subdued illumination. One road was wider and straighter than the others; the main street through town would have its share of pubs and yet they all appeared shuttered, judging from the lack of vehicles and the haunting silence. Somewhere in the distance a dog howled, his voice mournful and solitary. The sound lingered in the air as if caught in a wind current, not quite fading before the dog howled again, a conversation with itself in the gloom of night.

The car slowed to a gradual stop at each empty intersection.

"It has to be them," Dylan stated.

"They're looking for us," Alexei added.

"But how could they have known? I'm quite flummoxed. Even if they had been tipped off to the rendezvous point—and I don't know how that could have happened, quite frankly, either—nobody knew we were coming here. *I* didn't even know it."

"I'm tellin' you," Jack said, nodding toward his jacket, "it's that phone o' yours. You need to lose it, boy."

"It's a direct line. Encrypted."

"And I'll ask you again, would it be that same direct line—encrypted—on which you received your orders?"

"Alright." He reached into his pocket and retrieved the phone. Truth be told, he hadn't wanted to part with it until he knew Vicki was safe. But now that he had adequate satellite coverage, they were just an hour from the manor house. But what if Vicki had been trying to reach them? What if they'd left the manor house—how would he find her?

While he was debating what to do, Jack reached across the horse and yanked the phone out of his hand.

"What the hell?"

Jack popped open the phone and removed the card, tossing it onto the ground. Before Dylan could scramble off Dougal's back, he'd walked Ciara over it, crushing it with her hoof.

"Now what did you go and do that for?" Dylan demanded, picking up the damaged pieces.

Jack threw the rest of the phone into the woods before turning to Alexei. "Do you have one?"

Alexei grinned. "They already did that to mine."

"Okay then." He looked down at Dylan. "Get back on your horse, boy."

~~

Jack pried the hasp from the wood door with the speed of a man who had done it before. Behind them the horses grazed in the village cemetery, shielded from prying eyes by a stone fence that might have stood those grounds for hundreds of years. An owl hooted from the branches of a nearby tree, ruffling its feathers and rotating its head nearly all the way around as it observed the three men huddled into the tiny alcove.

"Ah," Jack said just before sliding the door open.

It began to creak. Dylan caught it, subconsciously holding his breath, and waited a moment for any sound of movement inside. Hearing none, he slipped inside, followed by the other two men.

Jack quietly closed the door and set the hasp on the floor in front of it. With a careful tap, the hasp moved under it, jamming it shut. "It won't keep a man out if he's determined to get in," he whispered, "but it'll slow him down for sure."

He brushed past the others and moved down the hall. "Ah, this warm air does wonders for my throat," he said, rubbing his Adam's apple before placing a palm on each wall. "Feel your way," he instructed the others. "She'll get awfully dark, she will."

Dylan urged Alexei to follow while he took up the rear. He didn't feel the warmth that Jack had mentioned; if anything, the stone felt cold and damp. He imagined a day in which the only heat might have been offered by a fireplace in the rector's office; a day in which women wore their muffs in the church pew, same as out. And as they continued down a hallway that curved first in one direction and then in another, he could easily imagine himself as having been transported back to that time. He shivered despite himself.

"Here," came Jack's voice through the darkness. "Stopping."

He heard the footsteps stop and the sound of men breathing.

"Ah, but what I wouldn't do for a light," Jack whispered. The sounds of fumbling reached Dylan's ears before a flash of light appeared. Jack lit his pipe and held it aloft for a moment, smiling slyly. Then he turned his attention to a closed door. He groped along the mull cover just below a stained glass transom. "Ah," he said again. The light was trickling to faint embers in the pipe's chamber as he retrieved the hidden key and unlocked the door.

A blast of cold air hit them full in the face as they entered.

"I thought we were outside again," Dylan whispered with an involuntary shudder.

"Oh, 'tis the ghosts of all those who worshipped here," Jack said, crossing his heart.

As they made their way deeper into the room, Dylan realized they were entering beside a pipe organ. Jack had moved a few feet away from them and after a moment, a light burst forth on a tapered candle. "Here," he said, "take this for me."

Dylan took the light by its processional candlestick, the metal cold against fingers that were chilled already. He realized as Jack made his way closer to the front that they were standing in the south transept. The organ comprised most of this area and behind that was the door from which they had entered. He stepped to the crossing to peer back at the nave. He had to admit that what little he could see was beautiful. The stone floor beneath his feet was smooth and intricately fashioned into an elaborate design that stretched through the center of the nave. On either side were rows of dark pews, above which was a curved ceiling.

A black ball morphed out of the shadows, hurling directly at his head. He ducked just as it brushed past him, ruffling his hair.

Alexei dodged and bobbed as it circled his head at breakneck speed. "A bat!" he exclaimed, nervously waving his arm.

"Christ Almighty!" Dylan said, jumping back as it flew toward him again.

"He'd be up here," Jack said calmly, nodding toward the stained glass representation of Christ on the cross.

As the bat retreated back into the shadows of the vaulted ceiling, Dylan turned around to find Jack pulling a rug from behind the altar.

"What would you be doing?" he asked, wiping his brow as he joined him.

"There's a door here," he answered, "leads down to a cellar. They've a landline there and I intend to phone Brigit."

"Now how would you be knowin' that?" Dylan asked.

Alexei knelt beside Jack. "Here it is," he said. "A catch." He sprang the catch and a wood door tilted upward. As Dylan stared at it, he realized the wood had been painted to exactly blend with the stone flooring.

The three men peered into the hole.

"I'll go first," Jack said, "on account o' you ladies bein' so prone to fright. Mick, hand the candle to the Russian. You'll need both hands to follow us. You'll need to pull the rug o'er the door as you pull it back down. Think you can manage that?"

"Aye," Dylan said. He handed the candlestick to Alexei, who held it above the trap door while he studied what little he could see.

Once the flame was away from Dylan's hand, it seemed the air had shifted. It had grown colder somehow, the shadows longer. The flying rat was nowhere to be seen, which gave him the willies all the more. And now the chill of the night and the long, tedious hours on the horse's back had permeated through to his bones. Oh, it would take a long, hot bath, a sizzling fire and a woman's curves to begin to put the warmth back into him for sure.

By the time he heard the soft fall of a footstep behind him, he couldn't turn around quickly enough. As he began to swivel back towards the nave, he was hit full in the head. He had a fleeting glance of Alexei looking upward from the cellar, his eyes widened in surprise, before Dylan fell toward the trap door. His head crashed against the header, ricocheting off it as he tumbled to the floor. The last thing he saw before complete blackness set in was a heavyset man standing over him holding an elaborate brass candlestick as though it was a baseball bat, Dylan's blood dripping from one end.

31

Vicki hunched behind the shrubbery at the corner of the manor house. The stone seemed to vibrate as though it was alive, despite the fact that it was cold and unyielding against her back. She had crawled, crept and at times, rushed past windows and doorways, terrified that at any moment she would be discovered and apprehended. Her surroundings were eerily silent; there were no signs of life from either inside or outside the manor house.

And now she found herself at war within herself.

Her body yearned to rush for the stables, toss open the doors and grab the first horse she came to. But her mind urged her to use her psychic gifts to discover where the men were and where her best chances of success might lie.

There was, perhaps, a misconception of what it meant to be psychic. Those within the CIA who did not have her gift assumed that she could turn it on or off at will. That she could see inside their homes, inside their offices or inside their minds. She would know things before they happened; could select the winning lottery ticket or know precisely what and where something would occur.

Yet it was both a gift and a skill, one that required relative silence in her spirit as well as her surroundings. It required letting go of the physical plane altogether, separating her soul from her flesh and blood, so it could wander away from the body that would otherwise confine her.

She closed her eyes. They pained her now; the biting wind had raked across them like gritty sandpaper. Yet when she closed her eyes, her spirit took advantage of the lapse and instantly seared her brain with the image, not of Brigit and Aislinn sleeping peacefully, oblivious to the danger that may lie just outside their door, but instead of two women clinging to one another in an unfinished room of some type. They were attempting to will their hearts to be still, their breath to slow, afraid that the slightest sound, the most insignificant movement, would give them away and seal their fates.

They knew.

She kept her eyes closed even as her mind shouted that they knew their home had been invaded and somehow they knew it meant the men they had entrusted their safety to were gone.

Now her thoughts invaded the image. She had moved across the entire front wall of the manor house without detection. She had hoped, perhaps, that an Irishman would spot her and realize that they were all in danger. Where were the other two men assigned to guard them?

Her soul searched for them, scouring the grounds around the house, the stables, the woods and the river. As if in reply, Toby whined as he scratched at the stable door in a plea to be freed from its confines.

Then in a flash, she saw one man lying on an icy stone floor. She tried to zoom in an effort to see whether he was alive, but in the next instant he was gone.

Was she imagining it? She wondered. She shook her head both in answer to her question and in an attempt to clear her mind of the images. The Russians. Where were the Russians?

The visions for which she searched were not forthcoming and despite herself, she sighed deeply.

They knew. Somehow, they had known where and how to intercept Brenda's transmission. That meant they knew the area of Ireland where they were staying. They had not gone to the village of Dylan's youth. Or had they? Was another team there now, and was Father Thomas attempting to escape just as she was?

Her cell phone grew heavy in her coat pocket, and instinctively she reached for it. But instead of dialing a number, she switched it into silent mode. It was only by the grace of God that it hadn't rung while the Russians had searched for them in the house.

She took a deep breath and stood where she could peer past the shrubbery and toward the stables. There was another option. Instead of rushing toward the main doors, she could make her way around the manor house until she could make a dash for the back of the stables. There, the doors opened onto the meadow where the horses usually wandered during the daylight hours.

Once she was inside the barn, she would call Dylan or Thomas or both. Then she would find a way to mount a horse and ride it bareback to God knows where. The situation was so ludicrous she would have laughed aloud had it not been so dire.

She took another deep breath and was just about to step out from behind the bushes when she heard the unmistakable sound of a car door closing followed by an engine rolling over.

She held her body flat against the stone even as it continued to vibrate, willing herself to become invisible. Her heart was hammering out of control, her face growing flush despite the cold. Slowly, methodically, she peered around the side of the house.

The vehicle was between her and the stables. It was faced in the opposite direction but a glance into the rearview mirror could easily reveal her presence. She was unable to see the driver from this angle and distance, and the steam from the exhaust pipe further exasperated her efforts. She considered using the steam as a cover; it was a long shot but she had no other choice.

A movement caught her eye and she peered beyond the car, her eyes narrowing. A man was moving along the tree line, his eyes riveted to the car. He was wearing a leather jacket and judging from the wide shoulders, he was a burly man. As he stepped into the waning moonlight, she caught a glimpse of his wide, pale face. She gasped as she recognized him from her vision.

He moved stealthily along the tree line, inching closer to the vehicle. A cap covered his head and was pulled low to his upturned collar and down to his brows.

Vicki's movements shifted to autopilot. In an instant, her brain registered the man from the village, a man Iakov called Kolya—the man assigned to capture Dylan, Alexei and herself. And in another instant, she was reminded of the vehicle idling just a few feet from her. Now she became convinced that the driver was one of Brigit's Irish friends, most likely warming up in his vehicle during a long night of frigid surveillance.

Before she even knew her plan, she was sprinting from the safety of the hedges to the passenger side of the vehicle. She threw open the passenger door and as she jumped inside, she rammed the gear shift into Drive.

At that moment, a shot rang out. She heard the sound simultaneously with the shattering of glass from the driver's side window. The car lurched forward, careening toward the side of the house before abruptly jerking toward the rear. Another shot and the back window exploded into the back seat.

Blood covered the dashboard and as she whipped her head around, she saw Kolya running behind them, his gun raised to fire again.

32

Dylan had never before heard church bells reverberating in his head but now he could not get the incessant pealing to stop. With each clang his head throbbed more violently.

"Now why did you feel the need to hit the boy so strongly?"

The voice echoed in his head like so many men speaking in unison, disembodied and distant yet somehow right on top of him. He felt something cold and wet brush across his brow before resting there. Struggling against the pain to open his eyes, he could vaguely make out a shifting, blurred shape leaning over him. His hand, almost of its own accord, reached up with honed precision to grab an out-of-focus arm as it neared his face.

"Don't be gettin' your knickers in a wad now, boy."

He strained to focus his eyes but the image above him was too fuzzy. God help him but he was going to be nauseous. Closing his eyes, he made a guttural sound as he strove to sit up.

"Easy now," the voice said.

As he came to an unsteady seated position, he slowly began to realize that he had been lying in a church pew in the transept. It was only a few feet from the altar and somewhere in the back of his mind the pieces began to fall into place like a shattered lake's surface returning to calm. No doubt he had been moved to the area where the choir normally sat. He became conscious of the object across his brow and realized it was being held in place.

"What the devil?" he said at last. His voice sounded hoarse, his throat strained, and though it didn't seem possible, the effort caused his head to throb even more violently.

"Ooh, it's a good thing to see you come to, it is," Jack said. He knelt so Dylan could see his face. His brows were furrowed with concern, his eyes dark. "You took a good one, right on the old head, you did."

Jack pulled the thin terrycloth from Dylan's forehead. It was soaked in blood.

At the sight of his own gore, the adrenaline surged through his body like an electric charge. He leapt from the pew ready to do battle but as shapes and figures swam before him in a vicious whirlpool, his knees buckled and he found himself grabbing the pew's arm to prevent himself from falling.

On the bench adjacent to his own sat a heavyset man in a thick flannel bathrobe, his own face bloodied. Alexei was beside him, helping to tilt his head back in a hopeless attempt to stem a wicked nose bleed.

"Son," Jack said with a slow smile, "meet Father Francis. This is his church."

"You're a man o' God and you almost killed me?" Dylan breathed. "What the devil's wrong w' you?"

"And just how was I to know you weren't here to rob me blind?" the man answered, groaning.

"You should've seen Alexei," Jack said excitedly. "I've never seen a man move so fast! He was up from the cellar quick as you please, grabbed that brass candlestick and would have killed the Father, had I not intervened."

"I didn't realize you were the priest," Alexei said apologetically.

"Well, it's all a wee bit o' a misunderstanding, wouldn't you say now?" Jack continued.

"A 'wee bit'?" Dylan repeated incredulously.

"Had I known it was you, Jack, I would never have hit the boy. You might've given me fair warning you were coming, you know."

"Oh, but I couldn't, you see. I was flyin' by the seat o' m' knickers. Didn't quite know I'd be here until just before..." He interrupted himself. "Ah, but where's m' manners? Let me introduce m' son to you, Francis! Aye, 'tis Mick himself."

Francis peered at Dylan. The area around his eyes was already turning black and blue. From the looks of things, Alexei must have cracked the candlestick over the man's bulbous nose and now it was hanging off to one side like the bone had been dislodged. For some odd reason that he knew he should feel guilty for experiencing, it made Dylan's head feel a tiny bit better.

Despite the pain the priest must have been suffering, he breathed incredulously, "Mick Maguire? So you exist after all. I thought you to be a figment of the old man's imagination." With the effort to both breathe and speak, his nosebleed worsened.

"I'm afraid not," Dylan said.

"Keep your head back," Alexei said, trying to stem the tide.

"Ooh," Francis said, his voice nasal now that Alexei was pressing against his nostrils, "but you were only a spark in your mother's eye when she left Eire." He took a deep breath through his mouth, revealing crooked and yellowing teeth. "You've been in America this whole time, have you?"

"He works for the United States Government now, he does," Jack said proudly.

"No," Francis breathed. "I just attacked a representative of the American government? Ooh, but I would ne'er—had I known—"

"I must use your phone," Jack interrupted. "I must reach Brigit out at the manor house. You see, we have Russian agents after us all—"

"Quiet." Alexei's voice was firm as it rose above the others. As all eyes turned to him, he held up his hand for silence. Nodding toward the far wall, they all focused their attention on the row of stained glass windows that ran the length of the nave.

As lights shone on the prisms of glass, they created wraithlike tentacles that sped across the pews and floor toward them in a rainbow of colors. Collectively, they held their breath as first one window and then the next received the full attention of the headlights. They moved deliberately before coming to a full stop at the last window.

"More company?" Francis breathed. "If I'd known to expect a party, I might've left out the wine."

The bleeding on Dylan's forehead had slowed and now he struggled to rise above the physical pain.

"Dear friend," Jack said, placing a hand on Francis' shoulder, "It's down in the hidey-hole for us, I'm afraid."

"Just like old times, 'ey?"

He nodded. "Ah, but I thought those days were behind me. Best you be comin' too."

Francis tried to snort but his nose would not cooperate. "Now, Jack, you know I never do."

Dylan tapped Alexei's arm. The Russian had remained transfixed, his eyes on the last window as his face had grown paler. Dylan tried to nod toward the trap door but the movement caused the room to spin yet again. Despite himself, he groaned as he rose. Who would have known that candlesticks could serve as such a weapon? He thought.

"These aren't like the others," Jack was saying to Francis.

"And how about is that?"

"They're Russians."

"Russians, y' say?"

"Sorry to interrupt your social niceties over there," Dylan said as he reached the trap door, "but the two o' you best be haulin' your arses down this ladder and be quick about it."

"Go," Francis said, pushing Jack toward Dylan and Alexei. "I'll hold 'em off, I will."

"No. It's too dangerous. I can't allow you to do such a thing—"

"Go." Francis rose on wobbly legs.

"Call the authorities, Father."

"The authorities?" A wry smile crept across Francis' face. "Now that would be a twist, 'ey?"

"I wouldn't be thinkin' that's such a grand idea," Dylan said. "We don't want questions about our actions—or about Alexei here."

"The boy's right. Best to leave the authorities out o' it," Francis said.

Alexei scurried down the ladder. "You're all wasting time!" he whispered hoarsely.

As soon as Jack began to make his way toward the trap door, Dylan climbed down the ladder into the darkened cellar. Francis followed behind and as soon as Jack's head had cleared the opening, he began to close the door.

"What about your nose?" Jack asked.

"A man can't have a nose bleed?" Francis retorted.

"I fear it's broke. It's lookin' a bit like the boot of Italy."

"Well, I don't suppose the Russkies will be examinin' me to find out now, will they?" With that, he slammed the trap door shut. As Jack dropped to the floor below, they heard the sound of scuffling above them as the rug was moved back into place.

The cellar was dark and dank but for some strange reason that seemed oddly out of place with their circumstances, Dylan found the fragrance of damp Irish sod comforting. As his eyes grew accustomed to the gloom, he realized that scattered throughout the ceiling were holes no larger than a quarter at best. Jack was making his way to one of them now, peering upward to get a glimpse of the nave above them.

Dylan found another opening in the low ceiling. The floor above had originally been thick planks, many of which were still in place. Others had been replaced over the years as the wood had decayed and then at some point, stones had been laid atop the planks. Whether by accident or design, there were knotholes scattered throughout the flooring that doubled as the cellar's ceiling, and the stones had been arranged to avoid those gaps. He had no doubt the stone's pattern had been designed to take advantage of these peepholes. Ireland had a long and bloody history, as most of Europe had, and the Irish people had remained resourceful at hiding from the enemy only to reemerge when least expected.

Now he watched as Francis' shadowy figure as he lit rows of candles as though preparing the sanctuary for worship.

The sound of car doors closing reached their ears. Dylan caught the eye of the others as he held up one, two and then three fingers. Alexei and Jack nodded their agreement. Three men then.

The double doors at the front of the sanctuary blew open just as Francis was closing the narrow door at the side of the transept.

Dylan watched as the three men entered almost shoulder to shoulder. The one in the center was slight in stature, easily six inches shorter than the others that flanked him. His face was pale, his brows almost nonexistent. His coat appeared thick but the heft did nothing to mask his narrow shoulders. But the moment they entered, he was barking orders; the others instantly followed his directives without question.

He stole a glance at Alexei. Though he didn't understand Russian, he hoped Alexei's expression might give away the man's meaning but his face seemed set in stone, his eyes riveted on the knothole above his head.

No matter, Dylan thought. Their intent was clear enough. They aimed to capture or kill the lot of them and he'd be damned if he allowed them to succeed. His arse wasn't much but it was his arse and damned if he hadn't grown quite fond of it.

As the two larger men fanned apart to move through the nave pew by pew, he knew they would tear the church apart looking for them. He turned his eyes away from the knothole and allowed them to adjust once more to the murky cellar. The ceiling was barely over six feet in height; too tall for a crawlspace and too short for a proper cellar. A hiding place, then. T'would make sense with the trap door at the altar, wouldn't it now? For a fleeting moment, he envisioned others throughout the centuries huddled as they were doing now, hiding from feuding lairds and Irish clans, Vikings, Normans and Brits, unionists or loyalists.

What was not immediately clear to him is what its inhabitants were to do once they were here. He made out a table and chairs set against the far wall and he made his way silently toward them. Jack was there already on an oversized black phone. He shook his head as Dylan neared; there was no answer at the manor house or on Brigit's phone.

The table was littered with soda cans and military rations that had seen better days and were now covered in a thick layer of dust. Taped against the wall were hand-drawn maps and lists of names that were difficult to decipher in the gloom. He picked out references to nearby places as if those that had hidden here had planned insurgencies or even battles in days long past. That's the lot of it, then, wouldn't it be? He thought. Living in a country with an ancient history where buildings stood for centuries, silent sentinels of bloodshed, betrayals and defense.

He realized that as he had moved along the wall, he had progressed beyond the altar. Closing his eyes for the briefest of moments, he envisioned the hallway they had traversed before arriving at the door to the sanctuary. They were somewhere beneath that corridor, which meant the horses and the enclosed courtyard would be at the far end.

Jack continued to press the button on the old phone to disconnect, only to redial a moment later. As Dylan turned to observe his efforts, his father seemed to morph into another; perhaps one in uniform frantically calling to reinforcements on a phone few knew existed, themselves late usurpers of a room in which scribbled messages might have been written in times past, to be smuggled past enemy lines.

Alexei had remained behind, his eyes still riveted to the scene unfolding above them.

Church bells clanged, splitting the silence with an onslaught that caused Dylan's head to instantly throb. "Jaysus," he breathed, the word barely making it past his lips.

Alexei's head jerked in their direction. Even in the dark, Dylan could make out the whites of his eyes, large and silently questioning.

Jack lowered the phone to its cradle, shaking his head one last time. "It's no use," he whispered quietly as Dylan joined him. "There's no answer, either at the main number or on Brigit's or Aislinn's mobiles."

"What the devil is the racket?" Dylan asked as Alexei joined them.

"That would be Francis in the bell tower. The sound is enough to wake the dead, 'ey?"

He stared at his father for a moment before his astonishment at the sound turned to understanding.

"Aye," Jack said, watching the emotions playing out on his face. "The closest Garda is still a distance away. The bells at this time of night will have all the villagers out o' their beds and in the streets like the town's on fire."

"A diversion then," Dylan whispered.

"They must know we're in here," Alexei said.

"But how?"

He shrugged. "They might have spotted the horses in the back, you suppose?"

"But the courtyard's walled."

"You'd be forgettin' the iron gate at one end," Jack said.

"But if they know we're here—"

"Then we'd best not be wastin' another moment," Jack finished. "Help me pull this table from the wall, boys. There's a door behind it and w' any luck the iron bar won't be rusted in place like it was the last time I was in here."

33

The man was shouting in Irish Gaelic, his language unknown to Vicki but his meaning quite clear.

"Get us out of here!" Vicki shouted.

"I've m' boot to the board!" he bellowed in return.

She clutched the grab handle on the dash. Her door was swinging open but she dared not reach for it. As the car swerved behind the manor house, more shots rang out behind her. Kolya was moving toward her side of the car and though they were fast putting ground between them, she ducked as they approached the edge of the building. She was in full view of him, her door swinging open wider as they entered the turn. The whistle of the bullet grazed past her ear, slamming into the dash before ricocheting off.

Then in the next instant, the door was swinging toward her. Frantically, she reached for it, pulling it to just as another bullet hit the metal.

The man was shouting again.

She stared through the windshield at the surreal terrain of looming evergreen trunks as the vehicle headed straight for the tree line. Then she was registering a star-filled sky and moonlight that focused with laser precision on a red-splattered dashboard.

Blood.

The car careened just short of hitting the trees, bouncing them shoulder to shoulder as the driver sped toward the narrow road. It was all Vicki could do to maintain her hold on the grab handle. She forced her eyes to drop to her body, where her jacket was splashed with blood. When she glanced in the direction of the driver, his jacket was also stained. Through a brain that seemed simultaneously on full alert and caught in a thickening fog, she wondered which of them had been hit—and where.

A cell phone slid across the console between them and Vicki grabbed it. "What's your emergency number?" Her voice was loud and strained in the confines of the small car.

"9-9-9!" the man answered, adrenaline propelling his voice into a shout though she was only inches away.

The car lurched onto the road, threatening to send the phone sailing out of her hands. Her frozen fingers managed to hit the number three times before the car gained momentum, spiriting them away from the manor house.

"What would be your emergency?" a male voice answered calmly.

"Gun shots at the Doyle Manor!" the man next to Vicki shouted in a thick accent.

She hit the speaker button.

"Jimmy?" the voice on the phone crackled back. "Would that be Jimmy Kelleher there?"

"Aye, it is!" he bellowed. "And the Doyle Manor just southwest o' Ardara has gunmen surroundin' it!"

"Gunmen! I'm on my way, Jimmy. Is anyone hurt?"

"Aye! I've been shot, I have!"

34

Brenda closed the door as silently as possible. The hunt for Brigit and Aislinn had become nerve-wracking. The ticking of the old grandfather clock in the main hall sounded like a constant, growing reminder that time was running out.

She had wandered from one room to the next along the main floor, believing that those who ran the manor house would have rooms close to the lobby, the kitchen and dining. But though she had opened one door after another and scoured the room within, she had come up empty handed time and again. She dared not call out to either of them; she had to assume at least one man and quite probably more were within the same house, searching rooms just as she was doing now.

It was an ancient home filled with unexpected drafts and unexplained noises; long, serpentine hallways and whole sections venturing off the main house as if it had been pieced together in ages past. The floor plan made no sense, particularly in the gloom, and it was difficult to determine whether she had explored every space on the main floor.

She reached the end of a corridor. A final doorway must be another servant's stairwell, she reasoned. She felt the Makarov's grip in her palm. It was reassuring. Heavy. Powerful.

She stood to the side as she had with the other doors, easing it open with her left hand while she aimed at chest level with her right. It was darker than most of the spaces she had examined; most had windows with draperies that were not pulled completely taut, allowing some semblance of light to ease around them. But this space was the color of tar, so dark that she could not easily determine whether she was peering into a closet or into a stairwell.

Surreptitiously, she eased through the doorway, using the toes of her shoes to examine the floor. She felt the hardness of what must have been stone. Ah. She was right; it was a stairwell. She continued to feel along the side in an attempt to judge the width of the steps.

The side of her boot brushed against something that gave way underneath it, and she recoiled. Over the sound of her instinctive gasp was a man's moan.

Damn this darkness, she thought as she knelt. Her back was exposed to the hallway behind her which accentuated her anxiety as if a spotlight was trained on her. She shifted the pistol to her left hand and felt along the body. With her prodding, he groaned more heavily.

"Oh, bugger."

An Irishman. Despite her unease, she almost smiled with relief from hearing the endearing Irish accent.

"Are you hurt?" she whispered hoarsely.

He gradually came to a seated position, drawing his legs against his chest. "Christ, I feel like m' noggin's been through a feckin' blender."

"Were you shot?"

"No. No, I don't think so."

She reached for his head, only to find his hands moving through his hair.

"I was hit w' somethin', don't know what. Knocked me flat on m' arse, it did, so fast I ne'er even saw stars before I was gone."

"Are you one of Brigit's friends?"

"Aye. That I am."

"What's your name?"

"Lorcan. They call me Lory. But I don't believe this would be the best time for pleasantries."

Brenda slipped the pistol into her jacket pocket. "Here," she said, "I'll help you to your feet."

His hands dwarfed hers. His weight was heavy as he relied on her help to get him upright. As he came to his feet, she shifted her hands to his forearms to steady him. They were muscular, even brawny, and she marveled at the force it must have taken to knock him out.

"Are you feeling okay?" she asked.

"Soon as the walls stop movin', I'll be fine, thank you," he answered unsteadily.

"Where are Brigit's and Aislinn's quarters? Their bedrooms?"

"Are you aimin' to get them out, then?"

"Yes."

"I was on m' way to them m'self when I was struck… They stay upstairs on the third floor."

She tried to glance upward but could view only blackness. "Looks like we have some flights to climb then."

~~

Brenda didn't know what was worse: being the first one up the stairs in pitch blackness or being the one at the rear. She felt exposed as she followed Lory, as if there was someone directly on her heels. Not one for nervousness, she nonetheless kept glancing behind her but she may as well have been trying to look through mud.

She was trying her best to remain as silent as humanly possible. Lory was nearly inaudible, his footsteps sure and quiet as though he was moving with the assurance of sonar. Despite the fact that she had found him nearly unconscious, his instincts were those of a survivalist, his movements measured.

In contrast, she was continually stubbing her toes as she tried to find the steps in the darkness, quietly cursing the short-sightedness of centuries-old architects that installed stairwells with no railings, especially when there was no consistency on the height of each individual step. The stone walls were moist as if the damp Irish air had completely pervaded their core, the edges sometimes jagged and always rough. In the darkness, the hospitality of the manor house morphed into antagonism.

Lory halted abruptly, causing Brenda to run into him in the shadows. He placed his hand gently over her mouth, not really muffling her but more as a signal to remain perfectly mute. She might have found it degrading under other circumstances, but there was something about his hand that oddly calmed her now. She had never been the type of woman who needed comfort or ever desired it and the unfamiliar emotion left her stomach in knots.

Instinctively, she slipped her hand into her jacket pocket. The Russian made pistol was reassuring, though she was certain she would never use it in the confines of the stairwell. There was too much opportunity for bullets to ricochet off the stone or hit the Irishman in front of her.

A door slipped open somewhere above them. Her first panicked thought was that someone was moving into the stairwell and would stumble upon them. Lory crouched further, removing his hand from her. She found herself stooping behind him on a step so narrow that she was forced to press her palms to the stones to maintain her balance.

A sliver of light illuminated the stairwell above them for the briefest of moments. It was enough to confirm that these stairs, like the others, were arranged in a spiral. But unlike more modern staircases that were open in the middle, this one wound around a stone cylinder. The walls were glistening. She was unsure whether a layer of black was soot or mold, and decided she didn't want to know until she never had to use this stairwell again.

The door slid closed with a small click. The two continued to crouch there for another moment, listening and waiting. Then Lory reached for her, pulling her upright as he rose. He tugged once on her, signaling that he was continuing his ascent.

A few moments later, he stopped once more. He half-knelt and whispered so quietly that she barely heard him, "We've reached the top."

Brenda swallowed. This meant that whoever they had heard a moment ago was on the same floor that they would be entering. She was acutely aware of the knife in her boot and the pistol in her pocket, and she wondered what weapons, if any, Lory might have. It crossed her mind to hand him one of hers but before she could act, he was cautiously sliding the door open.

35

The village may as well have been in the full throws of a battle. The hamlet grew ablaze with lights and the air roared with shouts as people left their homes and flooded the streets. As the horses left the protection of the stone walls and raced across open ground toward the forest, Dylan heard the unmistakable sound of a bullet whizzing just past his ear; he could have sworn he felt its warmth as well as it sliced through the air. Time seemed to slow so his senses were aware of every movement and every sound. He ducked, dipping his head to the far side of Dougal's long neck.

The gunfire served to ignite the villagers further, the church bells' incessant ringing like a call to arms against an invading force. As they entered the shadows of the trees and the horses were forced to slow, Dylan glanced behind them. He had expected to see the men fast on their heels; perhaps running after them or even attempting to navigate the rugged terrain in their vehicle. Instead, he saw no sign of them; in their place, he made out hundreds of villagers gathering around the church.

Jack pulled his horse to a stop a short distance into the forest. "That should keep them busy for a time," he said. Despite his calm words, his forehead was covered in perspiration and his observation gave way to a fit of coughing.

"Are you alright then?" Dylan asked Alexei.

The Russian nodded. "What about those people back there?" he asked, motioning toward the village. "I can't allow someone to get hurt on account of me. I have to do something."

"Oh, you needn't worry about them," Jack managed to say as he cleared his throat. "They've been protecting that village for centuries. Only this time it's but a few men and not an army. They'll be fine."

"Which way to the manor house?" Dylan asked.

"She'll be to the south," Jack said, turning Ciara away from the village. "We'll be there in the better part o' the hour."

As they each clicked their heels and set their horses on the path toward home, Dylan fought a growing unease that festered inside him. Being without his mobile was kin to leaving a limb behind; it left him completely cut off from both Sam and Vicki. Looming large in his mind was the refrain that reminded him there had been no answer on four different numbers—the landline at the manor house and Brigit's, Vicki's and Brenda's mobile phones. And he didn't feel good about leaving Vicki and Brenda at the manor house. He didn't feel good about it at all. He clicked his heels harder against Dougal, urging him onward.

36

There were times in Vicki's life when she felt compelled to control events and then there were times such as these when instinct caused her to hold on and pray for the best. The roads were narrow and twisting, coiling around the edge of the island at such sharp angles that at any moment she expected the vehicle to plunge into the Atlantic Ocean. Both of Jimmy's hands were held tight against the steering wheel and as she stared at them, she realized the blood on his right hand was growing.

"Are you okay?" she managed to croak.

"Hell no, I'm not okay!" he answered in a heavy accent. "I've been shot!" His voice sounded both incredulous and pained.

"Do you know where?"

"I can't exactly stop at the moment to examine m'self!"

She turned to look behind them. She expected to see headlights, the telltale sign of their pursuers gaining on them, but all she could see was the outline of the rugged coast behind them.

She leaned back in her seat. Her teeth chattered as much from adrenaline as from the cold; she held up her hand to find it shaking uncontrollably. The wind that whipped through the shattered driver's side window and back window was glacial. Jimmy had turned the heater up full blast, and now she placed her frozen fingers in front of the vent. He'd no doubt turned it up when he'd first started his vehicle to warm up, she thought, since neither of his knuckles had eased their grip on the steering wheel since they'd left. The warmth felt good but did nothing to stop her trembling.

Again, she glanced behind them. The Russians couldn't have followed them without their headlights on, she reasoned. Jimmy was obviously a native to this region but as he jerked the wheel yet again to stay on the dangerously winding road, she knew that even he would have plunged them to their deaths had he attempted the drive in complete darkness.

He glanced at her briefly before turning his attention back to the road. "They wouldn't be behind us," he stated flatly.

She nodded. That meant Kolya might still be back at the manor house. Her mind sped forward so quickly that she had to pull her thoughts back to put them in order.

The Russian had been outside. That meant there had been at least one other, who had broken the lock on the door, entered the house and was moving through it room by room, searching for her. They would not have known about Brenda—or would they? There was no way of knowing whether they assumed Vicki was a programmer and was attempting to upload the file herself—or if they knew of Brenda's arrival and her role in the operation.

She pulled out her cell phone to stare at the screen. There had been no calls from Brenda or from Dylan.

Through her terror, there was a sense of urgency to turn around and go back—and help her sister. But she dared not suggest it, and she dared not telephone Brenda. In her mind's eye, she pictured the three women hidden somewhere in the serpentine structure while at least one gunman hunted them down.

She had to trust her, she tried to tell herself. They had been in dangerous situations before. Brenda was resourceful. But despite her efforts, she could not escape the tension mounting inside her.

Up ahead, she spotted a few lights from a tiny village. It was impossible to know whether Jimmy was heading toward it, as the circuitous road had her looking directly at it one second and then it was off to their side in the next.

She hit the speed dial for Dylan.

A voice answered on the second ring. "The number you have reached is out of service. Please check the number and dial again."

Puzzled, she clicked off the phone. More slowly this time with care to select Dylan's number from her contact list, she tried again. The same voice answered with the same automated message.

She glanced again at Jimmy. "Where are we going?"

He locked his eyes on hers for so long that she was certain the road would veer once more and they would plunge over the cliffs. "We'd be heading for the Garda." After a moment, he turned his attention back to the road. "You can explain y'self to 'em."

"I see." She fumbled with her phone, glancing from the device to the dark Irish countryside and back. Then she hit the speed dial for Sam.

37

Lory held onto her hand as he moved into the corridor, his light tug indicating that he was moving to their right. The hall was bathed in the same inky blackness as the stairwell had been and she felt her toes brushing against uneven stones as they made their way down the hall.

She kept one hand on the wall as they moved. They came to a brief stop at one doorway but he did not open it. As he continued, she followed behind, her fingers racing over the casing before dipping onto the smooth wood and then back onto the casing on the opposite side.

I really must invest in night vision goggles, she thought wryly.

Then her next thought sent her heart pounding. What if the Russians had them?

Her thoughts were interrupted by the sound of a door opening and closing. Lory halted immediately, his arm held out to stop Brenda's forward progress. She pressed herself against the stone as if she could disappear within it.

The sound of footsteps reached their ears. They were almost imperceptible but as she cocked her head to listen, they grew louder.

Then Lory was pushing her back the way they had come, past the doorway, past the stairwell, into a vastness that seemed like a never-ending tunnel leading to the netherworld.

~~

They stood at the far end of the corridor, their bodies pressed against the wall as it rounded a corner. Somewhere along the route, Lory had moved ahead of her, his footsteps silent. He had halted at the corner, pulling her close to him, signaling to her to make her profile as thin as possible.

If the man at the other end had heard them, there was no indication; no running feet, no shouts. Another door opened and closed. He was moving methodically. His unhurried movement was grating on her nerves. She had almost rather that he rush them so she could shoot into the abyss and get it over with.

She felt lips grazing her hair. Then Lory whispered, "The door across from us is Brigit's. Aislinn's is at the opposite end, where I was originally headed."

She nodded, hoping he could feel her movement. Her lips were parched and she dared not speak.

A door opened and closed again. Footsteps grew louder as the man moved down the hall toward them. Lory squeezed her hand. She wondered if it was a sign of reassurance or a signal to remain silent, and she decided to interpret it as both.

Then the footsteps paused. Another door was opening and a second later, it was closed with a soft click.

Brenda could feel Lory moving swiftly away from her. A moment later, the door across the hall was opened with a slight whoosh of air and he was reaching back for her. Hurriedly, she followed him inside, closing the door soundlessly behind them.

It took only a moment for her eyes to become adjusted. The draperies here were not the heavy fabric used downstairs but a lighter curtain that allowed muted moonlight to reach inside. In an instant, she had taken in the standard bedroom furniture: the chest of drawers against one wall, a hutch against another, a dresser, a chair and ottoman—and an empty bed.

She raced toward the bed as if she could find Brigit within the folds of the thick down comforter. She had been there; the pillow contained an indentation and the sheets were mussed. The covering had been pulled back unceremoniously; slippers still sat beside the bed as if she had arisen too quickly to put them on.

Lory had moved into an adjoining room but returned shaking his head. "She isn't in the bath." His voice was a mere whisper.

She caught her first good look at the man. He was younger than she had expected; possibly her age. He was perhaps two or three inches taller and he sported auburn hair that teased his collar with the slightest curl. His eyes were large and light, either blue or green, she thought. And his jaw was squared, the slightest bit of stubble on his skin.

He seemed taken aback by her as well, but she couldn't tell if he was alarmed by her appearance, as she had no idea what she must look like after running all over the manor house and grounds, or if he had envisioned someone quite different.

Then her thoughts plummeted back to their immediate concern: Brigit and Aislinn.

As if he had the same thought, he turned abruptly away from her and appeared to be surveying the room.

Then with two quick strides, he was at the hutch, hurling the doors open. He yanked the hanging clothes from one side to the other in an attempt to determine if she could be hiding there but came up empty handed.

Brenda crossed the room to stand beside him. "If you were Brigit, where would you have gone?" she whispered.

He didn't hesitate. "To Aislinn."

"And if you couldn't leave this room for fear the man was right outside your door?"

Their eyes moved simultaneously to the windows. He raced to one while she rushed to another. They were locked from the inside. And glancing outside, she knew even if Brigit had managed to crawl onto the ledge, she would have been spotted immediately. There was no place to go that would have placed her beyond the visibility of the glass.

The sound was so discreet that she almost missed it. The door knob was turning.

She slipped her hand into her pocket, her fingers locking onto the pistol. She had no sooner pulled it out than Lory was pointing to the bureau adjacent to the door. "Behind there!" he whispered as he pushed her toward it.

It was ludicrous, she thought as she followed his instruction. Hiding behind the five-foot piece of furniture would buy them only seconds, and what were they when an assailant was determined to find you? But as she dashed toward it, she felt his hand over hers, sliding downward and pulling the pistol out of her grasp.

They reached the far side of the bureau as the door was opening. Lory stood behind the piece of furniture, both hands resting atop it and the pistol snuggly within his grasp. Brenda heard the faint click of the safety releasing.

The man was of average height but his dark leather jacket caused his shoulders to appear massive. As he entered the room, his back was to them, the door partially blocking their view. Brenda pressed her body against the wall behind Lory. Though she longed to grab the pistol from his grip, she knew it was no longer feasible. The die was cast. Instead, her lips moved in a silent prayer that he was as good a shot as she.

Having glanced in the opposite direction, the man was turning toward them. He moved slowly, silently, stealthily. One hand was on the door and as he turned he began to close it behind him.

The moonlight was catching his face as he turned.

Lory was completely still; so still that Brenda wondered if he would follow through. The seconds were ticking off in her mind in a mounting crescendo. In another instant, it would be too late.

He spotted them just as Lory fired the shots: not one but two, a double tap that Brenda had only witnessed once before—by a hired assassin. Before she could recover from her surprise, the man took two rapid steps toward them.

Lory fired again and then a fourth time but the man kept coming.

A bulletproof vest, Brenda thought in rising panic. She wanted to shout to Lory to fire at his head, but the words froze on her lips. Her feet seemed immobilized as well, her back plastered to the wall.

The man looked directly at her, his face ruddy and puffed, a snarl curling his lips. His arm jutted forward like a piston, a beefy fist gripping a pistol aimed directly at Lory, who stood between them. He fired as he simultaneously dropped to his knees.

Lory stepped away from the bureau, now in full view of the man. His pistol was still grasped within both hands as he took another step toward the Russian. The larger man had placed his left hand on his chest and was pulling it back to stare at the blood that washed over it.

The pistol was still held in his right hand. He fixed his gaze on Lori. With a wicked sneer, he fired again.

Brenda leapt to the side as another shot rang out.

When she looked back, the man was staring at her. He appeared surprised, his eyes widening in disbelief. Then he fell backward, his knees still locked onto the floor, fresh blood oozing from a spot midway between his brows.

"Take these two guns." Lory did not hesitate but bent quickly to retrieve the Russian's pistol still gripped within a brawny hand, "Hide them."

"Hide—? It was self-defense."

Lory locked eyes with her. "I said to hide them," he said firmly. "Someplace the Garda will not think to look." He turned back to the man who was bleeding out on the floor. "And I'll hide the body."

38

An officer rushed from the station as the car screeched to a halt near the entrance. Before Jimmy had the vehicle in Park, he was opening the door, his eyes sweeping across the shattered glass in Jimmy's lap and the blood that had saturated his right jacket sleeve.

"I've been shot," Jimmy said, tumbling out.

"Where?" The officer swept his arm underneath Jimmy's left shoulder, bolstering him.

"I can walk just fine," he said grudgingly.

"Maybe. Maybe not. But I'll be damned if I have to lift you off the pavement."

Vicki hurriedly exited the car and rushed behind the two men toward the station. It was a tiny office in a diminutive corner townhouse. As she grabbed the door for the men, she took in the gold lettering proclaiming *Garda Siochana* and the blue lamp beside the door with the distinctive Garda emblem. Fluorescent bulbs inside bathed the room in a stark radiance. After the darkness of the Irish countryside, it took her eyes a moment to adjust as the light seared into her pupils.

She found herself in a receiving area that might have been reminiscent of a 1950's small town police station except for two desktop computers on the other side of the counter. There were a handful of chairs in what served as a lobby but judging from the dust that had accumulated on the seats, it had been a very long time since anyone had made use of them. About halfway into the room was a long counter of polished wood; an ornate trim spoke of decades past. And on the other side of that counter were two desks facing one another. A desk lamp with a green glass shade was illuminating one desk while the other was darkened, the computer screen black. Off to one side was a short corridor, the overhead lights turned off.

The officer kicked a few chairs out of the way and Vicki sprang into action to help clear the foyer. Then he laid Jimmy on the polished tiled floor despite his objections.

"The physician is on his way," the officer said. He wore a name badge above one pocket that identified him as Duffy. "I called him just as soon as I heard from you." He nodded toward his desk. "Get me those scissors, will you?"

"Don't cut my jacket," Jimmy warned as Vicki hurried past the counter to the desk, returning with the scissors in hand.

She handed them to Duffy.

"Now you know the physician will do it if I don't." With that, the officer began cutting the sleeve at the wrist.

Under the bright lights, Vicki could finally get a good look at the man that had just saved her life. He was older than she had anticipated. His face was weathered and worn, his salt-and-pepper brows thick and unruly, his nostrils and ears also sporting grizzled hairs. An Irish cap hid his head but as he leaned back, it slid toward the floor, revealing a bald pate.

"Do you have towels?" Vicki asked.

Duffy nodded toward the hall. "In the facilities."

She dashed down the darkened hall. It was surprisingly short; one door on her left announced a single restroom for males and females, and two other doors remained opened, the offices dark. She turned on the light for the restroom, grabbed the single towel hanging from the rack and doused it with water. The liquid was so icy that it startled her, but she could not waste time waiting for it to warm. It would have to do. She wrung out the excess water and raced back to find that Duffy had retrieved a first aid kit and was kneeling again by Jimmy's side.

She began at his shoulder where fresh blood was very nearly spurting. From the angle, she wondered whether the Russian had fired the shot at precisely the same moment as she opened the passenger door, causing Jimmy to jerk in her direction. She no sooner had the wound wiped than it was covered in blood again.

"Clean it again," the officer directed. He tore open a package of Celox and moved closer to Vicki.

As she cleaned, he liberally poured the granules from the bag directly into the wound. Then he reached back to the first aid kit, grabbed some gauze and covered the wound. Pressing down hard on it, he peered at Vicki with sharp blue eyes. "Clean the rest o' his arm, will you? Just to make certain this is the only wound."

Jimmy groaned. "I won't be goin' to any hospital facility, I can tell y' that."

"You don't have a choice, boyo. The bullet may be lodged inside y' and I won't be stickin' m' fingers in to see."

Jimmy's arm was wizened. It was, Vicki thought, the

arm of a man who had once been much larger, perhaps much brawnier, and was now the limb of a declining elder.

"No other wound," Vicki said. "It looks like all the blood was coming from just that one."

"Hand me another gauze."

Vicki complied as Duffy tossed the saturated gauze onto the floor. Quickly accepting the one she offered to him, he returned to pressing on the wound.

"Not so hard, man," Jimmy said. "You're very nearly breakin' the bones in m' shoulder."

"I'd rather break your bones than have you bleed out on m' floor." The officer's voice was rough but he half-grinned at the older man, softening his words. His radio began to crackle and he caught Vicki's eye again. "Push down hard for me." As she moved into place, he released his grip and she leaned her weight into Jimmy's shoulder.

"Aye, this is Duffy. Go ahead."

"We've arrived at Doyle Manor. What do you know?"

Duffy raised one brow as he looked at Vicki. "How many?"

"At least two," she said. "Maybe more. When we left, one was outside. At least one was inside."

He relayed that information to the officer on the scene. "Do you know precisely where inside?"

She shook her head. "I'm afraid I don't."

He nodded, his lips pursed. "How many have you there?" he said into his radio.

"Five. And I thank you for telephoning the neighboring villages. There's more on the way. We've search lights being set about the perimeter now. It's dark as Hades out here."

Vicki leaned across Jimmy to catch Duffy's eye. "There's a dead man in the woods," she said quietly. "I think it's…" Her voice faded. She could feel Jimmy's eyes on her and her cheeks began to burn. "It is not one of the bad guys, I don't think."

The door whipped open, rushing in a frosty blast of air. "Where—?" The man's words were cut off as he knelt beside Jimmy. As the officer explained his actions to the doctor, Vicki rose. Not knowing what else to do, she retrieved the blood-stained towel. Intending to return it to the bathroom where she could rinse it out completely, she instead sat on the hard wood bench a few feet from the men.

She suddenly felt exhausted. It was as if her own blood had been seeping from her all this time, and now it had all drained out of her, leaving her so weary she could barely sit up. She vaguely registered the blood spattered across her jacket and pants. The men laboring over Jimmy appeared out of focus, their words blurred.

"Were you hurt?"

She hadn't realized the doctor had turned and was speaking to her.

"I'm sorry; what?"

"Were you hurt? Have you been shot?"

"No. I don't think so."

"You're awfully pale."

The officer rose. "Can you take off your jacket for me, please?"

Tiredly, she slipped off her jacket. Officer Duffy came to her side, pulling her to her feet and looking her over. "She doesn't appear to have been shot."

"Were you hit?" the doctor asked.

"No." She sat back down and pulled the jacket around her shoulders. "No one ever came close enough to me." Her voice caught in her throat and she self-consciously cleared it.

"He's ready to be moved," the doctor announced.

Duffy returned to Jimmy's side. "Can you walk, Jimmy?"

"Aye."

"Good," the doctor chimed in, "because it would take too long for a gurney to arrive. I'll be drivin' you to Killybegs Community Hospital m'self."

"I won't be goin' to any hospital."

"I didn't recall me askin' y'."

Vicki watched as they sat him up and then managed to lift him to his feet without putting further strain on his shoulder. She leaned her head against the wall as Duffy helped him to the doctor's car and saw them off. When the officer returned, his lips were pursed. He stopped for a moment to survey the blood-splattered floor before coming to stand in front of her. As she raised her eyes to his, he said, "Now then. It's time for you and I to have a bit of a chat."

39

It didn't take long for Brenda to discover Lory's approach to hiding a body. The Russian was hurriedly wrapped in the shower curtain and then placed into the dumbwaiter. She could still see his face through the clear plastic, his nose and lips flattened against it, his eyes not quite closed. Then Lory had pressed the button to lower it but had stopped it between floors before sliding the dumbwaiter door back into place. He did it so precisely and with such little thought that she was left wondering if this hadn't been the first time he'd had to employ such a method.

And somehow she knew, when this was all over, he would return to remove the body somewhere down below—perhaps even in the cellar she had walked through with Vicki—and the Russian would be taken away, perhaps to be found later floating downriver or perhaps he would never be found. Or perhaps he would be buried in the bogs somewhere for someone to find decades or centuries later.

For her own task, she set about opening and closing drawers and pretending to find the perfect place to hide the weapons. But in reality, she already knew the perfect place. They were not leaving her side. While Lory was busy with the Russian, she hid one pistol inside her left sock and the other inside her right. Her boots would keep them securely in place, along with the knife from the cellar.

Now she felt more confident.

By the time Lory was finished, she had cleaned up the blood from the hardwood floor and deposited the soiled towels in with the Russian. "What's next?"

"What's next is we find Brigit and Aislinn."

They met at the door. His hand was on the knob and his ear pressed against the thick wood. "I'm not hearin' anything," he said after a moment. "But the door's solid; I can't be sure no one is there."

"Well, there's only one way to find out." She smiled slyly.

"I must say, I do like a woman who doesn't scream and faint at the sight o' blood."

"Is that so?"

"I've done murder, you know. And you're a witness to it."

"If your words are meant to frighten me," she answered, "you've missed the mark."

In the semi-gloom, she watched as his eyes moved from her mountain of copper hair down to the high cheekbones, her jawline and her lips. They remained focused there and she slowly smiled. She'd seen that look, that movement, in a man's eyes too many times. After a moment, he looked her in the eye. He seemed to be studying her, perhaps trying to decipher the color of her eyes, just as she was doing with him. Blue-green, she decided. The color of the sea.

"Shall we?" he asked finally.

Before she could respond with the witty retort that was already on the tip of her tongue, he slid open the door.

After the dim light in the bedroom, it took a moment for her eyes to adjust to the total blackness of the hallway once the bedroom door was closed behind them. As she stood there motionless, she felt his lips against her hair just as she had before. She wondered how he would react if she simply turned her head and offered her lips. But before she could find out, he whispered, "Aislinn's bedroom is at the far end of the hall. That's where we're going."

Then without waiting for a reply, he took her hand and began moving silently, cautiously, down the corridor.

They were only halfway there judging from the number of doors they had passed before Lory abruptly halted. They stood frozen for a moment, and she sensed his head was cocked just as hers was.

"Did you hear that?" he whispered, his mouth close to her ear.

"Yes." It had been a heavy thump, as if something had fallen to the floor. A moment later, it sounded again; this time, slightly lighter but still unmistakable.

Lory gently but firmly pushed Brenda farther from the closed door but he remained just on the other side of it. In the murky shadows, she could barely make out his outline and with her senses hypersensitive, she understood his position: he would jump whoever came through that door.

They stood there for what felt an unbelievably long time, but in reality it might only have been a minute or two. She felt as though her breath had stopped, and instinctively, she reached for one of the pistols. With Lory's back to her, she was able to move in position behind him, the gun pointed chest-high.

When the door opened, it was so slow and silent that she thought she might have imagined it. But then she felt the draft as it opened wider and then wider still. And when the figure moved into the hallway, the faintest light from the room illuminated the outline.

"Brigit." Lory's voice was filled with relief.

She sucked in her breath. "Jaysus, but you frightened the shite out o' me."

"Is Aislinn—?"

"Aye. She's here."

"You were hiding in the library all this time?" Lory asked.

"In the attic."

"Ah."

"If you didn't know the stairs were there, you would never see them, hidden as they are."

"Congratulations, I'm sure," Brenda said as she slipped the pistol back inside her socks, "but don't you think you'd be safer staying there? At least until we can determine whether anybody else is in the house?"

"That was our plan," Brigit said, pulling Aislinn into the hallway with them, "but then we saw the Garda out the vent in the attic."

"The Garda?"

"Go across the hall, and you'll see them from the window for sure."

They hurried across the hall as if all danger was gone, throwing open the door and rushing to the windows. The front lawn was illuminated by several vehicles' headlights and another was quickly approaching along the coastal road.

"Fastest way out is down the servants' stairs to the second floor," Brigit said. "And then the main staircase will lead us straightaway to the front doors."

"Lead the way," Lory said. He gestured toward the hall. Brigit left briskly, followed by Aislinn on her heels.

As Lory and Brenda approached the door, he stopped and turned to her.

She found herself against the wall beside the door, her back pressed against the stone. His face was in shadows as he moved closer to her. She tilted her head upward in anticipation. But when his lips parted, she was met not with a kiss but a hoarse whisper.

"What happened here tonight will ne'er be spoken of. Are y' understandin' me?"

She tossed her hair. "I don't know what you're talking about. We looked for Brigit and Aislinn, and we found them. End of story."

He hesitated just a moment and then backed away, motioning for her to follow the others. As she started through the door, she stopped unexpectedly, allowing him to bump into her. With his body pressed against hers, she whispered over her shoulder, "But if you need help getting rid of any spoiled meat, I'll be on your team anytime."

Before he could answer, she was off, dashing to catch up with Brigit and Aislinn.

40

The hour's travel homeward had been perhaps one of the longest hours of his life. The horses were weary, their heads low, their ears tucked. It had been a long night for all of them and one he had no doubt that they each were ready to put behind them. His first order of business was to see to it that the women were safe. His second was to help Jack with the horses. And his third was to get them all as far from the manor house as possible. He had decided that no doubt the faster he could get Alexei into someone else's hands, the better all of them would be.

It seemed as though his mind had been racing in every direction at once, but the most compelling refrain was *go dark, go dark.*

Going dark meant cutting all communication with the CIA. It meant destroying the phone—which, thanks to Jack, was already accomplished—and staying off the grid for a period of time. Dylan might not know the island as well as his father, but he knew most of it well enough to know that getting Alexei off the island was to be a monumental challenge.

He could not expect another rendezvous and just the thought of explaining to Sam that the plane he'd sent had blown up before his eyes was enough to set his heart racing. How could he have missed the man in the lighthouse or the men along the landing site perimeter? Ah, they had spent too much time at the cottage in the Blue Stack Mountains, for sure. Had they moved out promptly, they might have arrived before those men. Alexei would be over the Atlantic at this moment, and he and Jack would have had a less eventful ride homeward.

To be sure, he told himself, the last thing he had expected had been for the enemy to know their plans. How could they? Jack's explanation of the phone's GPS only held so much water; sure, they could have used it to track them, had they known how to decrypt it, but these men had been in place before Dylan, Jack and Alexei had even arrived. Even if they had tracked their movements past the Blue Stack Mountains, there were too many possibilities along the jagged coastline for them to have known precisely where the rendezvous would take place.

So, he thought as they trudged up yet another hill that left only two possibilities. Either there was a mole in the CIA as Jack suspected—or the Russians were employing someone just like Vicki.

"What are these shenanigans now?"

Jack's sudden burst interrupted Dylan's thoughts. He hadn't realized the two men had stopped and now he pulled up his horse alongside them. They were at the crest of a hill peering into the valley and the coastline beyond. Nestled into the center of the valley was the manor house, looming and large against the stark Ireland winter, with the stables just off to one side. Dougal pawed at the ground, his tiredness forgotten as he recognized fresh hay and a good nap. But Dylan pulled back on the reins as his eyes darted across the terrain.

It was still dark, the Northern Lights long gone and the moon waning, that time before the sun begins to rise and the skies are the blackest. Yet the headlights from more than a half dozen vehicles had the manor house and its grounds lit up like summer solstice.

"I'm not believin' m' eyes," Jack breathed. "It's the Garda." He slipped off Ciara's broad back. "Hand me your weapons before they see us," he said. "I won't be goin' back to prison, I can tell y' that."

Alexei and Dylan handed him their weapons and ammunition. Dylan watched as he tucked them inside a satchel on Ciara's side.

"Vicki," Dylan breathed as he watched. He was itching to ride forward as was Dougal, who continued to paw at the ground in a blatant urge to push forward.

"Listen to me closely, boys," Jack said. His voice had assumed an air of authority. "I took the two of y's to see the Northern Lights on horseback. It's somethin' I've done before, and it won't be out of the ordinary. The girls didn't want to accompany us. You don't know where we were because you were unfamiliar with the terrain. We did not go near the Blue Stack Mountains. Do you have all that now?"

"Aye," Dylan answered as Alexei agreed. "Anythin' else?"

"When you get down below, hop off your horses at the stables. I'll tend to them whilst you speak to the authorities. I can hide the weapons in the stables."

"And what about me?" Alexei asked. "What if they recognize my accent?"

"Oh, they will for sure once you move your lips." Jack remounted his horse.

"You just broke up with your girlfriend," Dylan said, "and you came here on holiday by y'self to recover. You and I only met a day ago, so neither of us knows much at'al about the other. The fewer lies we'll have to tell, the better we'll be."

"And what if they check? I slipped out of Russia—"

"By the time they discover the truth, you will be out o' the country. I can guarantee you that." Dylan's voice sounded stronger than he felt. He was as impatient as Dougal to get to the manor house now, and without another word, he clicked his heels.

41

The guard narrowed his eyes. "And you don't know where you've been?" he asked suspiciously.

"As I've told you," Dylan said, trying to tamp down his growing ire, "the stable hand took this gent and I to view the Northern Lights. We did not enter any villages so I can't give you a frame o' reference and in the dark, I was quite disoriented."

Another officer joined them. "Good," he was saying into his radio. "Neither are hurt?"

"Would that be Vicki and Brenda?" Dylan asked.

"A man and three women," the officer answered. "We'll have their identities directly."

Before he had finished speaking, Dylan caught sight of Brigit and Aislinn as they exited through the double doors of the manor house. They were followed by Brenda, her copper hair wild as it was caught by the wind. On their heels was a man he had never seen before.

His heart sank as he realized Vicki was not with them. *A man and three women*, the officer's voice refrained in his head. Where was Vicki?

Despite the first guard's objections, Dylan started across the lawn, taking deep strides. Before he reached them, his attention had moved from Brenda to the man beside her in an effort to determine whether he was friend or foe.

He appeared to be around the same age as Brenda. He had deep auburn hair that curled just past his jacket collar. His face was wide and his jaw squared. As Dylan drew closer, their eyes met. The man's irises were large, and Dylan felt his anxiety easing. There was something about an Irishman's eyes; they tended to be large, much larger than any he had seen from other countries, except perhaps the Scots.

"Would that be Lory MacKenny?" the officer asked as he joined them.

Lory held out his hand. "Good to see you again, Brady."

"And what would you be doin' at Brigit's, 'ey?"

Before he could answer, Brenda slipped an arm around his waist. "Now don't go kissing and telling," she purred as she nuzzled against his neck.

Dylan took a step back. As Brenda and Lory continued their charade, his eyes scanned the house and yard for the umpteenth time in search of Vicki as the knot inside his stomach grew. Somewhere behind him, he heard Alexei repeating the same story he had—a tale that quite obviously the officer was not believing—and he heard Jack's familiar voice as he called a greeting to another officer.

He cut his eyes toward the stable. Jack had already brought Ciara inside and had returned to the grounds just outside the stable doors to retrieve the other two horses. Toby was bounding toward the investigators.

"Get that blasted dog out o' there!" an officer bellowed. "He'll be disturbin' the crime scene for sure!"

The guard nearest him cleared his throat. "So then. And the two o' you's were awakened by the sound of an intruder?"

"We didn't exactly say we were sleepin'," Lory said. His cheeks were flushed but whether it was due to the frigid weather or Brenda continuing to nuzzle him, Dylan couldn't tell.

"When you're quite finished with bein' horned up," Dylan interjected, "I'm quite concerned about Vicki, and these gents won't allow me into the house to search for her."

Brenda turned toward Dylan. Her eyes flitted past him quickly. He resisted the temptation to look behind him and a second later, she locked her eyes on his. "I haven't seen Vicki since midnight." Her lips remained slightly parted as if she wanted to say more and the slightest frown developed between her brows.

He felt as if he had been kicked in the stomach and as though all the blood flow had left his cheeks. A tingling sensation grew along the base of his neck. Their eyes remained locked on one another, the words left unspoken growing louder by the moment.

"I'm afraid all o' you's will need to come w' us," the officer named Brady was saying, "on account o' findin' Colin MacGill strangled in the woods there." He nodded his head in the direction opposite the stables.

"Colin strangled?" Lory breathed. "He's dead?"

Brenda squeezed his hand, a movement that Dylan instantly picked up on but which Brady appeared not to notice.

"Did you know Colin was here?" Brady pressed.

Before Lory could reply, another guard joined them. "We found bullet casings between the house and the stables. The crime scene technician is cataloguing them now." He raised his voice again. "Jack, get your dog out o' there, I say!"

"They might be from the weapon that shot Jimmy Kelleher." He turned back toward Brenda and Lory. "So one man strangled and another shot?" Brady mused. "And the lot o' yous wouldn't be knowin' anythin' about that?" His eyes narrowed.

"Jimmy's been shot?" Lory's face grew pale. "Is he—?"

"He's alive," Brady answered. "And we'll be requirin' a statement from him straightaway. So you'd best tell me all that you know."

"I knew that Colin and Jimmy were about to be joinin' us for a pint," Lory answered. "But when they never arrived…"

"We found other ways to occupy ourselves," Brenda finished. Her arm tightened around him.

"For Christ's sake!" Dylan interrupted. "My wife was in that house when I left her last night. And not a one o' you can tell me where she is or what has happened to her?" One hand balled into a fist at his side. "And if I'm not to be gettin' answers directly, I'll storm past the lot o' you to go through that blasted house m'self!"

Without waiting for a reply, he stepped toward the manor house but a surprisingly firm hand held him back. He turned to face Brenda. He opened his mouth but the words remained unspoken.

"She's not in the house," Brenda said in a low voice.

"She'd be speakin' the truth o' it," Brady said.

The sound of a vehicle's tires caused them to turn toward the road. Another Garda vehicle was making its way down the winding driveway.

"Looks to be Evan Duffy," Brady said. "And he's someone w' him. That wouldn't be the wife you're missin' now, would it?"

42

Vicki didn't remember when she had felt so exhausted. The events of the arduous night had depleted her strength and now she felt as though her body was somehow separating from her mind. As she sank ever lower in the passenger seat of the Garda vehicle, her thoughts continued to race.

Relief flooded through her as she spotted Brenda and Dylan standing outside the manor house. But in the next instant her heart began to pound as she glimpsed Alexei a few yards away speaking to a set of guards. Why wasn't he on the plane to America?

The lawn was lit up between the vehicles' headlights and sets of floodlights erected around the house. The woods where she had stumbled over the man were lit and several guards were inspecting the body and taking photographs. Where she and Jimmy had driven away, another set of officers were placing placards presumably at the locations of the bullet casings. There had to be some, she thought. The assailant certainly would not have taken the time to locate them.

Duffy pulled onto the lawn. He kept the engine idling and the headlights on as he eased his door open.

Dylan was at Vicki's door almost before she had it fully open. He pulled her into his arms, pressing his lips against her ear.

"Jack, Alexei and I went on horseback to see the Northern Lights. You two remained behind."

Before she could answer, an officer's voice interrupted. "So is this the wife you've been concerned about then?"

Dylan reluctantly pulled back. "Aye. And I'd like to know what happened here?" He shot a glance at Vicki.

"It's just what I'd be wantin' to know as well," Brady said, rolling back on his heels. "So how about the lot o' you comin' w' us for a wee statement or two?"

"Not so fast," Duffy said. "We've new orders."

"New orders?" Brady frowned. "From who?"

"The Commissioner."

"The Commissioner you say?"

"You heard me."

Vicki watched the wheels turning in Brady's eyes. He was filled with questions, curiosity that might never be sated. She wanted to tear her eyes away from him and look toward Brenda. She could see her unruly hair in her periphery, but she was unable to stop observing the officer in front of her as if a force beyond herself had taken control.

"Seems that the Commissioner was roused from his sleep by the Prime Minister."

"No."

Duffy nodded. "And we're to transport these lads—and ladies—to the American Consulate in Belfast."

Brady turned toward the others. "So you three Americans, prepare to go with—"

"Not just the Americans," Duffy interjected. "Is there one among you by the name o' Alexei Volkov?"

Alexei started forward. "That's me."

"The Russian too? What would the American Consulate be wantin' with a Russian?"

"You can ask once we get there," Duffy said with more than a touch of sarcasm in his voice. "You'll be drivin' a second vehicle."

"Fine."

"I've a list." Duffy pulled a note pad from his pocket. "Vicki Boyd Maguire," he read off, "Michael Dylan Maguire, Alexei Volkov, Brenda Anne Carnegie… And Jack Maguire."

"Jack?" Brady said incredulously.

"That's what I said."

"What the devil is he into now?"

"Whate'er it is, he's garnered the attention o' London, o' Belfast, and therefore, o' me. Now off w' you; go get the man."

"Oh, Vicki," Dylan said, pulling her into his embrace, "I'm so relieved to see you, darlin'." As his lips pressed against her, he whispered, "Jack can't be taken into custody."

"He won't be," she whispered back. "Sam's orchestrating this. We'll be fine."

As he pulled back once more, she gave him a quick wink meant to reassure him. But his eyes were clouded with doubt. A feeling began to creep through her, chilling her more than the icy temperatures ever could. There would be no chance to talk inside the Garda vehicles and because there were five of them to be transported, they would be separated into two cars. There were too many unanswered questions on the tip of her tongue and from the look in Dylan's eyes, he felt the same.

43

Jack shuffled from one foot to another. "I'm not understandin' why I'm to go to Belfast," he said again. "I've got m' job to do here." He looked to Vicki and Dylan with imploring eyes, but it was Lory who answered.

"I'll take care o' the horses, Jack. Don't you worry about a thing."

"And Brigit and Aislinn will be just fine without y'," Duffy said. If his words were meant to be reassuring, his tone was not.

It was the way of it then, Jack thought. His throat was raw from the night's ride and he'd spoken more in the past twenty-four hours than in the twenty-four days before it. He was tired and he ached. He knew better than to try to disappear. They would find him, sure enough, and it would make matters just the more buggered.

Still, he did not relish the thought of a ride with the Garda and he'd just as soon never set eyes on Belfast again.

"So, here's what's to be," Duffy was saying. "Mrs. Maguire, Mr. Maguire, and Miss Carnegie, you three will ride w' me. The two o' you's—Mr. Volkov and Jack 'ere—are to ride with Brady."

Jack made his way to the second vehicle as directed, taking his time to breathe the morning air once more, just in case it would be his last for a while. Mary, Mother o' God, how he loved the stables. He worried about Ciara. He knew Lory would care for her, sure enough, but it wouldn't be the same as the one that brought her into the world, now would it? Who would slip her a carrot or two in the slow hours o' the afternoon or make certain her blanket was about her proper on the coldness o' nights? Who would greet her with an extra rubdown when the frost was still on the grass and coo to her?

He caught a glimpse of a vehicle rounding the hill and he narrowed his eyes. Dawn was breaking; it was that time of the morn when headlights were still needed but the promise of another day was just on the horizon. There was the thinnest sliver of red beneath a cool blue, the kind of sky that could go either way—fair or foul—and 'twas nothing to do but wait for the gods to make up their minds about it.

Brady opened the back passenger door. Jack motioned for Volkov to go first and the Russian nodded as if Jack had done it out of chivalry but it twasn't that at'al but a desire to keep his feet planted on the land he'd come to love just a wee bit longer.

The profile of the vehicle wasn't right, he thought, narrowing his eyes in an attempt to focus on it more clearly. He glanced at the vehicle in front of him. Duffy was watching it approach as well. Vicki and Brenda were hesitating at one vehicle door. He caught Dylan's eye at the other door, but they were too far apart for him to impart any type of message. And what message would that be? He wondered. Things were amiss and yet Vicki had assured them it wasn't and what was he but just another cog in the wheel.

Turning to peer again at the incoming vehicle, his heart sank further if that was at'al possible. It was a Garda van. He hated the vans more than he hated the cars, truth be told about it. The vans were outfitted with extra devices to keep the human cargo from escaping, and that's precisely what they were was cargo. It was a terrible feeling, it was, for a man to be locked up with no say in where he goes or how he does it.

Duffy and Brady were making their way toward it as it slowed to a stop just a few yards away.

Jack recognized the uniform of the driver as soon as he emerged. He could pick out the rank insignia from half a mile away, he could. It was an Inspector and he would no doubt take charge of the scene faster than the wind could snuff out a flame.

A moment later, the three men made their way between Brady's and Duffy's vehicles. The five joined them at Brady's front bumper.

"I'm Inspector Howard," the man said in a flat British accent. He appeared to be in his mid-forties. The cap covered most of his hair but a few salt and pepper strands were visible near his ears. He kept the chin strap in place as the wind howled. Funny, Jack thought, he hadn't noticed the wind so much before the man had appeared. Ooh, they were ill winds. He could feel it now. It caused his hackles to be up and he had to tamp down the urge to flee.

"I'll be taking the five of you to the American Consulate myself. I've brought the wagon so you can remain together." He nodded toward the van as he pulled a piece of paper from his jacket pocket. "Let's confirm everyone's identities, shall we?"

As the others provided their names, Jack kept his eyes fixed on the inspector. He never looked at the note paper in his hand to compare them, as if he already had the list memorized. His eyes were gray and he kept them narrowed. Veiled was more like it, Jack thought. As if the man had something to hide.

"John Maguire," he announced when it came his turn. He thought Inspector Howard peered at him just a moment longer than he had the others, and he shifted from one foot to the other.

"And we've two Americans?" the inspector was saying. "Vicki Boyd Maguire and Brenda Ann Carnegie." The two sisters nodded and he continued, "And two British subjects—"

"Begging your pardon," Dylan said. His voice was polite but one brow rose. "I am not a British subject. I was born in New York and I am an American citizen."

The inspector nearly snorted. "With that accent?"

"I've spent most o' m' life in the Republic o' Ireland—not Northern Ireland, mind y'. But I've m' passport so you can verify what I say is true."

As he pulled out his passport from a jacket pocket, his eyes met Jack's and Jack nodded so slightly that he hoped his movement was imperceptible to all but Dylan. American citizens were treated differently than the Irish and the boy was smart enough to know it and play the card early in the game.

"One British subject," Howard said, glancing so quickly at Dylan's passport that it should have been impossible for him to notice the details. "And," he almost scoffed, "a *Russian*."

"They'll be waiting for us at the American Consulate," Vicki said. Her voice was calm but firm and she jutted her chin slightly upward as she spoke. "*All* of us."

Howard attempted a smile but it seemed to Jack more of a smirk. "We'd best get going then, 'eh?" He turned to Duffy and Brady. "One of you is in charge of the crime scene, I take it?"

"I am, sir," Duffy answered but Howard was already moving toward the van.

"I swear to God I don't like this at'al," Jack breathed. He felt the others' hesitation as well as they slowly shuffled toward the van.

Howard opened the rear clamshell doors and gestured inside. Vicki and Brenda entered first. As Jack waited for Dylan and Alexei to join them, he peered past their shoulders. The interior was like all the others he'd been in for sure. There were two sets of rear doors; the outer clamshell doors contained windows with a grill across them, while another set of bars resembling a jail cell with another door in the center were just inside. It was built for the safety of the officers; the outer windows so they could keep an eye on the inmates while opening the outer door, and the inner cage in the unlikely event that one of them had loosened their ties. A bench lined each windowless side with plenty of positions in which a man could be handcuffed.

Every bit o' blood that coursed through Jack pleaded with him to flee while he still could, and it took every ounce of courage within him to ignore the call and place one foot and then another on the step and turn his body so one shoulder at a time could slip through the smaller barred door. In the front of the van was a single grilled window that kept them apart from the driver.

As he settled into the seat nearest the back door, the inspector clanged the inner cage door shut. He seemed ready to lock it but Duffy interjected, "They're not prisoners," before adding belatedly, "sir."

Howard chuckled. "Habit." He closed the outer doors.

Vicki began to speak but Jack motioned toward the ceiling. "He'll be listening."

"Is there a camera?" Dylan asked, inspecting the ceiling.

Jack shook his head. "Not in this one."

The unmistakable sound of the outer doors locking reached their ears and Jack tried to calm his nerves. It wasna natural for a man to be caged like a wild animal, he thought.

The driver's door opened and Howard's voice came through the speaker. "The outer doors are locked for your safety," he said in a chirpy tone that sounded forced.

"My safety my arse," Jack whispered.

The engine roared to life and a moment later, they were clinging to their seats as the van bumped its way down the drive toward the road.

~~

The hum of the engine and the smoothness of the M1 had lulled Jack into a fitful sleep, interrupted every now and again as his head or his shoulder nudged Dylan adjacent to him or the bars on the opposite side. Even with five bodies in close proximity, the air was frigid as if the air intake had been turned on full blast and his coughing spells were getting the best of him.

Unable to remain asleep, he did what the others appeared to be doing: looking at everyone else.

Brenda sat across from him and at the end closest to the driver. Her face was hard, her lips tight. Her arms were crossed in front of her, her hands tucked under her arms in a possible effort to remain warm. Jack met her eyes but once; they were veiled, the eyes of one who had been in a tight spot before and liked it even less than he. Oh, she was a fighter, he thought. He could see it from where he sat.

Alexei was beside her and almost directly across from him. His brows were furrowed. For all his broad shoulders and possible weight-lifting, Jack surmised, he was unaccustomed to circumstances such as this and didn't quite know what to make of it. He caught Jack looking at him and attempted a forced smile.

Jack leaned a bit forward as if he was attempting to stretch his arms to his legs. He peered at the end of the bench where Vicki was leaning her head against the divider that separated them from the driver. She appeared as though she had been waiting for the opportunity to connect with him. Her lips opened slightly but he shook his head once and she closed them again. Her eyes, however, spoke volumes. She was fae, he thought, Lord help them, fae as his wife had been and fae as her mother, the woman Dylan called Mam. And the look in her eye confirmed what he had suspected as soon as he'd identified the van.

He could not make out Dylan's expression without appearing obvious so he settled back into his seat and stole a glance at the monitor in the ceiling.

The van slowed.

Curious, Jack peered as best he could out the rear window. They were entering a roundabout and at the second junction, they should continue eastward. But they turned too quickly, taking the first instead. Shite. They should have remained on the main road once they'd reached Donegal some time earlier, a smooth main motorway that should have taken them straightaway into Belfast.

He leaned back in his seat. He felt all eyes on him. Of course, he thought. I'd be the only bugger among us who knows the route to Belfast.

"We're headed southward," he whispered to Dylan. His voice was barely audible and for a moment, he wondered if his son had heard him.

Dylan turned as if looking out the rear window. "Is it right?" he mouthed.

"No."

Jack tried to get a bearing on their location. There was an indirect route that could go south off the motorway before taking them into Belfast but it made no sense that the inspector would take it, as it would add time to the trip and for no good reason. He closed his eyes, attempting to draw a map in his mind's eye. They turned at Kesh, he thought, headed toward Enniskillen.

Oh, shite bugger feck, he thought.

The sun rose slowly in Ireland in the winter; she slept in, lazy and insipid as if she had to muster her strength to combat the long, cold nights. The skies at mid-morn were like flannel blankets with just enough color to tell a man that dawn had passed but too high to provide any warmth. And as they bounced toward Lisnarick on the route to Enniskillen, the winds howled down from the north, buffeting the van like it was no more than a tin toy.

The farther south they traveled, the heavier his jacket became. It was time. The men each wore jackets; they would know what to do.

He slipped his hands under his armpits as if to keep warm, though he knew he was far enough removed from the driver that he would not see his movement. Methodically, he slipped one hand lower until it slid into his pocket. He could feel the cold metal against his fingertips. He preferred the Glocks, he did; they were some of the newer pistols added to the old farmhouse stash. Fairly lightweight, not so easily detected, but accurate and sure.

Slowly, silently, he slipped the Glock from his pocket, pushing against Dylan's side as he moved. The younger man's fingers seized it, sliding it quietly into his own jacket.

Jack glanced across the aisle at Alexei and nodded. The Russian's head barely moved as he nodded in return. God knows I hope the gent can fire a pistol, he thought as he dipped into another pocket, and he doesn't shoot one of us.

He eased the second pistol into Dylan's hands. The movements were so unhurried that he wasn't certain but that Dylan had kept the second one himself until he saw Vicki ease it underneath the window separating them from the driver. Brenda grasped it with a sure hand and Vicki pointed quickly at Alexei, careful to keep her movements as close to the metal divider as possible to avoid detection.

Brenda waited so long to pass it along that he was growing concerned that she intended to keep it for herself. And that would not do at'al, he thought. The women would need the men to protect them. And there would be the three of them to the inspector, not bad odds. Then why was he beginning to feel that same unease that had pervaded his senses during the entirety of his imprisonment?

The van slowed once more and as the driver turned his head to peer out the side window, Brenda slipped the second Glock to Alexei. A split second later, it was hidden inside his pocket.

They exited the main road and turned onto a narrow, winding road.

"Where are we?" Dylan whispered hoarsely.

"I believe we're headed toward the Lower Lough Erne."

Dylan almost jerked his head in his father's direction but caught himself. "Why?"

"Other than the old castle," Jack murmured, "it's an isolated area."

"What's it near?"

"There are several islands in the Lough. They're uninhabited."

"Why is he takin' us there?"

Jack peered across at Brenda and Alexei. Though they both were watching Dylan and himself, he knew they could not hear their whispered words. Just as well. "I'm thinkin' he aims to kill us."

They found themselves holding onto their seats as the van lurched on increasingly rural roads that seemed more suited to cattle than vehicles.

As Vicki was pitched into Dylan, she said, "They found our contact at the American Embassy in Moscow."

"Oh?" Dylan's reply was curt but he peered at her with interest.

Jack leaned forward so he could hear her better. She glanced at the monitor above them as if signaling that she knew the driver was listening. "He was tied to a tree," she said, her voice slightly breaking, "in Siberia. He'd been eaten by wolves."

"Ooh," both Dylan and Jack said in unison.

Oh, feck us all, Jack thought. He had heard stories years ago of one of the cruelest forms of execution in Russia. The person was brought into Siberia, where the temperatures were subarctic; stripped, gagged and left tied to a tree. Helpless to escape, they either froze to death or they were eaten by wolves.

He glanced across the aisle at Alexei as he crossed himself. The Russian was wiping perspiration from his brow, though it was still frigid in the van. His face was white as a sheet. Obviously, he knew of the practice as well, Jack thought. The only reason he had known was the prison guards in England often threatened to send them to Siberia, taking delight in telling them precisely how the Russians executed prisoners there. And Vicki had said their contact at the American Embassy, which boggled his mind. Were not diplomats and their staff protected?

His thoughts were interrupted as they pulled to a stop. Inspector Howard opened his door and called out in greeting.

They were not alone.

Brenda reached swiftly to her ankle, raising her pants leg just enough to extract a pistol tucked within her sock.

She handed it to Vicki, who quickly slipped it into her pocket. Brenda was still reaching for her alternate pants leg when the door abruptly opened.

44

Vicki was the last to step out of the van. She found the others surrounded by three men carrying semi-automatic rifles. Her eyes locked onto Dylan's briefly before he tore his eyes away to look first at Jack and then Alexei and finally coming to rest on each of the strangers as if assessing each one.

One of the men slipped Inspector Howard a white envelope. He opened the thick package, obviously thumbing through a stack of bills before shoving it into his pocket. "Nice doing business with you," he said with a slight tip of his hat.

The man who had given him the package murmured something inaudible. His face was oddly familiar and with a start, Vicki realized she was staring at Iakov, the man from whom the other Russians had taken their orders. It was an unsettling experience to come face-to-face with someone she had seen in a psychic vision. He looked exactly as he had then: roughly her height and perhaps all of a hundred and thirty pounds soaking wet. And yet the memory of his cold-blooded murder of one of his own men loomed large in her mind.

She glanced at the other men; Kolya was not among them.

Howard was making his way back to the van. Panicked, Vicki looked around them. They were standing on a tiny peninsula at the edge of a body of water; it was obviously not the ocean but an inland lake. To her left was a small island and what appeared to be piers jutting into the water. Directly in front of them was a much larger island with just the hint of stone ruins visible through the shifting mist. Beyond that she glimpsed the edge of a third island.

"That way," Iakov said with a heavy accent, pointing his rifle in the direction of the island directly in front of them.

Vicki hesitated, taking her cue from Dylan and Jack. Dylan held out his palm in a gesture meant for the sisters to move forward first. As she began to walk past him, he fell in line beside her.

The air was thick with tension and unsaid words hung on fingers of mists that danced and intensified, merging into hands and then bodies like apparitions. Somewhere behind her, she heard Jack's hacking cough.

From out of the vapor she spotted a rope bridge that dangled above the current between the peninsula and the island. A large flat rock beckoned on the isle, leaving her guessing whether a helicopter intended to land there. As visions of their abduction and transport to Moscow loomed in her mind, she balked, taking a step backward before Dylan caught her.

"It's okay," he said loud enough for the men to hear. "Just do what the men say."

In the distance, she heard the sound of a motorboat engine roaring to life.

She heard Alexei moan and turned to see him stumbling over the craggy ground, blood spurting from his temple. The guards stood nearby, grinning; one was putting his rifle back into position, the butt bloodied. "Dylan," she pleaded.

He squeezed her hand with his left hand, his right tucked securely into his jacket pocket.

She swallowed hard and reached her own hand into her pocket.

"Halt."

The directive had come from Iakov, who was moving closer to them. He fixed her with a cold, hard gaze devoid of a soul, his light gray eyes almost blending into the surrounding white.

She tore her eyes from him to peer at the others: two men with bulked shoulders that each stood at least six inches taller than their boss. Both wore caps pulled low to their brows. One had a wicked scar across one cheek that had permanently split his upper lip. The other grinned at her when their eyes met, revealing yellowed, crooked teeth.

Iakov looked toward the road behind them and she followed his gaze. At first, she was uncertain of what held his attention; she could see only the fog settling in over the rural Irish countryside like a soft blanket. But then she spotted the glint of taillights, two red bobs that dipped and climbed over the rough terrain. The Garda van.

She looked back at Iakov as an icy smile spread across his face.

The detonation rocked the morning air, sending a plume of black smoke and flames into the sky. Vicki cried out instinctively, but her voice was drowned out by the explosion. Pieces of the van were raining down; still aflame, they set the ground afire as they landed. A jagged piece of metal sliced through the water not far from where they stood, and she found herself hugging the ground, afraid to run and terrified to remain where she was.

The gunshot near her ear might have deafened her had her eardrums not already been filled with the lingering sounds of the car bomb. She opened her eyes to see everything unfolding in slow motion. Brenda was saying something to her and pointing but she could no longer hear her voice, let alone make out her words. Jack's back was turned to her; he bobbed in front of her, his head bowing forward before jerking back. Alexei was enveloped in a shroud of mist and smoke; his mouth was moving but like Brenda's, no sound was escaping. Dylan was gone and then he was back, running toward her as hot embers peppered the ground beneath his feet.

Then the noise was everywhere. Brenda was shouting in one ear and Dylan in another as they each grabbed an arm and yanked her back to her feet. Automatic gunfire sounded like firecrackers. Jack was bellowing, the syllables running into one another until he was incoherent. Alexei was yelling and pointing, dipping to the ground only to reappear, his feet slipping and sliding from under him.

"Go!" Brenda screamed. "Go! Go! Go! Go!"

She had no sooner come to her feet than both Dylan and Brenda were shoving her toward the lough. Her feet discovered a mind of their own as they flew along the bank parallel to the water as Brenda propelled her forward. And then Dylan was gone and the gunfire blended into a solid chorus. As the rope bridge came into view, the sound of a motorboat grew louder amid fresh shouts in a language she could not comprehend.

45

Jack's instinct was on high alert, the adrenaline building to a crescendo that was surging with increasing intensity. His eyes moved between Dylan and Alexei as they stood near the water's edge. The three Russians standing in front of him were not the only ones; he was certain of that. He heard the motorboat's engine, heard it coming in their direction, and heard the distant sound of men's voices from the mainland.

He had the advantage of knowing the area well. Behind him was Lower Lough Erne, one of the largest lakes in all of Ireland. It was formed by the River Erne which flows north instead of south before curving toward the Atlantic Ocean. The currents often ran swift and sure like those of the ocean, making it ideal for the avid or extreme sportsman but deadly for those not ready for her powerful waves.

There were more than a hundred islands within the lough, 154 to be precise; some he had explored and some not, some privately owned and others maintained by the Irish government. During the high summer months when tourism was at its peak, this shore would have been littered with visitors who took the ferries to some of the largest islands. Behind him was Abbey Davy's Island, the site of a medieval monastery that was now little more than stone ruins. And to the north of it was the larger White Island, best known perhaps for the stone figures and church ruins that dated back to 800 A.D. Though that was impressive enough, he supposed, the church and figures were actually built upon a far older monastic settlement.

The island was mystical; some said magical, with monolithic pagan creatures interspersed with Christian figures. The mists tended to swirl and sway over White Island as though they were spirits still alive, and many who graced those grounds came away with stories of hauntings and sightings. Some might have been too fantastic to be believed but so many had now experienced them that it was undeniable something lurked there that remained largely invisible to the naked eye but never undetectable by the attentive soul.

Now the tourists were gone and the lough nearly deserted; deserted enough, he thought, for the five of them to disappear without a trace.

He caught Dylan's eye. The movement was nearly imperceptible, moving between Jack and the man nearest him, followed by a slight nod of the head. Jack dipped his chin slightly in response. Satisfied, Dylan looked next at Alexei.

So there he had it, he thought. Three assailants, one for each of them. All he needed now was the signal to attack.

The van's explosion was like a favor sent from the gods. There was barely a good riddance paid to the Inspector before the three of them were moving in tandem as if they had been a well-oiled machine. Jack didn't bother pulling the pistol from his jacket pocket; he fired straight through the leather with nary a doubt. Before the man nearest him could hit the ground, he caught his rifle, wrenched it from his grasp and fired another shot with the larger weapon straight through his skull so he could meet the devil all the sooner. Then he was off, rushing toward the sound of the other men approaching, firing at will.

Through the mist, he caught sight of Brenda firing her weapon pointblank at a man and then firing again as he went down. Jack kept moving, never waiting to see if his bullets found their mark, trusting in only the seconds he had and determined to make the most of each of them. He felt like a young man again and even his throat ceased to be buggered as he dodged this way and that through a swirl of mist and smoke.

After surging ahead, he doubled back to find in addition to the man he had killed, another lying beside him. The smaller man that had been in the middle was gone and Dylan's figure moved in and out of the mist as he searched for him.

Jack shouted to him that there were more coming; the only escape was toward White Island.

He had spotted the rope bridge when they had first arrived; was surprised to see it, truth be told. The island was dotted with similar bridges; they were temporary and usually erected by fishermen during the high fishing season and dismantled directly after. The fact that it was there most likely meant the Russians had pilfered it. No doubt they had planned to march them across to the island and it wasn't lost on him that it would serve as the perfect spot for a helicopter to land and whisk them away, if they weren't killed instead.

He shouted to Dylan and Alexei to get the girls to the bridge. It seemed counter-intuitive, he knew, to flee into the fast-moving lough to an island where they could easily be trapped, but they would simply have to trust him. There was no getting past it. Once across, they would cut the ropes. It was the only thing to do with their enemy surrounding them where they were.

He darted back and forth, firing and dodging, until he had moved closer to the bridge. With a single shout, he waited for Brenda to turn toward him and then he tossed the rifle to her. She had proven herself to be a woman who could fire a weapon and kill a man. Their lives depended on it.

The rope bridge rose nearly one hundred feet above the surface of the water. Unlike those that catered to tourists, this one was the type that was thrown together by salty fishermen with no fear of heights, the winds or the current. It consisted of fishermen's nets woven together to span the length between the main shore and the island; then a hodgepodge of wood planks were plaited in the center, two abreast, to form a surface perhaps eight inches wide. If a plank happened to slip through the net, it could easily plummet to the waters below, taking anyone walking it down with it. There was also no rope to serve as railing or by which a man could steady himself.

Brenda was the first to take it. She stepped onto it without hesitation but when it swayed dangerously, she nearly lost the rifle he'd tossed her.

"Hurry!" he shouted but his voice was carried away by the mounting wind.

As if suddenly realizing that there was no handrail, she bent low and used one hand to steady herself while the other held onto the rifle.

Before she was more than a few yards out over the water, Dylan was pushing Vicki onto it. His mouth was moving but in the noise and confusion, Jack could not decipher his words. Vicki appeared not to hear them at all. Dropping to her hands and knees, she began scurrying across the footbridge.

With every movement either made, the ropes wavered and danced frenetically as if they were in the full throws of a seizure.

Dylan tossed a rifle to Jack and then grabbed the one Alexei had been using. They stood nearly shoulder to shoulder, firing at the figures that popped out of the mist like apparitions. In between the bullets, Dylan barked at Alexei to follow Vicki and Brenda.

Then no sooner had Alexei begun to follow than Jack caught sight of Dylan dropping to his knees. He threw himself in front of his son, continuing to fire, the bullets expending so quickly that in another moment he would be out of ammunition.

"Get up!" he bellowed. "Get up!"

Dylan's jacket was covered in blood, thick and flowing. He struggled to his feet, slipping once before he managed to stand upright again.

"Go!" Jack shouted. "I'll hold 'em off!"

Somewhere in the back of his mind, he knew the others were making their way across the water; ten stories up in winds that buffeted them like an infant's sheets on a clothesline, the lot of them clinging to nets designed for a solo passage.

46

Vicki was nearly halfway across when the men began firing from a motorboat below. The constant barrage had forced Brenda to stop completely and now Vicki was bottlenecked at her heels as her sister rolled dangerously over onto her back. Despite the peril from below, Vicki remained on her belly, slipping her arms through the netting to wrap around the narrow strips of wood that were the only things preventing her from plunging into the fast-moving current.

Three more were approaching behind her; she could no longer see them but felt their presence with every shift and wobble. When Alexei bumped into her feet, she cried out, afraid the man would attempt to crawl over her and plummet them both to their deaths below. He halted but the net continued to sway as Dylan and Jack moved closer.

"Brenda!" Vicki called out. She forced herself to raise her head.

Her sister was lying on her back, her head barely extending over the plank width, peering at the boat below. Beyond her, the horizon swayed and bobbed with nauseating intensity.

"Brenda!" she called out again.

"What?" Her sister did not look at her but continued to watch the boat.

"They want us alive."

"Is that why they're shooting at us then?"

Vicki felt the pistol tucked in her pocket, the hard metal between her body and the plank. "You have to move, Brenda. No one can get across until you do."

"I'm a bit pinned down at the moment." Despite the need to shout to be heard through the whistling and moaning of the wind, her voice was surprisingly calm.

Vicki tried to catch her sister's eye but Brenda had moved the rifle into position. The boat had stopped below, two men laughing at the five stranded on the ropes as they continued shooting. Their shots were not aimed but appeared to be intended more to frighten them into dropping into the water than to kill them outright but as a bullet whizzed past Vicki's ear she called out to Brenda again.

The rifle was across Brenda's body. One hand was on the grip while the other was extended along the bottom of the barrel in an attempt to steady it against the buffeting winds. Her movements were painfully slow and meticulously steady.

The men were firing at those bringing up the rear. The combination of Jack's, Dylan's and Alexei's continued shouts and their return fire served to remind her of their dual efforts to reach the island while simultaneously being forced to fight back. With a lump in her throat, Vicki realized that the Russians only wanted three of them; Brenda and Jack, at the front and the rear, were completely expendable.

The seconds passed as the five continued to bottleneck until each was holding onto the netting beside the other's feet.

Vicki heard the rifle firing at almost the exact moment that the boat below burst into flames. The blaze from the ruptured gasoline tank shot so high that she could feel the heat searing the ropes. The recoil caused Brenda to lose her balance, sending the weapon careening through the open netting to the current below. Her sister's arm and shoulder slipped through as well and Vicki grabbed her by her ankles as she shouted for her to hang on.

"Go!" Jack was yelling behind them, his voice rising frantically. "Go! Go! Go!"

Brenda scrambled back, disentangling herself with such speed that the netting swung out dangerously, threatening to plunge them all into the lough. The men from the boat had either leapt into the water or were propelled there by the force of the blast. One was screaming in agony as lit gasoline floated around him like demons coming in for the kill. The other was swimming toward White Island; only the top of his jacket was visible above the water and as Vicki watched, it caught fire until he, too, was screeching. As his hair erupted in flames, he disappeared beneath the surface only to reappear and reignite a moment later.

In the next instant, Brenda had rolled onto her stomach and was scrambling across the bridge as rapidly as possible, appearing almost crablike given the gusts of wind that seemed intent on turning the net inside out. The ropes were drenched and moldy from the constant damp, the mists rising to make them slicker as Vicki tried desperately to get across. Alexei grabbed at her ankles more than once, nearly causing them both to plummet. And somewhere behind them Jack was shouting for them to hurry, his voice rising with intensifying desperation.

Then Brenda was scrambling onto the cliff face, heaving herself upward and onto the flat protruding rock. She reached back almost immediately to grab Vicki's arms with bloodied hands, hauling her off the rope. It wasn't until Vicki had reached firm ground that she realized her own palms were bloody and raw as well, sliced through from the coarse and unforgiving rope.

Somewhere in the distance she heard the unmistakable sound of helicopter blades. Rising onto legs wobbling from their exertions, the two sisters waited at the edge of the craggy rock, shouting for the men to hurry. A blur of color rose behind them through the mists before disappearing and rising again as the Russians gained ground behind them. The sisters fired their pistols in an attempt to keep the enemy pinned down and buy the others precious time.

The sound of the blades was increasing. Brenda and Vicki's eyes met with the same anguish mirrored in both. It was now obvious that at least two more men had entered the bridge, oscillating it with such force that it was obvious their intent was to dislodge them.

"Hang on!" Jack was yelling.

Dylan's body was covered in blood, soaking Jack with it as his father ventured across behind him. But then Jack stopped. The gap between Dylan and Jack widened as Brenda and Vicki shouted for him to hurry.

"Hang on!" Jack yelled again.

Alexei was perhaps three feet from the rock when one side of the netting gave way. He rushed to intertwine his right arm through the net even as the left bent. When he gathered the strength to haul himself forward, the planks that were no longer kept in place by his weight slipped through the net, plunging to the water nearly a hundred feet below them.

"Get my legs!" Brenda yelled as she collapsed onto her stomach.

As Vicki hurriedly moved behind her and grabbed her ankles, she fought the futility of trying to hold onto her. Wedging her knees into the rock grooves until she cried out in pain, she held onto her sister while Brenda struggled to grab hold of Alexei.

Then the other side of the netting gave way in a blur of men and blood and sky and water. Vicki heard Dylan's anguished voice as he cried out, his bellow seeming to echo in the wind. Then the shots and voices abruptly stopped.

Brenda's legs were slipping out of Vicki's grasp. They were water-soaked and slick as oil and Vicki felt herself sliding toward the rock's edge in a desperate attempt to hold onto her. Brenda was screaming now, her words incoherent, her head plunging over the side.

Then a hand appeared and another until Alexei's head popped over the side of the cliff. Vicki painstakingly hauled her sister back as the Russian continued to emerge. No sooner had he scrambled onto firm land than he was turning back, rolling onto his stomach as Brenda had.

On the ground where Alexei had emerged was the top piece of a shoe heel. It seemed ludicrous that in a desperate moment like this, Vicki was drawn to it as though it was a powerful magnet yanking her toward it. And yet everything around her faded into the background; the men's frantic shouts, the pistols still firing, the helicopter approaching the makeshift landing pad behind them. It was as if she had entered another realm.

In the center of the broken heel was a round metallic object. Her eyes seemed to travel in slow motion to Alexei's shoes, the soles exposed as he leaned further into the abyss in a frenzied attempt to reach Dylan and Jack.

Brenda was shouting to her and Vicki felt as though she was snapping out of a dream. She lunged forward to help them, but not before she snapped up the heel and slipped it into her pocket. She knew exactly what it was: a tracking device, one that had helped to lead the Russians to them every step of the way.

As she grabbed the netting with both hands, she stole a look at Alexei beside her. His face was strained, his muscled forearms bearing most of the weight as they heaved the rope higher, inch by inch.

The helicopter was coming into focus now, arriving through the mists like a giant gray monster, the dual rotor blades swirling the moisture onto their bodies as it approached.

It had all been a trap, she realized with a start. The Russian defector, sheltering him at the manor house, luring Dylan and Jack to a rendezvous point that he knew would never take place—it had all been a brilliant work of deception. Even the microchip she still carried might be nothing more than a series of meaningless files.

As Brenda, Vicki and Alexei were pressed shoulder to shoulder, Dylan and Jack clung to the netting below, the planks that hadn't yet escaped poking through like a child's pick up sticks. All were bloodied. The waves were roiling, lapping at the men like a shark attempting to swallow its prey. And now, flying directly over their heads was a Russian helicopter, the side door slid open to reveal armed men ready to pluck them off the island and whisk them off to Moscow.

47

Dylan's left shoulder was useless. He had been forced to climb the net by wrapping his legs around it, shimmying upward until he could grasp upward with his right hand once more. He knew he was shaking Jack like he was an apple in a tree but there was no other way.

They were hanging eighty feet above the water. They had been plunged into the cliff face when Jack cut the ropes, a sensation that felt as though they had been driven into a concrete wall face first. Blood poured from the wound in his shoulder as well as from his nose and face and he fought the urge to faint from the loss of blood.

Then the netting was being hauled upward as though Vicki, Brenda and Alexei were seasoned fishermen and Dylan and Jack were helpless fish ensnared in the net. By the time he reached the top, his legs felt like sticks of butter, boneless and powerless.

The sisters dragged him farther onto the craggy island, each uneven stone and dormant piece of underbrush razor sharp. He caught a glimpse of Alexei, still leaning dangerously over the cliff, his arms like pistons as he heaved Jack to safety. Above them, a helicopter was circling the island in the final approach to the pseudo landing spot.

Exhausted, the five were strewn across the tip of the island, each one's breath more labored than the last, the blood oozing onto the land like the dying vestiges of lava.

Despite the fact that the others were rallying despite their exhaustive states, Dylan found himself unable to move. His body wanted nothing more than to drift away into a deep, dreamless, bottomless sleep but his mind was racing like a disembodied voice urging him to get up.

The helicopter seemed to be moving in slow motion now, its approach steady. Men's faces on either side emerged; perhaps strapped into the aircraft or holding on with one hand, the other held a rifle as they prepared to land. The two men that had been behind Jack on the rope were coming, it was certain of it; it was only a matter of time. And although Iakov had disappeared when the firing had begun, he knew better than to count the man out. They were all advancing on them.

The skies were gray and white like a black and white film, the heavy clouds tumbling with the threat of rain. The winds were moving fast, ushered in from the Atlantic; a lazy wind, the kind that wasn't to be bothered going around a man but one that would cut right through his body instead, chilling him to the bone. It caught the helicopter in a rogue gust, nearly keeling it before it was righted once more.

Somewhere in the back of his mind he registered the cold, hard stone beneath his back. He was bleeding out but he was powerless to do anything about it. Even the figures of the others were no more than indistinct blurs now, their voices disintegrating.

Too weak to blink, he watched the aircraft bob and then hover above the landing pad.

He was dying, he thought. The clouds were opening, beckoning his spirit to move through to the other side as a soft rain began to fall.

A swoosh of air and adrenaline surged through him as if he'd been jolted with a defibrillator. "Jaysus." He tried to bolt upward but his body had a mind of its own; his left arm flopped uselessly and he found himself trying to force his torso higher by kicking his heels against the rock until his knees had inched closer to his body.

Jack and Vicki came to his aid, lifting him off the ground. He swayed and almost fell back down but they were on either side of him, half carrying him toward stone ruins that seemed too far away and too exposed.

Then the sky seemed to open up in front of them as a ball of fire sliced through the clouds. It might have looked like a jet plane's condensation trails except for the outline of red-orange.

"Hurry!" Jack was shouting, though there was no need for his frantic order. They were all making a frenzied dash for the ruins of a megalithic church. No sooner had they reached the archway than the Russian helicopter exploded. The missile had found its target, shattering the aircraft into a million shards. All five were knocked off their feet as metal rained down around them. With all the strength he had left, Dylan threw himself across Vicki's body in a final, wretched attempt to shield her against the onslaught.

It felt like an eternity and it felt like only a moment before the sounds of a second helicopter rose above the mellay. The sound grew thunderous and as he lifted his head, the welcome sight of two American Black Hawk helicopters came into view. Then everything seemed to be fading. The distinctive sound of the rotor blades waned and as he dropped his head against Vicki once more, he wasn't certain he had seen them at all.

48

The soldiers placed Dylan on the gurney and raced across the uneven terrain toward the waiting helicopter. The medic was quickly gathering the supplies for the IV while another was recording his vital signs. He had lost consciousness shortly after throwing himself across Vicki, his weight nearly suffocating her. As the medic cut his jacket and shirt from him, she realized in a rising panic that he had been shot through the shoulder at close range and had lost a substantial amount of blood, judging from the pools on the ground where he had lain.

Sam was wearing an earbud, his palm covering both ears so he could hear over the sound of the rotor blades. The island had become a flurry of frenzied activity as they were hustled toward the waiting aircraft. Every second counted.

Sam pointed at Alexei and then at Brenda. "You two!" he shouted to be heard over the din, "in that second aircraft there! Now!"

Brenda stole a quick glance at Vicki but did not question his order. As she turned toward the second helicopter, Alexei grabbed her by the elbow and they both made a dash for the aircraft.

"Vicki, you and I are going with Dylan," he said, hurrying her toward the first aircraft.

"Wait," Vicki said.

"We don't have time. We've got to get out of here."

"Stop, Sam. Listen to me." She fished out Alexei's shoe heel from her pocket. "He was wearing this."

He stopped in his tracks to take the heel from her. He inspected it for only a second before declaring, "It's a tracking device."

"I know."

He tossed it onto the ground. "Let's go."

"But Sam, that means he led the Russians straight to us."

"I know what it means."

"But—"

"It means he's either a spy for the Russians or a double spy." His steady eyes met hers. The helicopter carrying Alexei and Brenda was already lifting off. "It doesn't matter now. He's on his way to a carrier in the North Sea. After an interrogation there, he'll be brought back to the States. He'll never see Russia again."

As the helicopter made a turn before heading away from the island, Vicki said, "But, Brenda—"

"Her mission's done."

She stared at the aircraft as it grew smaller. "But—I never had a chance to say good-bye." Her voice was barely over a whisper. Sam didn't appear to have heard her; he was rushing toward the helicopter. She turned to find Jack looking at her curiously. "Sam!" she called.

She motioned for Jack to follow her as she sprinted toward Sam. He had reached the helicopter doors and was ready to board.

"What about Jack?"

"Jack?" He looked beyond her as if seeing him for the first time. "Oh, the stable hand."

"Sam, he's Dylan's father."

"Dylan's—what?"

"That's right. We can't leave him."

"Get in," Sam ordered him.

"Whoa." Jack held up both hands. "And where would you be goin'?"

"Does it matter?" Sam barked.

"It does to me."

Sam grabbed Vicki's hand and hoisted her into the aircraft. Two men were tending to Dylan and two armed soldiers were watching the surrounding terrain. "Sixty seconds," one of them shouted.

"Germany," Sam answered before climbing aboard. "Now get in."

"No," Jack said. "I think I'll stay right here, thank you very much."

"Jack, you can't!" Vicki pleaded. "Please get in!"

He waved them off. "I'll be fine. Phone me and let me know how m' son is doin', won't you?" His voice broke.

"You have to come, Jack!"

Jack moved toward the door as the pilot announced they were lifting off. "Don't worry, Vicki. I must get back to Brigit. She needs me. And I'll mail your luggage to you."

"Sam—" Vicki turned to him. "Please—"

"He knows what he's doing," Sam said. "Sit down and strap yourself in." He grabbed onto the handhold. "We're sending in another team," he shouted to Jack as the helicopter began to lift. "They'll make sure you get home."

Reluctantly, Vicki sat down and strapped on the seat belt. As Sam joined her, she stared out the open door.

Jack had moved safely away from the aircraft and was standing all alone. He waved to her with a smile on his face but Vicki felt as though her heart was breaking. He looked so forlorn there, and she couldn't shake the thought that they were abandoning him.

As the helicopter rose higher, she saw the rope bridge clinging to the cliff face, the other side flapping in the water near the opposite shore. The lake was still on fire, the gasoline from the motorboat forming a black film that looked like an undulating whale from the sky. The opposite shore was littered with bodies, and the Garda van was still blazing a short distance away.

Then she spotted a line of cars speeding toward the island with lights flashing.

"Sam—" she said, her voice catching in her throat.

He had his hand over his earbud. He glanced at Vicki and then out the window. "They're ours," he said briefly before turning back to his call. "Yeah, that's right. Take him anywhere he wants to go."

As the helicopter veered into a turn, she caught one last glimpse of Jack. He was still standing where they'd left him. As the cars reached the opposite shore and came to an abrupt stop, he lifted his hands to the back of his head like a criminal under arrest.

Then as the mists rolled in and the turn was complete, she lost sight of him.

49

Dylan was sitting up in the hospital bed despite Vicki's efforts to get him to rest. His left arm was in a sling, the bullet removed from his shoulder and bandaged. His first words as he'd been rolled into the military installation's hospital room after surgery and the recovery room were to inquire about Vicki, and his second was to ask about his father. He was genuinely relieved when Vicki appeared by his side, and troubled over the fact that he was separated once more from the father he had just found.

Always the unemotional professional, Sam finished briefing him on Alexei. "So we'll find out whether he blew your cover," he was saying, "or if there are other forces at work here."

"So he's to be interrogated," Dylan said flatly.

"Oh, he already is," Sam said. He glanced at his watch. "No doubt about it… We'll most likely treat him as an enemy combatant; probably transfer him to one of our Black Ops…"

Dylan nodded.

Vicki pulled a chair beside the bed, sat down and took Dylan's right hand in hers. She had been to a Black Ops site once and now the specter of men in cages loomed large in her mind. "What if he didn't know he was wearing the device?"

Sam scoffed. "In his shoe? Yeah, I'd like to know how it got there without his knowledge."

"I have the file, Sam. I don't know if there's anything on the chip."

"We received the file from Brenda."

"You did?"

"Yeah. Good information, too. The latest on the Russians' stealth technology."

"Can you share any of it with us?"

"A little. Both countries have been working with metamaterials—materials that bend light around an object so it cannot be seen. Then the Russians had perfected a skin partially made from several types of metal coatings much like the process used in mirrors. They were able to combine the metamaterials with the mirror reflection and the colors of the aircraft to trick the eye so it was not readily visible."

"But aren't metamaterials the same as a mirror reflection?" Dylan asked.

"Not at all," Sam answered. "Metamaterials bend the light around an object while the mirror coating reflects it. It's a tricky procedure but they were getting it right—to a point."

"That would take care o' the naked eye for sure," Dylan interjected. "But what of our own detection technology?"

"That's why we needed their plans. Our equipment couldn't see it, either. They were using a newer generation of stealth technology; their planes were so effective at redirecting electromagnetic waves from our radar, sonar and infrared devices, that the aircraft could literally be above our heads and we might never know it was there."

"But what I'm not understandin'," Dylan pressed, "are the scores o' people that *did* see it. Was it a flaw in their design?"

"We're not sure yet. Using the plans we received, our people will create a smaller version for test purposes. We're working now on the assumption that they wanted us to know they had the capability."

"But why would they do that?" Vicki asked. "It takes away the whole element of surprise."

"Ah, but that only works if you have the power to back it up. You see, Russia—for all its want of showing its might—is hurting financially. It's been hurting for quite some time. They have a crumbling infrastructure, a declining economy."

"So if they made us think they were capable of battling the west, they thought it would somehow insulate them?"

"Quite possibly. That's why the plans were so valuable. They obviously made their military might their top priority and they wanted the world to know it."

"But why?"

Sam shrugged. "Your guess is as good as mine. They've always seen the United States as a continuing threat to communism. And they're probably alarmed at the rapid rise of India, China and parts of the Middle East—like Dubai in the UAE."

They grew silent, each with their own thoughts.

"Then Alexei's mission might have been to set us up—"

"Yeah. There's always that possibility." Sam sounded bored. "We'll figure it out. It's for somebody else to put together the pieces of the puzzle now."

"When Brenda sent you the file, she received a message in Russian."

"Our computer tech detected infiltration just as the file had completed uploading. He was able to close the connection from our end but obviously, once they had compromised the line, they could backtrack to Brenda's laptop."

"But the file came through intact?"

"Just made it. Had the Russians been a few seconds faster… But they weren't."

"It makes a good deal o' sense to me," Dylan said, "for Alexei to be a double agent. What's been troublin' me is how he knew his contact in Moscow was to meet us in Donegal. The Russians knew we would be there; they knew of the hand-off."

"Dylan's right," Vicki said. "They were there waiting for us when we came out of the pub."

"We're still looking for that operative—the one from Donegal," Sam said. He looked tired. He pulled up a chair on the opposite side of the bed and sat down heavily. "He's most likely in Russia right now. We have assets there, too, and they are trying to find out all they can."

"Do you think Alexei was present when the Moscow agent was abducted?"

"One of the questions they'll be asking him during interrogation," Sam answered. "It's possible the Moscow agent disclosed the rendezvous point. He wouldn't have known it would be you two picking it up; only that someone would. He would have assumed the chip would be handed off to someone else; that's usually the way it's done."

"So, Alexei would have contacted his Russian handlers," Dylan said, "perhaps he had a camera and had a photo of Vicki and me without us bein' the wiser. Face recognition might've identified us both, and from there, we became their focus."

"Yep. And Vicki, you did the right thing by calling me when you did. We were able to train the satellites on you at the Garda station, so we had you in our sights from the time you left to return to the manor house... Fortunately, we had a carrier in the North Sea and were able to turn them around and send them toward Ireland."

"Thank God you got there when you did," Vicki said. "I don't even want to think about what might have happened—"

"Word of advice," Dylan interjected. "Don't."

"Speaking of that," Sam said, clearing his throat, "you two are going to have to lay low for a while."

"What does that mean?" Vicki asked.

"It means," Dylan said, his eyes narrowing, "now that our cover's blown, we're vulnerable to bein' picked up by the Russians any day, any time. Is that right, Sam?"

"I'm afraid so." He waved away Vicki's objections. "We'll get to the bottom of it. But for the time being, you two need to pick a different spot for your honeymoon. We'll fly you anywhere in the world. New passports, new identities."

"But for how long?"

"Oh, it won't be long."

"Our house—" Dylan began.

"I promise you'll get back there. And I'll take care of the angelfish until you do."

"Speaking of which—"

"I kind of hired somebody." Sam paused. "Benita's niece. Nice young lady. Hard worker. I've been teaching her how to care for the fish." He cleared his throat again. "Now back to you two. You've been cleared to leave the hospital tomorrow, Dylan. Pick a place."

He rose and started for the door. "I'll leave you two lovebirds to discuss where you want to go." He stopped with his hand on the knob and turned back to them. "By the way," he added, "almost forgot to tell you. We did a recon over the first rendezvous point. Strangest thing.

Three men were dead at the bottom of a cliff. You wouldn't know anything about that, would you?"

Dylan shook his head. "No," he said in a hushed voice. "No, I wouldn't."

"Hhmm. Thought it was interesting, is all. Their car was parked not far from the landing site, but they were found in the opposite direction, as if all three had simply walked off the edge of the cliff. Their necks were all broken, probably due to the fall."

He waited a moment for Dylan to respond. When he didn't, Sam opened the door. "Honeymoon's on the U.S. government. I'll be back tomorrow to find out where you want to go."

A NOTE FROM THE AUTHOR

Thank you for reading the 6th book in the Black Swamp Mysteries Series. I hope you enjoyed it as much as I enjoyed writing it.

Please consider writing a review on Goodreads (https://www.goodreads.com/book/show/33972653-cloak-and-mirrors) and recommending the book to your friends. They can view the book's trailer, read an excerpt and click through to amazon and other vendors through the book's page at http://pmterrell.com/cloak-and-mirrors/.

For advance notice of upcoming book releases, please sign up for my newsletter at http://pmterrell.com/newsletter/. Your information is never shared or sold and I promise to guard it as carefully as Dylan Maguire's next CIA mission.

I also post weekly at http://pmterrell.blogspot.com/ (http://pmterrell.blogspot.co.uk/ in the United Kingdom and Ireland) and if you follow my blog, you'll get the inside scoop on all the places mentioned in the book, the inspiration for the scenes and plots and of course, on Vicki and Dylan.

I enjoy hearing from readers. Contact me through my website (http://pmterrell.com/contact-me/) or through these social media sites:

Facebook: https://www.facebook.com/pmterrell.author/
Twitter: https://twitter.com/pmterrell
YouTube Channel: https://www.youtube.com/user/terrellpm
Pinterest: https://www.pinterest.com/pmterrell/books/
LinkedIn: https://www.linkedin.com/in/pmterrell

p.m.terrell

Other Books by p.m.terrell

Black Swamp Mysteries:

Exit 22 (2008)

Vicki's Key (2012)

Secrets of a Dangerous Woman (2012)

Dylan's Song (2013)

The Pendulum Files (2014)

Cloak and Mirrors (2017)

Other Books:

Kickback (2002)

The China Conspiracy (2003)

Ricochet (2006)

Take the Mystery out of Promoting Your Book (2006)

Songbirds are Free (2007)

River Passage (2009)

The Banker's Greed (2011)

The Tempest Murders (2013)

The White Devil of Dublin (2014)

A Thin Slice of Heaven (2015)

www.ingramcontent.com/pod-product-compliance
Lightning Source LLC
Chambersburg PA
CBHW070915260626
47162CB00007B/2684

* 9 7 8 1 9 3 5 9 7 0 3 8 5 *